Margo Daly and Jill Dawson

Margo Daly co-edited the anthology *My Look's Caress* before leaving her native Australia in 1991. Since then she has worked as a travel writer and researcher, as co-author of the *Rough Guide to Australia* and contributor to the *Rough Guides to France, Europe, Thailand* and to *More Women Travel*. She is currently writing her first novel. Jill Dawson is an award-winning poet and the author of two novels, *Trick of the Light* (1996) and *Magpie* (1998), and has also edited *The Virago Book of Wicked Verse* and *The Virago Book of Love Letters* and two books for teenagers.

SCEPTRE

Wild Ways

New Stories about Women on the Road

Edited by
MARGO DALY and
JILL DAWSON

SCEPTRE

Extract on p.83 is from the poem 'Monterrey Sun' by Alfonso Reyes, translated by Samuel Beckett. This English translation © Samuel Beckett 1958. Published in *Translations of Mexican Poetry*, ed. Octavia Paz, Calder and Boyars, London 1970. Reprinted by kind permission of Editions de Minuit, Paris.

Every effort has been made to trace copyright holders in all copyright material. The editors regret if there has been any oversight and suggest the publishers be contacted in any such event.

Copyright in anthology © 1998 by Margo Daly and Jill Dawson
For the copyright on individual stories see page 226

First published in 1998 by Hodder and Stoughton
A division of Hodder Headline PLC
A Sceptre Paperback

The right of the contributors to be identified as the Authors of the Work has been asserted by them in accordance with the Copyright, Designs and Patents Act 1988.

10 9 8 7 6 5 4 3 2 1

A CIP catalogue record for this book is available from the British Library

ISBN 0 340 69517 X

Printed and bound in Great Britain by
Mackays of Chatham PLC, Chatham, Kent

Hodder and Stoughton
A division of Hodder Headline PLC
338 Euston Road
London NW1 3BH

For Sally and Lewis,
Kathleen and Paul

CONTENTS

INTRODUCTION $\int$

Women these days are big on adventures. The 1992 film *Thelma and Louise* captured the Zeitgeist – heralding the beginning of media joy and discomfort with the Bad Girls phenomenon – when its two sassy heroines, played by Geena Davis and Susan Sarandon, abandon controlling husbands and boring jobs to whoop it up on the great American freeway. Finally gals got a look in on the road trip – a story where protagonists are either out-running one thing (typically the law), or searching for something else (typically themselves), and exploring friendship along the way, for this is essentially a 'buddy' story. That the road trip had been for so long a macho preserve seemed suddenly writ large.

Discussing the ideas for this book over a coffee in a sunny North London café, we searched for women in the definitive road novel – Jack Kerouac's *On the Road* – but found that Mary-Lou, Camille and the rest weren't great travellers themselves but part of 'the experience' of the road for narrator Sal Paradise and his buddy Dean Moriarty, described in terms of breasts and their kooky smiles, or their 'smoky blue country eyes'. So no surprises there. No great role models either.

Of course, as well as being a male domain, the road story has traditionally been an American form. Ever since Mark Twain's *The Adventures of Huckleberry Finn* American writers have decided to 'light out for the territory' (with the road for Huck Finn being the Mississippi River), mostly in terrible fear of being 'civilised' – generally by women, and in Huck's case, by his Aunt Sal. Women have been the civilising (read: restraining) force for many a road trip protagonist and in American literature the frontier has been something that males pushed at while women tried to settle and keep the men at home.

We two editors have both travelled. We have driven cars across wide open landscapes. One of us is Australian, one English. We have had the usual disasters and mishaps, some particular to women, some to travellers everywhere. But we felt hungry for stories of other women's road trips and decided that one way to get them was to commission them; and what of the road story which is neither American nor written by a man? What happens to the genre when the writers are women from Scotland, Jamaica or Australia?

Naturally enough the stories we received were surprising, contradictory and challenged the form in ways we expected and plenty of ways we didn't. This is not a collection of Anything Boys Can Do We Can Do Better. Things are a little more complex than that. The women in the stories collected here are more likely to seek the freedom to *do* something, rather than freedom *from* something. Typically in male road stories what is sought is freedom from domestic responsibilities, freedom from women and children, from relationships, the stultifying influence of the home. In *Wild Ways* the children or lovers occasionally come too and some of the women don't just bond with their companions, they fall in love with them. Another distinct feature is the amount of times the driving itself is of issue – hard to imagine guys like Dean Moriarty worrying about their parallel parking.

Although the writers are not American, some of our stories are set in road fantasy land, America. Big landscapes lend themselves to road travel and some of our protagonists drive across the USA, or motor from Canada right down to Mexico, with sunsets all the way. The vast Australian landscape is road trip-worthy too, and in one story the characters drive through New South Wales in search of Big Things; in another they travel in a drunken haze from Melbourne to Hanging Rock after a flight from New York. They fly alone from London to Western Australia to face a father's funeral and trace scars they've left behind. They drive across a futuristic Jamaica wisecracking to the end. They bus from Mexico to Guatemala with some guy they've picked up along the way. They wander alone through the streets of Beijing, misunderstanding everything, searching for human connections.

They tell stories to each other in a hotel in New York, curtains drawn, wearing their knickers. They stay put in London thinking of travel, and what it means to be a young woman today, plotting and planning to pay their own way across the world.

Thus not every story in *Wild Ways* is a road trip, but each features a new generation of independent women travellers, and several are in the form of a travel diary – perhaps a glancing reference to the diarist as a female tradition. The style of the nineteenth-century Doughty Dowager Diarist is a recognised one – for instance, the diaries of Isabella Bird in the Rocky Mountains or *The Journals of Susanna Moodie*, roughing it in the Canadian wilderness. These ladies in their long skirts, wading through rivers and bravely fending off mosquitoes with their smelling salts have also been, at times, figures of fun, never quite losing their aura of respectability. Travelling alone is possibly no less dangerous for women than it was back then, but in every other respect the world of travel has shifted; in film and television remote corners of the world are made inviting; it is hardly surprising then that the women in these stories are fascinated by these places, long to take off and take part, to party with the best of them.

The diarist in Emily Perkins' story *Can't Beat It* has been aided by an Arts Council grant, which permits the writer plenty of opportunity to consider – or send up – the role of the artist as traveller, or the traveller as artist. This theme is picked up by other writers, and the cult of the seasoned traveller or the insecurities and conflicts of those who are afraid of travel is explored by Joanna Briscoe and Bidisha. Fantastical journeys – Leone Ross's final journey or the relentless journeying of Bridget O'Connor's sci-fi match-maker – mingle with 'real' journeys: two friends desperate to have adventures but with a young daughter in tow, sisters revisiting painful betrayals, along with journeys of escape, journeys in an alcoholic daze.

We wanted this to be an international collection. The writers here come from Australia, New Zealand, England, Canada, Scotland and Jamaica; many of them have spent a lot of time travelling, living abroad or in migration. That a large percentage of the contributors are not living in their country of origin gives the collection an apt, 'countryless' feel. It is sometimes not apparent – nor important – where journeys start from, or the nationality of the narrator or characters. Readers are forced to suspend prejudices about a particular country or culture or to take up new ones, the ones the characters suffer from. How do Australians see themselves, their own mythology? is one of the questions posed by Margo Daly's story, *Big Things*. How do indigenous people respond to the traveller and what impact do international travellers have on the culture they visit? are tantalising lines of enquiry for Kathy Page, Louise Doughty and Gail Jones.

That fiction is an ideal medium for these vexing, layered questions to be explored is evident in the stories which arise. Not a collection of travel yarns, *Wild Ways* is above all else, a *demonstration* of the short story – with travel as its subject – by a selected group of contemporary women writers, already published and experienced in the field of fiction. The short story is a tricky medium. Frequently understimated, denied status or seen as poor cousin to the novel, a practice ground for bigger things, we as editors were determined to showcase writers who can actually handle the form. Some of the writers included here have published acclaimed short story collections (Bridget O'Connor, Ali Smith, Catherine Ford, Emily Perkins, Gail Jones), many have won prizes for individual stories (Jean McNeil, Kathryn Heyman, Jill Dawson); all would, we feel sure, acknowledge the singular charm and challenge of a good short story, its unique capacity to create its own brand of intimacy between the reader and the fictional world it conjures up.

Some have claimed that the thing that makes a short story distinct from a novel, that is to say, the brevity of the form, is directly imitative of the modern experience of being alive. Everything is fleeting, inconclusive, unexplained, possibly illusory. And so it is that the short story form lends itself beautifully to a journey, with its impressions, its moods and flavours, some with a clear destination, others meandering and meaningless, all concerned in some way to convey the texture of transition, of feeling foreign and feeling at home.

Few in this day and age need persuading of the seductive joys of travel. That is, in theory, at least. In practice, there is plenty still to fear; not least the ubiquitous mosquito bites, stomach upsets and violent (or punitive) men. *Wild Ways* captures a uniquely modern experience – travel stories for women raised with the expectation that they too will have adventures, on their own and with friends, easily as many adventures as their male contemporaries, and nothing much can stop them.

Margo Daly and Jill Dawson

Can't Beat It

Emily Perkins

Emily Perkins was born in Christchurch, New Zealand, in 1970. She grew up in Auckland and Wellington and once spent three long months in a town called Palmerston North. In 1994 she moved to London. Her first collection *Not Her Real Name and other stories* was published by Picador in 1996, and she has been widely anthologised.

∫

Can't Beat It

Here we are in the United States of America! We are *so* excited. It's like a dream. It's like the movies. It's *just* like the movies. Except there are more fat people. At the airport everyone was fat. Cecilia stuck out like a sideshow freak, Skeleton Woman. I'm travelling with Cecilia Sharp, art star and supermodel. She is here to make Art – paintings especially – and I am here to record it. The Official Diarist and Record Keeper. Not, as Cecilia pointed out on the plane, a record holder, or record breaker. No. Well, that's all she knows. Maybe there'll be time for some Art of my own.

Everything is so American here. It's beautiful. There is a fake waterfall in the lobby of our hotel. (Lobby, see, not foyer. I'm practising.) Our food at dinner was just like the food on the aeroplane – smooth, vibrant colours, perfectly formed, tasting of nothing in particular. Plastique. We ordered a bottle of wine and the glasses came with parasols in them. And this isn't even a tourist part of town. The hotel receptionist is called Mindy. I wanted to say Nanoo Nanoo but Cecilia said she'd be on the next plane home. We can't have that.

There was graffiti on a wall outside the airport saying Welcome to Amerika. Tomorrow we hit the road!

We spent a lot of money today. We had to buy a car. It's fantastic. We bought a used car off of a guy called Morty. I love America. It's a blue convertible automatic. What could be better? I can't say how much it cost. We've decided not to itemise our expenses. People back home might not understand.

Cecilia has to do most of the driving, for now. I tried but the wrong side of the road thing freaked me out too much. Cecilia is more confident I suppose, so she's okay with it. It even spooks me sitting in the passenger seat and not doing anything. Where is the steering wheel? I keep thinking. Who is controlling this thing? Then I remember Cecilia on my left and I'm reassured. Kind of.

We bought a car, and some maps, and a carton of cigarettes – I don't smoke, but Cecilia tells me American cigarettes are the best in the world. She smokes Kents, because Audrey Hepburn used to smoke them. Cecilia does look a little bit like Audrey Hepburn. Gamine, they call it. I didn't point out that Audrey Hepburn died of throat cancer. You don't say that sort of thing to Cecilia.

So, we packed up all our stuff – my notebooks, Cecilia's Super 8 camera and book 'for ideas', film. (Cecilia is an abstract expressionist. It seems to make life difficult for her.) And our clothes – one whole suitcase for Cecilia's shoes, don't get me started – and Cherry Cola, and off we went. Perfect.

It seemed like all day just to get out of the city. The freeways are terrifying. I thought maybe we should have oxygen masks – not being used to the pollution – but Cecilia said I was crazy. She's chain-smoking Kents.

We're in a dirty little motel off the side of the highway. We had our choice of the Honeymoon Deluxe All Nighter Suite (vibrating heart-shaped bed and specially soundproofed walls), the Businessman's Pleasure Weekend Bargain (48-inch TV screen, mosquito netting, mural of harem on wall), or the Nuclear Family Shelter (four beds, no windows). After carefully reviewing our options, we chose the Nuclear Family Shelter. 'We're from New Zealand,' we told our host (Marvin), an irony which I'm afraid was lost on him.

Tonight we plan to find a diner to eat in, and hopefully a waitress named Merle.

Our first drugstore! Cecilia bought 'a pack a Trojans'. They were the most American things we could think of. I recorded the event on our Super 8 camera. The guy asked what kind, and Cecilia said Ribbed, buddy – for her pleasure. I was so embarrassed. She's a real showoff that way. If this was the seventies she'd be doing performance art for sure.

The drugstore was in a small town called Table. Cecilia pronounced it to rhyme with Schnabel. Luckily we weren't there for very long. It's hard to say what people do in these places. I expected a nuclear power plant or an ammunitions factory or something. No sign.

The land is kind of desert-y between towns. The towns, so far as I can gather, are all pretty much the same. Tonight we plan to go to a bar and drink beers. But not Budweiser, Cecilia tells me. 'Bud's for losers.' Apart from me filming her in the drugstore, we haven't gotten a whole lot of Art done. Cecilia's kept the Trojans though. She plans to use them later, 'in a piece'. I hate to think.

Screaming hangovers. Less said, the better.

In honour of our American friends, and for the purposes of easy assimilation, I have decided to change my name for the duration of our visit. Henceforth, I will be known as Marcie. Cecilia refuses to change her name under any circumstances, and keeps quoting annoying bits of literature to justify her position. If she's not careful I'll start calling her John Proctor. She has agreed to humour me, however, and calls me Marcie in public. I am pleased with the choice of name. It conjures up appropriate images of blonde hair, big teeth, and a non-threatening intellect. Also, it sounds better if you say it in an American accent.

I am trying to train Cecilia in the American style. 'Don't spit your chuddy out on the footpath,' she says, and I have to tell her that it's gum, not chuddy, a sidewalk, not a footpath, and that everybody does it. She is a sullen student, but not slow. Mainly I think she resents the all-pervasiveness of Amerikan Kulture. I explain that it's exactly what we came here for and she nods, scowling, lighting another Kent. 'America's better in New Zealand,' she says. I don't agree. I think what worries her is the cities. She knows that when we get to one, every second waitress will be an art star and supermodel. She's a big fish from a small pond who has just been dropped into the Atlantic. I feel for her. But she's just going to have to get over it.

We are in a town called Truckee. We are in search of a laundromat. Soon we will be in the desert and we may have to sleep in the car. Totally road.

We've had a week devoted to Art. I have been driving through the desert. Cecilia has been making secretive notes in her exercise books. Today we filmed an interview, discussing her artistic intentions. I *say* interview – it was more like a monologue. We filmed her sitting on the car bonnet in front of an oasis – she thought it was an appropriate setting, the 'life-giving water in the arid desert', the 'fluid feminine', that sort of thing. Here's a sample:

'I really want to tackle *paint*, you know, really *directly*, in a really direct kind of way.' (She runs her fingers through her hair and scowls.) 'But it's important to be somewhat elusive as well, elusive without being evasive . . . It's like this road tour.' (She gestures expansively.) 'Here we are taking a very *thrusting* action, a very direct and straight*forward* tradition if you like, and . . . well . . . we're drifting with it. We have no direction – or do we? We're playing here – at least I feel *I* am, – with the idea of a non*linear* narrative, with sub*vert*ing the road, using mimicry and yet attaining something entirely *original*.' (She smiles.) 'And entirely feminine. And what is the feminine if not a frontier? We are rewriting the desert here, and I aim to capture that on canvas, the *essence*, the . . . It's like – a worn, dusty old piece of rope – that's been used for tying steer and towing trucks – and suddenly it's stretched and pulled and ex*tend*ed, until there's a lot of *space* within it – until it's more hole than fibre, if you like, and you look at it again, and it's a lace tablecloth. You know?' (Lights a Kent.)

I mean. Call me simple. But really.

'In a way, we're paying homage to Kerouac and to Cassady – they refused to accept a strict, narrow time structure; they also rejected the suffocatingly moralistic society of the fifties, with its creeping Victorian shadows. They paid a price for this attempt to stand outside the patriarchy – their early deaths are testament to that. And *yet* they also colluded with phallocentrism – look at the benefits they reaped, the fame, the 'freedom', the access to naïve – I don't say stupid – women. So we must look further than these men. We look to the road itself and pay homage to that, to the passive, 'female' land that must bear the *scar* of the road that man has carved through it, the burdened road, burdened land that carries its traffic in much the same way as the female carries the male . . .'

And on and on and on. I left the camera and the tape deck running and went for a little walk towards the horizon.

I think the work will be very popular, anyway. I myself have written two poems (not in the beat style) about the desert. I am struck by, more than anything, the sky. It is a lot higher than the sky back home. The clouds are different too, only clean white streaks with no grey or depth to them. Looking at the sky too long is like taking drugs, or being trepanned. I could develop agoraphobia. I feel very very small.

Every night we open a bottle of champagne and toast the Queen Elizabeth II Arts Council of New Zealand for making this excursion possible.

'Are you two girls from South Africa?'

That is our most commonly asked question. We deny it emphatically, though Cecilia says once we're in the Southern States, maybe we should say yes.

We haven't seen a lot of people, mostly old men. They're just like movie extras, exactly. Our dream is to find a movie being made and be extras in it. Cecilia hopes to be discovered. She would make a good movie star, with her skinniness and her bones. They say the camera adds ten pounds. That would bump me up the scale to obese. I was an extra in a New Zealand film once, when I was at high school. We had to walk across a road, behind the movie stars who were acting an argument. The first time I did it, I tripped over. The second time, a car came and I had to run across. There was also a lot of waiting around. Of course, that's why they get paid so much money. When the movie came out I went to see it with my family. In my scene Bruno Lawrence kept shifting around so you couldn't see me in the background.

We think the chances are good that we'll stumble across a

movie being made in the desert. For practice, we make Super 8 films of each other going into gas stations. Sometimes I go in first with the camera, like a tourist, and when Cecilia walks in later I film her. Other times we go in together, or Cecilia comes in with the camera to find me already there. Our acting routines include: Swedish tourists who speak no English; old college buddies who are delighted to bump into each other; a couple fighting; Thelma and Louise.

I am keen to buy a pistol and stage proper girls-with-guns scenarios, but the Brady Bill has just been passed and we haven't got time to wait around five days in one place. Just as well, Cecilia says, guns are asking for trouble. America seems to be the kind of place you don't have to ask for trouble, it'll just come right on over and find you. Anyway, we are gunless. It keeps us clean. Not literally – I haven't washed in three weeks. My hair's been through the grease cycle and back again. I can't tell if I smell, any more. Cecilia assures me that I do. She sprays herself with Evian three times a day – 'toning and moisturising in one'. I am surprised to find that I like not washing. Did Martin Sheen wash in *Badlands*? Did Billy the Kid wash? Did Jim Morrison? No way.

God this is a beautiful country.

More sun. Sunburn. Cacti. Tumbleweeds. Kents.

We've given up on the movie set. Our next hope is to see a mirage.

Cecilia's been reading this diary. Go away, Cecilia. She said this morning, 'Why don't you use proper descriptions? Why do you have words like "kind of desert-y"? I thought you were supposed to keep a record of this journey. I thought you were a writer.'

We had our first fight.

I called her a snoop, she called me talentless, I said at least my art wasn't competely inaccessible like hers, she said how dare I call my scribbling Art, then I struck the final blow and reminded her who got the most money off of the Arts Council. She said, What did they know anyway, they're a bunch of parochial philistines, and I said it would be a shame if I had to put that comment on record in the journal I'm submitting to the Arts Council on our return.

That shut her up.

We're getting near a city, which we'll probably avoid. Cecilia's pretty twitchy. The towns are closer and closer together. There are more young people in them too, girls with white high heels and Farrah hair pushing twin strollers. 'Look, Marcie,' says Cecilia, 'there goes your sister.' Or we see a real fat pig crossing the road with his pants halfway down his backside. Cecilia toots the horn. 'Marcie, aren't you going to wave to your husband?'

I'm getting sick of America. It's all the same and the food's crap.

Conversation hasn't been going too well, so we bought a car stereo. It's the best thing ever. We play Bruce Spingsteen exclusively. I thought some of the lyrics would go against Cecilia's feminist stance, but she sings along regardless. Bruce. The Boss. What a babe. At night, even when the tape deck's turned off, I can still hear his voice rolling around and around in my head. We try and make out his shape in the unfamiliar stars above us. Constellation Springsteen. Sometimes we just find his belt, or his leather jacket. We love him. We don't care that he can't dance.

I had a frightening thought. We have been in America nearly a month, and what have I got to show for it? Five poems and an erratic diary. Cecilia's still making cryptic notes for her paintings. It's true, she is a real artist. I'm never going to get a grant again. Writing seems futile when you're in the desert. Here you are in the middle of the heat and the space and the most overpowering sky in the world, and there's nothing to say. Experiencing it is everything. But somehow I just don't think that's going to wash, back in Wellington.

Cecilia's undergoing some strange personal epiphany. This morning she hauled her suitcase full of shoes into the back seat of the car. I thought she was going to polish them, even though we're nowhere near New York, the place she's been saving them for. But as I drove, still having to concentrate to stay on the right side of the road, she started throwing the shoes overboard. One by one she threw out first each left shoe, then each right. I asked did she want me to get the camera, but she just said keep driving. So I drove.

Tonight, at the diner in Pick, a woman walked in wearing a pair of high heeled silver sandals with white bobby sox and jeans. Cecilia's drunk fifties housewife shoes. See, she said to me over the table, they've found their true home. And she's right. Cecilia might not be at home in America, but her clothing certainly is.

Today, totally out of the blue, Cecilia said, 'I reject fame. I reject the idea of an elite group of so-called *masters* who deserve eternal celebration. Fuck the Arts Council. What is art? What is an artist? What am I? I mean, fuck them. Who do they think *I* am, to give money to? They don't *know* me. Do they? They don't—' And then she stopped. It spooked me, I'll be honest here. It came out of nowhere. I mean, I didn't ask her or anything.

I really didn't think that communication could deteriorate any further between me and Cecilia, but it has. While I'm living on cheeseburgers and Cherry Cola, The Razor has virtually stopped eating. She's on to her fourth carton of Kents. 'Go easy on that gum you're chewing,' I say. 'Could be a couple of calories in there.' She responds by addressing me only in Pig Latin, a comment I suppose on my junk food diet. 'Utshay upay,' she says.

Another source of disagreement is my driving. 'Utpay your ootfay ownday,' says Cecilia, snapping gum; sixty-five mph is 'ootay owslay'.

I never would have come to the desert if I'd have known Cecilia would turn into a gibbering loon with an eating disorder. I saw a page of her exercise book with a sketch of me on it. Not flattering. I am a scratchy squat figure with stringy hair and a frown, titled simply, Marcie the Hog. Thanks, Cece.

Meanwhile, the desert keeps on going, blue and brown, flat and hot. The closest we've got to a mirage is the constant heat shimmer on the road ahead of us. I don't even notice the towns, not unless we stop for gas or cheeseburgers. Glasso, Pick, Ideal – it seems like we've been through a million of them.

First the communication breakdown, now the car. Neither of us is in the least mechanically minded. Why didn't the Arts Council put us through a car maintenance night school before we left? It looks serious – the car started whining and then hissing and then smoke came out the front. We stopped and had to wait two hours before a ute came by and we could hitch to the nearest town. Now here we are, stuck in Bony, population five hundred and twelve. Our mechanic, Mitch, sent a towtruck to get our car. He says it'll take at least three days – might have to get a part sent in from Ragrug. Mitch looks like a cross between Lorne Greene and the Devil. He offered to have us stay at his trailer home, just out of town, but we declined. We're staying in the Bony Motel for Weary Bones, run by a woman named Marcie. She got so excited when I told her my name, I thought she was going to give us a reduced rate. Marcie is surprisingly politically aware. 'I think it's just wonderful how you folk are letting the Africans vote now,' she says before we have a chance to correct her. 'That President de Klerk is a real gentleman.' Marcie's husband is a big Puerto Rican man, Carl. They have a teenage son, also Carl, who is very good-looking. I caught Cecilia eyeing him in a predatorial way. One thing – this car disaster has brought me and Cecilia back together. This is a relief. United, we are much better equipped to handle Bony, Mitch, and Carl Jr. I might even take a shower.

An amazing stroke of luck! Tomorrow night a bar in Ragrug is holding a Jack Kerouac lookalike competition! Apparently Jack and Neal used to pass through here quite a lot. Marcie tells us there's a retarded girl in Ragrug whose mother, before she died of ovarian cancer, used to swear was Neal's lovechild. Cecilia and I are ecstatic. Cecilia tried to be strict and tell me we didn't come all this way to get boyfriends, but she didn't mean it. What about that unopened pack of Trojans in the glove-box of our car? Besides, this is *perfect* for her frontier/feminist/beat project. She'll get at least two paintings out of it.

I should say: it hasn't rained once the whole time we've been in America. Bizarre.

Can't wait for tomorrow night! Mitch is driving us.

Well. Here goes.

The competition was in a bar called the Lone Dude. When we arrived with Mitch, there was hardly anyone there. We ordered some whiskey sours and waited. I was nervous – I smoked one of Cecilia's cigarettes. She said it didn't suit me. It just about made me sick up. Mitch said he didn't think smoking was pretty on a lady, anyhows. Cecilia spent the rest of the night aiming her smoke for his face.

Gradually a few men started drifting into the bar. They bore more resemblance to Allen Ginsberg than to anyone else. They arranged themselves in a careful, almost choreographed way, around the walls of the bar, leaning on one elbow as if we were all in a movie. I desperately hoped these weren't the contenders. Cecilia asked Mitch if this was a gay bar. Queers? he said, downing his whiskey. Could be. Never can tell with these cowboy types.

A guy came and stood in the middle of the bar and said, I'm Fat Matt, welcome to the first annual Jack Kerouac lookalike competition, prize as much bourbon as you can drink, here come the boys.

The 'boys' all traipsed out of a door in the back of the bar. There must have been about a half dozen of them. Most of them looked kind of like Kerouac circa 1965: drunk, puffy, rotten. Cecilia and I clapped halfheartedly, to be polite. Mitch said, Fuck this shit – hell, I look more like the man than any of these losers. We only just managed to talk him out of paying the $5 entry fee and getting up there.

Well, we were disappointed, but then, secretly, we had known we were going to be. It was one of those things. The Ginsbergs stayed leaning against the walls, faces impassive. We ordered more whiskey sours, doubles.

Then everything began to happen in slow motion. The back door opened. Through it walked the most beautiful man I have ever seen. You know that photograph of Kerouac taken in Cassady's house, in a chair reading with his workboots on? He looked exactly like that. I couldn't help it – I stood up and wolf-whistled. Cecilia kicked me.

I couldn't imagine the next bit happening, but it did. Fat Matt presented him with two huge bottles of Wild Turkey. He carried these over to our table, where he greeted Mitch like a long-lost brother. This is Mack Maverick, said Mitch, my long-lost brother. This here's Marcie and this is Cecilia Sharp. They're all the way from South Africa. We drank more whiskey. Mack made a toast to Nelson Mandela. I watched Cecilia carefully to see if she was watching me. She's always running me down for being 'boy crazy'. It's just not true. It's not as if there's anything wrong with boys, most of them. Cecilia can't just rule out a whole gender. I usually tell her she's being essentialist and she quietens down. Anyway, I started to worry about Mack watching me and Cecilia watching each other so much. He might have got the wrong impression. It's amazing how easily people can do that. So I smiled at him and downed my drink. I said, Do you like Bruce Springsteen? Then he leaned across the bar and hollered, Hey Mailer! Put my music on! He turned to me and said, Marcie, may I? and as the Boss sang some low and mournful tune, Mack Maverick and I gazed into each other's eyes and danced.

The Arts Council's going to kill me. I'm getting married! So much has happened. Our car was fixed, just in time to be our getaway vehicle when we got thrown out of Bony. Carl Sr caught Carl Jr in bed with Cecilia. It was not a pretty sight. Carl Sr I mean not—. Well none of it was, actually. Cecilia got very very drunk and said a lot of things she was ashamed of in the morning. I think she quite enjoyed it though, leaving Carl Jr standing teary-eyed in the dust as we drove off. She didn't even put up much of a fight about Mack coming with us. On our first night under the stars when I pointed out to him Bruce Springsteen's belt, he asked me to marry him. We have to wait for his divorce to come through first. It's a long story, Mack says, one he'll tell me all about some day. Cecilia is very suspicious, I can tell. She'll be muttering under her breath, and I can catch words like 'Bundy' and 'Dahmer'. She's taking the car on a *pilgrimage* to Texas to look for the Rothko Chapel. She says she wants to feel cleansed. I suppose I understand. It is hard to feel clean in this weather, so hot and still like an earthquake's about to happen. We don't need her, Mack says. We can buy our own car and hit the road again.

Who knows if the documentary on Cecilia Sharp, Abstract Expressionist in America, will ever be finished? Probably we should bury it in the desert for aliens to find. Cecilia says I *am* a record breaker now – I get the gold medal for the shortest courtship in history. I will miss her a lot. I'll miss New Zealand too, I guess. Mack's kind of a drifter, but he can always get work on the railroad somewhere. He says he can't wait to introduce me to his best friend. Of course. God America I love you. Land of pilgrims, you know. Land of dreams.

Lady Chatterley's Chicken

Louise Doughty

Louise Doughty, born in Melton Mowbray, is a London-based novelist, critic and broadcaster. Her novels, *Crazy Paving*, *Dance With Me* and *Honey-dew*, are all published by Simon & Schuster. The material for this story was gained during a trip to Guatemala with her younger sister. (They ran out of money, got lost, bribed soldiers with their watches and ended up hitch-hiking across the no-man's land between the Guatemalan and Mexican border.)

Lady Chatterley's Chicken

They hitched up together in Puerto Angel. He was a good shag.

'I'm a good lay,' he had said hopefully, over *cocos naturales* at the beachside café. His head was bent to sip coconut milk through a straw.

'Shag,' she replied.

'What?'

'A good shag. In England, we say shag.'

'No kidding?' He tried the word out for size. 'Sha . . . g. Shag . . .' rolling it round his mouth like a toffee.

It was then she decided to go to Guatemala with him. His innocent enthusiasm won her over.

When they had finished drinking, the woman came over to their table and sliced their coconuts with a machete, then broke them into chunks so they could eat the meat inside.

'Isn't this perfect?' he garbled. He gestured out to the bay, where sun sparked on the water with phosphorescent ferocity. A small grey warship was tied to the end of the jetty with steel hawsers. It rolled gently in the surf, like a captured whale. Several tiny boys were climbing hand over hand along the hawsers, then shrieking and letting themselves drop into the sea. A couple of Mexican marines sat on the jetty, smoking and watching the boys indulgently.

He was right. It was perfect. She felt an ache of impatience to enjoy its perfection alone. She had come to travel around Latin

America, not to explore this good-natured boy with his shiny white smile and cotton T-shirts and air of perpetual anticipation. But then, she had been in Mexico for three months without – as he would call it – a lay. What harm could a little casual sex do? At least he was ordinary, and safe.

'No questions,' she said, before adding hastily, 'and especially no answers. I don't want to know what your dad does for a living or how your mom bakes cookies and I don't want to talk about my family or England.'

He looked at her, puzzled, then realisation spread over his face. He gave a broad smile. 'So you'll come with me, hey that's . . . great. Great. No questions I promise . . .'

'Or answers . . .'

'Or answers, except, my mother doesn't bake cookies. Actually, she teaches physics.'

In her hut at the Puesta del Sol, they made hot, efficient love. She had left her bikini to soak in the sink on the wooden veranda, floating amidst a light scum of sand, industrial oil and Boots Factor 6.

Afterwards, they lay still. She listened to the lizards croaking in the eaves.

Felipe Martinez woke early, while it was still dark. His brothers were sleeping on the straw mats beside him but he could hear his mother stirring on the other side of the curtain. She would be wrapping her blue woollen shawl around her shoulders, moving quietly in the dark so as not to wake his father, feeling with her feet for the clay jug and splashing water over her face. He lay still and listened. The sounds were comforting.

Usually, he found it hard to rise in the mornings but this morning was different. He was to start work for his uncle and it would mean taking the truck up to Sololá. For the first time, he was to be allowed to take the truck on his own.

He would have to help his father deliver the baskets first. There were over forty to go to different shops and houses. It would take several hours but if he ran he could be back in time to get the truck to Sololá before lunch. He pulled the blanket up to his ears, enjoying the rough warm feel of it, treasuring the few minutes of the day before the beginning of work, while it was still possible to think of the things there were to look forward to.

He could hear his mother breathing hard. She would be gasping on to the glowing chunks of charcoal left in the fireplace from the previous night. She would kneel there for ten or fifteen minutes before it caught. The price of matches had gone up that week and if his father caught her using a match there would be trouble. He heard her sigh with satisfaction. Then there was a clanking sound as she filled the clay pot from the jug and set the water to boil for cinnamon tea. A rattle came as she lifted down the tin from the shelf, the one with the flour for *tortillas*. Next to Felipe, his brother Hector stirred.

Hector and Felipe shared a mat as they were closest in age. 'Is it time yet?' Hector murmured. 'No,' Felipe whispered, 'not yet.' When their mother began slapping the *tortillas*, they had to rise. Felipe closed his eyes for a few moments more, relaxing, smiling with anticipation.

The next day, as they waited for the bus, she rehearsed the names of the towns they would pass through en route to the Guatemalan border. Her finger traced the route on her tiny fold-up map; Santiago Astata, La Gloria, Pijijiapan. She hummed the music of those names inside her head, as if they formed a film score to accompany the sights they'd see: the women and their bundles; the plastic rosaries and crucifixes obscuring the bus drivers' rear-view mirrors; the boys selling *refrescos* by the roadside.

At Salina Cruz, they hit a bus strike.

Salina Cruz was an oil refinery town set in a sparse landscape of wide scrubland plains. The yard where the bus parked was empty but for a couple of wrecks in one corner. There was no through service to the Guatemalan border for the rest of the week. They would have to find a local bus to the next town and hope the situation there was better.

While they waited, squatting in the yard, he told her about the novel he was working on. He loved English literature, he said, even though his father had persuaded him to major in business administration. He had read Austen and the Brontës and James Joyce – all that stuff. His novel was going to be a satire on the sexual mores of upper-class England between the wars. He was going to call it *Lady Chatterley's Chicken*.

They were half a day from Puerto Angel, and already she was desperate to be rid of him.

He talked incessantly, even when she was wearing her Walkman headphones. As their bus skirted the Chiapas, he told her about how close he was to his father, what a great guy he was. It was his father who had told him to go out there and get around a bit.

As they crossed the plains, where the *maguey* plants sat in huge, motiveless clusters, he explained to her that there was no way he was settling down until he was thirty. He thought there should be a law against it until then.

As they swung through the tight-cornered backstreets of Arriaga, he elaborated upon why he thought it was important for someone like him to have plenty of new experiences.

On the edge of the town, the bus stopped in front of an unbarriered railway line. For several minutes, it sat chugging. He took advantage of the low tone of its engine to lean close to her and talk softly in her ear.

'Honey,' he said, 'know why we travel? It's like El Dorado, looking for gold. We're all out there looking for that thing that's going to turn our lives around, that unexpected thing. Could be anything. Might be something that happens to us, or maybe . . .' He snuggled up to her, pressing the length of his thigh against hers and breathing into her ear. 'Maybe it could be just meeting someone . . .'

She feigned a coughing fit. He moved back and said. 'Jeez, you a smoker or something?' As she leaned forward he thumped her back with his large open hand.

There was the distant grumbling motion of the approaching train, then a sudden blare of noise as the great filthy darkness of it thundered upon them. He craned his neck forward. 'Christ that was close. We were almost parked on the tracks.' He leaned back. 'See what I mean? Anything could happen anytime. We were almost killed by these guys.' He waved his hand around the bus to encompass all of its Mexican passengers. She leaned her head against the window and closed her eyes.

Later that day, they came to a village. At first glance, it seemed an ordinary village, with small adobe houses in neat lined rows and a few brown, contorted bushes. It was only as they drew through it that she realised it was completely deserted. The houses were shuttered. There was not a single person to be seen, not even a dog.

The bus had slowed down. The rest of the passengers had fallen silent. The noise of the engine echoed. It was an empty sound.

They drove into the centre of the village. As they passed through the tiny *zocalo*, she saw that it was lined with tall walls made of rough stone and cement. A large building to the left was fronted by a wall on which were set long spikes. On each of these spikes was a plastic doll's head – some with plastic hair, most of them bald – all with inefficient grins and painted lashes. As the bus chugged slowly through the square, a woman dressed in black suddenly darted out from an alley. She ran towards the bus, waving her arms and calling out.

The bus accelerated and swept past her. As it pulled away, they could hear her behind them, shouting.

He leaned towards her and whispered. 'Creepy village, huh?' She shivered.

At the time, she believed she had shivered with irritation. Later, she wondered whether it had been a premonition.

By the time Felipe entered the kitchen, his father was dressed and sitting on the side of the bed drying his face with the rag from the wall. Esperanza, the only girl in the family, had risen from her mat in the corner of the kitchen and was helping with the breakfast. She was eight this year and had already learnt how to make *tortillas* as well as her mother. As the men of the family hauled themselves to their seats, she brought the tea, *chile* and salt over to the table. Felipe's father was quiet, as he always was in the morning. Felipe watched him anxiously from the corner of his eye. If he showed signs of bad temper it was possible that he would change his mind about letting Felipe drive the truck. Then, his father lifted his head and caught him looking at him. He gave a slow, deliberate wink. Felipe smiled with relief.

As they began to eat the *tortillas*, the thin wail of the baby next door began. The Gomez baby was sick. Felipe's mother said it would not last the rainy season.

The basket deliveries did not take as long as Felipe had expected. Gustavo Gomez was taking some mats across the lake to Santiago Atitlán and offered to take the baskets in return for a lift up to Sololá later in the week. When Felipe and his father returned, Felipe ran into the house to pick up the keys and ran out immediately to the truck, waving the keys in the air. His father shouted after him to take care.

They crossed the border at dawn. A solitary official stamped their passports in a deserted emigration hall, cancelling their Mexican tourist cards and bidding them good morning. As they walked towards the exit, a cleaner who was brushing the hall stopped, straightened and pulled a bundle of *quetzales* from the inside of his overalls. He offered them one per thousand *pesos*. They tried to haggle, but sensing their exhaustion, he insisted on his price.

The two countries met in a valley, cleaved by a tiny trickling river. A small stone bridge lead into Guatemala, where the road plunged upwards through dense lush greenery dotted with palms. In the distance, the early morning mist was rising from a huge volcano. A rim of gold gleamed at the corner of the white morning sky.

It was in Guatemala City that she decided she could stand it no longer.

They checked into a hotel two blocks from the bus station. The whole of the ground floor was an open-plan foyer, bar and television room where several men sat in chairs grouped around a large black and white set from which a Western was blaring. Enquiring about rooms, she had to shout above the sound of ricocheting bullets. As the receptionist handed over keys, she pointed to the sign above her head which informed them that the hotel bore no responsibility for their belongings or their personal safety while they were there – and would they please not spit.

Their room had two single iron beds. The walls were bare but for a wood-framed picture of a Jesus with calm, European features – a glow behind his head, hand raised in benediction. The narrow window was covered by a grey plastic blind.

They had not had sex since Puerto Angel, so they had it on one of the narrow beds, striped by the sun through the blind. It was mid-afternoon. Afterwards, he propped himself up on one elbow, naked on the rough woollen blanket. He watched her while she sat on the edge of the bed and re-arranged her clothing, fiddling with her bra strap.

'How old are you?' he asked suddenly.

She did not reply.

'Twenty-eight?' he continued. 'Thirty-two? I'd say you're the wrong side of thirty. Know how I can tell? This flesh here.' He raised a finger to her back, near the shoulder, just above the shoulder blade. 'It's kind of loose, you know, as though it isn't quite stuck right to the bone underneath. That's how you can tell with women.'

She stood up without speaking, to pull on her knickers and shorts.

He swung his legs off the bed in a swift, angry movement. 'And another thing, how come English girls never shower after sex?'

He grabbed his towel from the bottom of the bed and strode across the room to the bathroom. She heard the sound of him urinating, then the rattle and fizz of water from the shower.

She sighed. Then she went over to her bed, and began to pack.

She had almost finished by the time he emerged from the shower. He stood dripping onto the bare lino, roughing up his hair with a towel, naked. She noticed the strong muscles of his feet, the ankles, and felt a pang of regret.

'What are you doing?' he said, lowering the towel.

'Going to Panajachel,' she said. 'I want to see the lake and the volcanoes. Guatemala City is horrible. I'm not spending the night here.'

He sighed. 'Look. I'm sorry I was mean to you. It's just, I find it really difficult sometimes. It's not your fault. But, you know, you're so mysterious and wrapped up it just drives me crazy. It isn't easy when you never talk about anything. I don't know anything about you. I'm not used to operating this way. Hey, you know, usually girls want to know everything about me and with you I just talk like an idiot. I've always had a big problem with commitment up until now. I'm way too young for any of that stuff. I guess you've kind of sensed that. But it's my problem, not yours. There's no reason why it should make you uneasy. I'm just a regular guy.'

She was fingering through her money belt. 'You'll have to pay the full whack for tonight. So I'll leave you my half.' She dropped some *quetzales* on to the bed. 'It's a bit under. I don't have the right change.'

As she moved to the door, he crossed the room swiftly and took hold of both her arms. His hands were damp. His thumbs exerted a slight pressure on her biceps. She looked at the floor.

'Come on . . .' he said, dipping his head to try and look her in the face. 'You're tired. It's all that sleeping on buses. Hey, I really like you . . .'

She waited until he released her, then, without speaking, she turned and left.

She went to Antigua first, the old capital. Her guide book said it was much prettier than Guatemala City. It was also possible to do day trips from there, to the markets at Chichicastenango.

She stayed in Antigua for two nights, until she felt it was time to move on. On her last evening, she sat alone on a stone bench in the *zocalo* and ate guava-flavoured ice cream from a rough brown cone, tipping her face to the dying sun. She kicked her heels in the dirt and watched hummingbirds hover in the branches of a nearby pomegranate tree.

She had been in Panajachel for three days when he turned up.
I don't believe it, she thought. *I'm being stalked – in Guatemala.*

She was staying at a place called Mario's Rooms. Mario was a ten-year-old boy, the only male in a household of women it seemed; mother, sisters, a couple of aunts. A wooden café formed the front of the hostel. There was a garden out back with a stone well, a few wooden shacks and an open shower. She was paying three *quetzales* a night for one of the shacks.

On her third morning, over a hot-cake breakfast in the café, she had got talking to a Guatemalan called Sergio, a tall bearded *mestizo* who lived on the far side of Panajachel, with the other Spanish-speaking families. He and his kind looked down on the Indian families like Mario's, he said, with their multicoloured tunics and their multiple dialects. Even so, he didn't agree with what the army had done a few years ago. It was wrong to try and wipe people out like that.

She told him about a roadblock they had encountered on the Pacific Slope Road and he laughed. It was typical of the army, he said. They loved holding up the traffic. Probably it was just a vehicle check, but you never knew. You never knew when you might get hauled off. The people on their bus would have said a prayer of gratitude. The presence of foreigners ensured their safety. Nobody did anything to tourists, Sergio said, the army had instructions to look after them. If any of the local people robbed or hurt a tourist it would be . . . *thitch*. At this sound, he made a circular motion with his hand, then a pull – a rope around the neck.

Sergio was something of a local character, it emerged. He knew everyone in the village, and made it his business to make friends with all new arrivals. He was very concerned that she was travelling alone, convinced that she must have a broken heart.

'Perhaps I have no heart,' she replied, as she scraped the last of the maple syrup from her plate, wondering if her daily allowance would stretch to a fruit salad to counteract the self-indulgence of the hot-cakes.

'How far are you going?' he said. 'Nicaragua? Costa Rica? Costa Rica is expensive. If you're going through Colombia you must be very careful. There, the army doesn't look after *turistas*, no one does. You get on a bus at the Colombian border and you stay on it until you reach the other side.'

How far am I going? she thought that afternoon, as she sunbathed by the edge of Lake Atitlán. The volcanoes on the far shore were a deep, fathomless grey. She tipped her face to the sun. *As far as I can go . . .* she murmured to herself. I'm going to go so far south it starts to get cold again.

Sergio thought her travelling alone was dangerous. She gave a small ironic grimace. The only bother she had faced so far had been when she had acquired company. Thank God she was rid of him.

Funny to think that when she had gone as far as she wanted, she would catch a plane straight back to Gatwick. It would be more logical if she had to travel back the route she had come, reversing all those experiences, one by one. Her tan would slough off and she would become pale again. She would put on the weight she was losing because of diarrhoea. She would have to un-fuck that strange American boy . . .

The afternoon was old and golden by the time she climbed the path back up to the village. A few yards away from Mario's Rooms she stopped to talk to one of the Indian women selling *serapes*.

She was squatting by the roadside – she saw him as she looked up. He was standing in front of the café, talking to Sergio. Sergio was nodding and gesturing towards the lake.

She lowered her head again but it was too late. He had turned and seen her.

Later he said, 'God, you know, you gave me a real fright walking out on me like that. It really brought me to my senses. It made me think and I really realised just how much I wanted to be with you. You want to know something really weird? It brought back all these memories, it really triggered something. When I was little, my mom left us, me and my dad, she just went off someplace. I don't know where. And after a week when it looked like she wasn't coming back, my dad went right off and brought her back. She didn't see me for a while though. She hid in their room crying and Dad said she was real upset to have let us down like that. Isn't it weird that I didn't remember that till now . . .'

Sergio had told him where she was staying and he had simply walked through the café and put his rucksack in her shack.

She had a choice, she realised. She could cause a scene – appeal to other tourists, tell someone to fetch the local police – or she could bide her time, choose her moment.

She had checked out the buses on her arrival. There was one through to Huehuetenango mid-morning. From there, she would be able to find out about buses south. She might have to go back through Guatemala City, although she wanted to avoid it if she could.

She made sure they stayed out late that night. They ate in a *palapa* shack, sitting at one of two tables while a woman served them plastic platefuls of fried fish. The woman's husband and his friends sat at the other table and played cards. Several children watched a portable television with bad reception in a corner of the room. A black pig snuffled sleepily around the dirt floor.

She encouraged him to drink too much local beer. When they got back to the shack, she feigned an attack of diarrhoea. By the time she returned from the toilet, he was snoring. She climbed carefully into bed beside him. She hardly slept.

In the morning, she was already dressing when he woke. It was a muggy day. As he rose, bleary and hungover, through layers of sleep, she went over and knelt beside the bed, kissing him lightly on the forehead. 'I'll get some breakfast,' she said, cheerfully. 'Won't be a sec.'

She had her money belt which also had her passport and plane tickets. There was some clothing and spare toiletries she would have to leave behind in the room, but most of her stuff was in her big bag, stored behind the till in the café. Mario required that you left belongings with him as a deposit.

She was feeling smug as she boarded the bus. She had timed it just right. Even allowing for the wait while the bus filled up, he would look in the café and down by the lake before he came up to the crossroads. She congratulated herself on managing her escape so smoothly.

Then, she heard a shout.

He was running down the road towards the bus. His face was furious. She closed her eyes.

What would happen when he reached her and dragged her off the bus? Could she call for help? There were no other foreigners on the small bus. Would any of the local people intervene?

He had been right, she thought. Travel was a pilgrimage in honour of the unexpected, some extrinsic event which would put a life in order. People like her – and him – travelled in the expectation that these events would be pleasant, benign. It was the difference between them and the people whose countries they scoured. People less fortunate expected the unfortunate. *It serves me right*, she thought bitterly, and she had a brief vision of all that was waiting for her if she could get away – if only he would stumble and fail to reach her. If only the bloody bus would leave.

The truck was waiting at the end of the *barrios*. It belonged to Felipe's Uncle Emilio, his father's half-brother, who lived in Sololá and owned his own shop. Uncle Emilio bought some of their baskets and asked for the occasional delivery or errand. He paid their father poorly and none of the family liked him, but work in the fields was scarce. He had taken a liking to Felipe. If he worked hard, he might take him into his house. It would be one less mouth for his mother to feed and a good start for him. The whole family was hoping for it. As Felipe started the truck, his mother ran down from the house to remind him of some errands he had promised to do in the town.

Coming down the hill into the village, he gripped the large steering wheel and whistled between his teeth. The truck bumped beneath him like a live thing, swinging and grinding as he negotiated the holes in the road. He pulled round the hair-pin bend just before the *banco*. To turn on to the Sololá road he had to pull out round a stationary bus. He glanced over his shoulder to make sure he had cleared it.

There was no way Felipe could have seen the *gringo* as he ran out into the road. He caught only a brief glimpse of a pale face looking past the truck, shouting in anger.

There was a thumping noise against the side of the truck. Felipe's foot shot out for the brake and he was hurled forward against the steering wheel. The truck skidded and swung and he was thrown sideways against the door. There was a moment of blackness and brief pain in his head.

As he staggered down from the truck, the crowd came running. People leapt from the bus and gathered round the *gringo*, pushing each other out of the way to help. Felipe wriggled past two men to see the body where it lay, face down in the dirt. One arm was dragged at an unnatural angle across the man's back. A pool of blood was pillowing his head.

Felipe sank to his knees. Around him, people shouted. Someone clutched at his arm, to detain or reassure him, he didn't know. Soon, the soldiers would arrive.

Felipe closed his eyes. Above the commotion, he could still hear the puffing noise his mother made to light the fire in the morning, her steady optimistic breath: the sound of someone who knows calamity may be around the corner but refuses to admit defeat.

A Hundred Years as a Snail

Catherine Ford

Catherine Ford was born near and lives in Melbourne, Australia. She studied literature and drama at university and trained as an actor in America. Her first travel experience was a year spent moving from hotel to hotel through Africa, Europe and South America with her parents at the age of eight, in 1970. She has spent a lot of money and energy being anywhere in the world but Australia, but now happily stays at home with her family. Her first collection, *Dirt and other Stories*, was published in 1996 and she is now writing a novel.

j

A Hundred Years as a Snail

'For the first time I know that I am truly loved,' says my sister Rose, 'and I love him so much I'd wash his feet and dry them with my hair, if I had any.' We lie side by side on a hotel bed in the afternoon in New York. We've got on our new underpants – mine bound in white elastic, hers with lace in an apricot shade. We have pulled the curtains across, against the light and the sirens, and turned on the bed lamps. 'He and I are equals,' she says.

We have been in the room less than a day and already she has washed out her socks, singlet and underpants in the basin and hung them over the heater to dry. My sister can make even a hotel seem homely and this afternoon the room smells sweet, as though an infant has been sleeping in it.

On a pillow between our heads is her right hand, resting. Her ring finger bulges at the tip and she says it feels as though it might burst, but it is only red and tight because she has gnawed at the quick.

'If only there was a way for him to stay with his wife and love me as well,' she says, 'without having to tell lies or feel guilty or treat her meanly.' She looks at her finger and prods the knuckle. 'I suppose that's out of the question. I suppose she'd hate that.' She sighs. 'Why is everything so rigid, where love and sex are concerned?'

This doesn't require an answer, and besides, it makes me

anxious just thinking about it. I turn my ear to the pillow to hear the rumbling noise I've discovered rising and falling away, very faintly, below us. It must be the subway – even though under my head is the pillow, under that a comforter (as they say), a mattress, a wooden board, and under that, two storeys of hotel.

'I stayed in this hotel once before, with Spencer,' I say. 'Remember him?'

'He was a strange one. Tell me about him to take my mind off my finger.'

It started in Europe and it started with another sister. I tell Rose, 'Patty and I were staying in a boarding house in London. It was an awful place, the toilet paper wouldn't absorb anything, it was shiny, and the whole place smelled of roast lamb, day and night. A man with a hairpiece ran it, an old poofter, and Patty called him Rug Alert. All the rooms had names. Our room was called Sad. Can you believe that? A room called Sad?'

Rose gets up from the bed and gets out her Instamatic from her suitcase. She goes into the bathroom, lowers the toilet lid and arranges a towel on top. She places her hand on the towel and says, 'Photograph my finger.' I go in and take three in different positions.

'Keep going,' she says, lying down again. I take a deep breath.

'Then Spencer decided to come to England, to see me. I went to the airport to get him and – this is terrible – in the car park I wanted to turn and run. I wanted to go back without him.'

I look at Rose. She says, 'I know what that's all about. The exact same thing happened with me and Keith Mortimer.'

'He of the furry boots?'

We cover our mouths and laugh and make our legs turn this way and that.

This sister, lying with me, has had a lot of experience. She once sat on a beach and counted how many men she'd been with and she got up to a hundred and twenty-three. She was only slightly older than I am now. It was, she said, because of our father that she was like that. (What exactly had he done, our father?)

'So Spencer arrived,' I continue, 'and he moved into Sad with me, and Patty had to move into another room, next door. It was awful. I was with *him* and she was on her own. I was awful.

The night Spencer arrived I convinced him that the only way he would get over his jet lag was to remain in bed, in the room the whole evening, while I went out with Patty to see a band.'

Rose laughs.

'I locked him in and left him there.'

'Was he sexually hopeless, I mean, what was it about him that you liked?'

'He was funny. He was very, very funny. But he hadn't had a girlfriend in a long time. I could've been anybody.'

Rose says, 'My finger is throbbing,' and around the infection I can see the ridges of her fingerprint raised and white. She bites her lip.

'Go on,' she says.

I tell her about Patty, how she got her nose out of joint because I was no longer with her. I tell Rose, 'One day Spencer and I went out by ourselves. When we got back that night Patty was watching television in the entertainment room by herself. She wouldn't look at us or talk to us for ages, and then she said, "Well, are you going to France or aren't you?" We shrugged our shoulders. "Well, when you've made a fucking decision let me know," she said and she stormed up to her room. We were shocked. We hadn't done anything.'

Rose turns on to her front and studies her fingernail. 'That girl doesn't have an inner life, that's her problem. She suffers from boredom. She only wants to be with people who are hip and that cuts out about 95 per cent of the population. No wonder she's lonely.'

She pauses and blows on her fingertip. She says, 'I need a drink. I want a martini just like Grandpa says to make them: pour the gin, then carry the glass past the room in which the vermouth bottle stands and Bob's your uncle. We're going to get room service.' She picks up the phone. 'Watch this. This is how things are done in this city.' She says into the phone, 'I want a dry martini and a Heineken in room 202,' and hangs up. 'If we talked like that in our country, we'd get a knuckle sandwich, but here it's expected. It liberates everyone to talk like that,' she says.

Even in her lace culottes and singlet, little apricot frills around her smooth and feeble-looking joints, and with her finger pointed at the ceiling, my sister is in command. I respect her, and to tell the truth she frightens me a bit.

'Keep on with your little story about you and Spencer,' she says and lies back on her pillows.

'Um, I think I was up to France,' I say. 'Yes, the next morning Spencer and I decided to leave, to get the ferry to France. I went into Patty's room and she was lying in bed holding the sheets right up under her chin, clenching them and peering over them as though she was naked and ashamed. I said to her, "We've made a fucking decision, we're going to France, goodbye." She was frightened and she cried. She said, "But what about us? What about New York?" I said, "New York? I don't care if I never see you again," and I left her there.

'We travelled to France, him and me, on the ferry. I couldn't look at him, I believed he had become the most ugly man I had ever seen. I hated the shape of his head, the cut of his hair, the big brown coat he always wore. I could have died for shame. We sailed and I had left my sister behind in her bed, all by herself.

'In France we were a couple. I was only twenty and he was more than thirty. He couldn't speak, he wouldn't speak the tongue. And when I tried the sound was all wrong as though my tongue had swollen in my mouth, had grown so large and sour it sat like a slug, unmovable. I despised him. In restaurants he would never say the words on the menu, he would just point, and in the street he would often stand completely still, unable to walk in any direction. He would simply stand there, looking confused.'

'Poor bastard,' says Rose.

'After three days he and I went to the Pompidou Centre. We were about to enter the doors and Spencer says to me, "My God, look who it is, it's Patty," and sure enough across the square came my sister, running towards me and calling out, "I knew I'd find you here – can you imagine this, in a city the size of Paris?" I could not. I turned white and fell to my knees. This was not a coincidence. She was again at my side. And once we were inside, she said to me, quietly, "I am so lonely, I can't be on my own, I am in a tiny room in a horrible hotel and I'm only there because I have to be. I know this is odd, but I knew I'd find you. *Don't leave me.*"'

The hotel room feels warm. My ears are hot and my cheeks prickle. Rose is the first person I have told this to. I am ashamed. I look at her. She says, 'This is entertaining. Go on.'

'This is how it was, with Spencer and me. Once we went to a large department store and arranged to meet at a particular door at a particular time. I didn't turn up. I bought three grey linen suits and half a dozen pairs of silk underpants. I went crazy in there. That evening when I returned to the hotel he told me he stood outside the shop door for four hours. He was so angry. He strode up and down the room and drank from a bottle of scotch. He kicked the TV set. He said, "What's going on, why are you so cold to me?"'

'I suppose he thought he was Sam Shepard,' says my sister, smirking.

'And that was that. He said he would go back to England. He was broke and needed money. I gave it to him. He was ashamed but he took it anyway and caught the ferry back again. Patty and I took a train to Italy. We eloped. I was not with him: I was with *her*. We were sisters, and I was married to her. We sat, sides touching, our heads bent and we laughed into cupped hands as the train went through the suburbs. We giggled all the way to the country, and when the buildings became fields we got out our baguettes and ate them, looking out at the fields without speaking. We made a carpet of crumbs.

'After some time, in a fit of madness, Spencer and I called each other on the phone. We apologised. He said he missed me. He said he was going to fly here to New York, and that I should fly here too and we could try again. I agreed, out of what . . . I don't know. We ended up sharing a room in this very hotel. Here he was in his element. He could speak the language here, he could sit in bed and watch TV and order in food because that was American. I asked him, "What is it you want?" He wanted to have a show on television, he wanted to tell jokes, and he was funny enough but he was too strange for it to ever happen. He watched *King of Comedy* four mornings in a row on cable.'

Rose says, 'This is the land of opportunity.'

She goes and looks at herself in the bathroom mirror and holds up her finger. 'I am in a lot of pain,' she says. 'I need more than a martini. I think I need an operation.'

We go to the hospital. In the cab my sister leans forward to speak. 'Take me to an emergency centre.' She pronounces it 'senner' and rests back. We hurtle along the mighty avenues at great speed. She looks out her window. Her face is pale and her finger is red. She rests it on her knee and I look at it. She seems small and her finger is bloated. It is disproportionately large, like a dream limb.

We sit in the tiny white emergency room. She fills in a form. We admire the black staff in their uniforms. We are like stick-figure ghosts against the wall, looking out at their blackness; especially my sister who barely registers as flesh. A doctor takes her details and tells her to wait.

'Keep going with your story. Then what happened? What were we up to?' she says.

'One night he and I were walking, looking for a place to drink. We couldn't decide where to go to sit for a while. We couldn't even agree on this, on the littlest of things. And then he just walked off and left me on the corner of some huge intersection. I was scared. I didn't know the place. It was night. I walked on tiptoe. I was afraid of doorways and men. The buildings were too wide and high. There was a lot of rubbish on corners, and lamps threw upside-down cones of yellow light. It was like a drawing in a comic strip. I had to stay the night in the apartment of a person I hardly knew. And when I went back the following morning he was sitting up in bed watching the television, watching Rupert Pupkin trying to get on television, again. He said, "What happened to you, where did you go?" and I said, "No, Spencer, where did *you* go? You left me alone in a strange place. You are meant to be my friend and you left me by myself."

'I also said, "I can't stand your laziness, your indecision. You watch too much television. I can't stand it any more." I got out my suitcase and opened the drawers of the chest. He knew what I was doing. He'd watched enough television. He got up out of bed and said, "No, don't do that." I went to the wardrobe and took a coat off a hanger and put it into my case and went back for my shirts. He took the coat out of my case and put it back on the hanger, back into the wardrobe. He did the same with my T-shirts, my underpants. I worked faster and faster to get the clothes into the case before he had a chance to take them out again. I said, "Stop it, I'm going, just leave me alone," and I pushed him away.'

I look at Rose to see if she's still with me, still listening. She's resting back in the chair, her head against the wall, her hand on her chest over her heart. I do the same with my hand.

'I'm listening,' she says.

'And I closed the case and we sat on the bed and he cried and put his head on my lap. He held on to me and said, "Please don't go, I'm in love with you, I don't want you to go." And I placed my hand on the crown of his head. I looked at his strange-shaped head and said, "No you don't, you don't know anything, you're not in love, this isn't love."'

'Gosh,' says my sister.

'And then I got up with my suitcase and I walked out, out of a room in this very hotel, and he followed me out to the elevator and tried to hold open the elevator door, to prevent it from closing. And I left.'

My cheeks are red and hot. How long ago all this was. Why am I telling my sister? She is barely listening, this I know.

A doctor comes and takes my sister behind a plastic curtain. Her legs disappear with a sideways swoop and I see the doctor's legs remaining perfectly still.

Then, through the door, come two women. One is old and stooped over in large grey woollen clothes. The other, much younger in smart clothes, handsome, with spectacles, holds her elbow and ushers her to a seat. The young one looks around, her hand on the old lady's thigh. A doctor comes out and says to the old one, 'What can I do for you, ma'am, what's the matter?'

The old lady speaks very slowly. 'My right leg feels like there are rags tied around it and are dragging behind me when I walk around the apartment.'

The doctor goes and gets a little black hammer. He hits her knee with it. It doesn't move. He tells her to wait and goes back behind a curtain.

The old lady says, 'Thank you, my darling, for bringing me in. I know you lead a busy life, you and your husband. I hear you through the wall, doing things, leading your lives.'

The young woman laughs. She turns her head to survey the

room and says, 'Oh yes, we're in the middle of a law suit, in the middle of the Christmas rush, in the middle of organising our daughter's birthday. I have a few chores. But I am alive, I'm well.' And she smiles a handsome smile at her old neighbour. They both look towards the curtain, and through the gap beneath it at the backs of the doctor's legs.

The old lady says, 'I'd rather live ten years as a fox terrier than a hundred years as a snail.'

A knife and a finger, side by side. The knife enters the finger and a rush of fluid pours forth. A bursting open, an emptying. Out it runs. The flesh sags, the flesh resumes. There is a split and then a joining up. I have a glorious thought of amputation.

My sister comes out from behind the curtain like a spectre, tiny and sad. Her finger is in a white bandage. It looks like a huge par-boiled sausage. She holds it up for me to see and shuffles her feet towards me. Her tiny voice says, 'I have three little stitches, dissolving ones.'

Back in the hotel I put my sister to bed. I make the room soft and comfortable. I close the windows. I place her hand on a fluffed-up pillow and draw the sheets right up under her chin. 'There, there,' I say. Her eyelids flutter then close.

'Read me something while I go to sleep,' she says. I read from the newspaper. I speak the words. I make my voice small and undulating and after a while I stop saying words and make a sound like, 'mer, mer, mer'. After a while of this, she drifts off. I go out into the corridor and get into the elevator and go down into the lobby and think back. I try to remember when I was here with that man. I think to myself, 'Which room was I in back then?'

Its Own Place

Joanna Briscoe

Joanna Briscoe was born in London in 1963. Her first novel, *Mothers and Other Lovers* (Phoenix), won the Betty Trask Award. Her second novel, *Skin* (Phoenix), was published in 1997. She has stories in several anthologies and has written for the *Guardian*, *Sunday Times*, *Observer*, *Independent*, *Vogue* and *Elle*. She lives in Bloomsbury, London and has lived in Paris, but often writes in New York and at American artists' colonies, and now travels as much as possible.

Its Own Place

Oh, how wild we were. We rode bucking rivers. We tasted the transient talk of moonlight ring-flared in alcohol. We corralled young Berber men.

Home was a tent of blanket and camel sweat, or a ticker-tape of Route 75 motels boasting roaches and axemen, and the mornings in the desert with sunlight buttering our arms like sex, sand spiders, running dogs, camel-back insomnia on the trading routes and honey mouthed with strangers.

We were very free that time. We broke in boys in northern geysers, we span along those roads of the world so long and straight you hallucinate – it's like planing on a boat, the blood-rush hurtle when you fly, you don't care, the crash might come as you soar into the air churned silent with bird and cloud.

'Let's do all the things,' she said. 'No one'll ever know.'

'Because we're lost,' I said.

We trailed *postes restantes* rarely visited, on the road for a year, buying and junking vehicles and layers of clothing. We escaped from life in coffee spoons through our pledge one night, early on in the northern Indian desert, to suck it all dry, river raft every boiling rapid, fuck everything going: buckaroos, garage attendants, camel drivers, youth hostel maintenance staff. We would crack open our minds so they gaped like coconuts, our bodies brown and scratched only there to carry us, no matter how torn, how berry-stained or engine-mauled. We

were at the mercy of trade winds, frozen goods trucks, sweet
strangers.

'He was like silk,' I'd say.

'He was like a bag of dry vegetables.'

We cackled and howled in the starlight, grinding ourselves
into the night's bed, to become one with the sand. The stray
dogs nosed our rum vomit in the mornings.

We liked the camel drivers best, with their facial hair and
cynicism, slinking into the desert areas near Pakistan where the
maps were unwritten and landmarks were all in their heads and
their camels' feet.

We had our pledge. Young French students. Days in the sun.

We soared across worlds. A net of dreams.

Anti-malarials are eventually forsaken for alcohol and quinine;
every land has a way with a foetus; the gut can accommodate a
cupful of new organisms.

Driving through time zones, Eastern Standard became Pacific,
and we burned tyres thin, we saw crotchety dawns in need of
a shower, stained with petrol leaks. We laid down a past of
strangers and bruises in five continents. We took the sulphur
baths of Provence and dried out in the wild thyme; we swam
fish bare off the Galapagos; we shook off the old choreography
of cereal in the mornings with men as familiar as breathing, and
made harum scarum scrawls of food, day, love.

On the road, we broke the skin of dawns, barrelling along
through that half-light and stopping, the engine burned, for
breakfast at five with the truckers. After coffee, we turned
the radio up loud to wake the sun, the volume rising with
the heat, slapping our knees with a drum tattoo as the sound
cracked and spinnakered in its distortion, hitting the accelerator
as we hollered and yodelled and sang fake Western swoops and
harmonies, a dozen strangers hopping in for a ride during a
single day's driving, and in India, we wove between rickshaws
as elephants cantered along the verge and camels pulled up in
the lane beside us at the traffic lights.

You learn a different language of the limbs. The joints pour into a squat. The legs drift. The spine straightens. The mind becomes numb with new virtuosity. We had never known freedom, though we had sensed it in a variety of placebos.

I flew from Kathmandu to Mount Everest one dawn. She was lying beside her October love, a Nepalese rafting guide. I was to meet his colleague from New Zealand in the evening.

'*Bon voyage*,' she murmured. She opened one eye to squint up at me. Her lips were peeled and raspberry with sun.

I would fly to the mountains, then we would meet up near the Chinese border and plunge down the country to the Terai to offer our skin to its mosquitoes and tigers.

So I shot to the top of the world. A soar of snow, a pour of blue. Free, free, how free.

And this is how it was.

I flexed my stomach in, out, in, out, as we glided through the snow bloom of that morning in the Himalayas. My gut gurgled with the tensing of my muscles. I had hoped I might be sick in Nepal, like other people, vomit away pounds of body fat, and suffer cramps and nausea to emerge flat stomached.

I cannot have youth hostel conversation, that laid-back dialogue free and charming as wind: those intense friendships formed of code and cool personality. I fear our car will explode as we bullet along the roads. I freeze when the hitch-hikers we have picked up banter with us, the horizon in their eyes as they turn their sky-blank irises to the window, hand up to shade the sun, and she talks back to them, so easily, as fluently as the road ribboning ahead, surfing over my small nervous laughs from the back. Surreptitiously, I ease my nose towards my armpit to check. I recall long-lost embarrassment, carried by the birds outside the window or my own diseased synapses, and I press further into the seat.

So there is Everest. Here my brain. I see the greatest sights this world can offer, and my mind's worms squirm.

This is how it really was.

We picked up men in deserts from Rajasthan to California, the world a playground, taking them to our own tents, or behind our private dunes, and she emerged in the morning with her mouth grated pink and curved to sleepy contentment, while I teased and played with them a little to ward off complaint, turning my face from them to groan in attempted pleasure. Those men were beer-stained and hard. I lay tangled with the thin legs of drifters, and I froze, and laughed with her in the mornings, a headache tensing in the sunlight.

Every day, I see stray hairs growing near my belly button, and they make me despair, crowning a stomach that's a little pot of French brie and Nepalese curd, and I can't get into the Goa mood, I'm terrified the drugs will damage my brain or make me spill untethered revelation. I remember – in a neon motel, on a houseboat – the terrible humiliation of some knowing comment, a lifetime ago, that made me die inside; I recall embarrassments I had tried so hard to dig below earth, that now erupt, and I howl in wolf tones a snatch of song or an exclamation, in my yelp of remembered shame, oh earth pour over my head, oh kill me right now.

In November, we left our rafting guides and we had our car adventures again. Such sights we saw. How we were winged.

The hair warms and crackles to silk in the sun. We travel along the roads that map the world again, sunglasses on, eating up petrol stops, meeting hikers, our skin stripping in that road life that's like the desert, erasing the past for the endless hot now. Shooting into those last fluorescent suns, the evening mosquitoes hovering, tinny radio songs, I try, very hard, to lose myself. In anticipation of suddenly, as if by a magic pill, unstiffening and entering their normality, I hold my breath; I dive from the top board into the water; I go on the roller-coaster: I make a comment, a passing comment, tossed off at last among the loose-limbed strangers, and it sails in its own silence, and crashes, and my small laugh and explanatory noises to follow are a buzzing of bees in a void.

I could never live. I could never absorb the now-now-now. I could understand it only in the photographs afterwards, a myth kicked in at last in silver bromide, but when I crouched on that ruin or that storm fence at the time, I could only think of unwashed clothes, sun-damaged skin, of how I would manage the collapsed spine of my map, and how I might scar my face on a truck round the next corner. My suspension is wrong. My stiff skeleton jolts over the bumps, while the others flow, they melt, they shuffle their hair, with tans and plaits and dungarees, bare scuffed skin, cross legs, the stars and moon and the greatest joke told in abbreviated references and shared with a joint.

Each day she discovers more, and finally realises, and will leave me on the roadside like a bag of kittens. Increasingly, there is the silence of our knowledge that I'm along for the ride as though I'm a paying guest, or a flattering shadow, in contrast to her wildness.

I had tried so hard. I had hoped for epiphany. I came for the ride because I loved her. I came because I thought I could change, change again, and make her love me back. I look at her sugary skin, I hear her laugh with a strange man, and I shrink and glory in her from the back seat.

I had hoped to learn how to live, to become like her, to be with her. The mind is its own place. I flew one bright dawn to the top of the world, but I was pulling my stomach in.

Tofino

Jill Dawson

Jill **Dawson** was born in the north of England and now lives in London with her young son. Her first novel, *Trick of the Light*, was published by Sceptre in 1996; her second, *Magpie*, is to be published in 1998. An award-winning poet, she is also the editor of three anthologies including the bestselling *The Virago Book of Wicked Verse* and *The Virago Book of Love Letters*. In 1995 she completed an MA in Writing and in 1997 was the British Council Writing Fellow at Amherst College, Massachusetts. She has travelled extensively in Canada and the United States and owns a log cabin and seven acres in Washington state.

∫

Tofino

Tofino. Sounds like a cross between a casino and some kind of sweet. Candy, as they would call it, now. Mum has her finger on the place in the map and they are both on the floor on their hands and knees, bums in the air, in a position of worship. 'The West Coast,' she says, needlessly, one purple nail-varnished finger tracing pink lines to the edge of Vancouver Island. As if Ann can't read. 'But Nickie, is it the right season?' Ann asks and Mum looks as if she is considering this. 'Is there a season for whales?' No, they decide, there probably isn't.

'God, I'm knackered.' She leaps up, plonks herself on the bed nearest the window. 'Don't you think it's time you were in bed, Poppy?' She never tells me to go to bed. That would be too . . . parental. She only ever asks, allows me to take responsibility for my own wellbeing or some other such crap she read somewhere once.

'I'm not tired. I'm reading.'

I switch on the lamp nearest to the middle bed and I don't even have to look up to see the glance they exchange. 'Stephen King. Can you believe it.' Ann goes into the bathroom. Sounds of gurgling and teeth brushing.

'I might just pop outside for a cigarette,' Mum says, opening the door and letting in a blast of strange warm air. It folds through me, this air; I feel churned up, like a cakemix being spooned over. I want a grey winter morning and the smell of damp newspaper. How long now until we go home?

She leaves the door half open, blows smoke out towards the other motel doors, out towards the car. 'God, listen to those things. Crickets. What are they called again? They sound beautiful.'

She is always annoyed if she doesn't know something. Waits – I almost hear her wait – for Ann's correction. Sound of Ann's hasty swallowing.

'I think they call them cicadas out here.'

Ann, her face shiny and free of make-up, is pulling back the nylon coverlet on the bed nearest the door. I'm not watching her, my face down, chin in my elbows, supposedly reading, but I'm wondering how long it will take her to ask if the door could possibly be shut, if you don't mind, Nickie. I imagine her bottom lip, the teeth just touching, holding the small line tight. I can't stand this for long. One, two, three. I try counting then give up.

'Mum, shut the door for God's sake. You're blowing smoke in here.'

Ann is rubbing moisturiser into her face, sitting up in bed, her hair dragged back into a spiky pony-tail. Of course she doesn't sigh but I hear it like she does.

'You OK, Poppy?' Ann asks, breezily. I grunt, closing the book and putting it on the table next to the bed. At least Mum takes no time at all to leap into bed, doesn't even take her make-up off, most nights. A subject of a brief discussion, early in the trip. Ann (concerned, but not bossy, not too Avon Lady): 'Don't you worry about your skin, Nickie, going to sleep in your eye make-up?' Mum (slightly caught-out, truth be told she's never spent this long in close proximity with another woman and had all her little foibles noted; that's if you don't include me, of course, which I don't): 'Oh, I don't think it does too much harm, once in a while. Saves putting it on again in the morning.' And then over-doing it, justifying herself just a tad too much: 'I think taking it off every night probably does more harm. Dragging the skin.' It's the closest she's come to disagreeing openly with Ann. And on such an important subject, too.

There is a tense moment, broken by me, coughing so hard they both look at me in horror, Ann leaps up to smack me between the shoulder blades, dislodge the tortilla chip stuck there. Mum makes a pretence of borrowing Ann's Neal's Yard geranium and almond deep-cleansing something or other to take her make-up off a few times, but she can't keep it up. Here we are four weeks later, and she's back to sleeping with panda eyes.

Maybe I'm watching them too much. I don't have much else to think about, out here. Seven days until we go back to England. Six, actually, because as Ann is pointing out, it's gone midnight.

The morning breaks in with a scream. It's Ann, standing in her T-shirt and knickers, staring at the cover on her bed and shrieking. My heart jumps out of bed, me with it.

Mum is a bit slower to respond. Her spider-head of locks appears from under the covers and a worried voice, clogged with sleep asks, 'God what is it?'

Ann is quick to recover herself. 'Look at that,' she is saying, and she sounds calm now, but affronted. We stand at the end of her bed, and stare. The cover is a pattern of yellow and green swirls, very seventies, this is a motel, after all, and it takes us a while to work out what Ann is pointing out to us. Then I see it. A giant green locust, the size of a fist. Huge legs. Absolutely still, like it is concentrating on something. I'm sure Ann's shrieking scared it just as much as the rest of us. It has that look, as if it's thinking I know I'm a great hulking thing that *can't* actually blend into the scenery and disappear that easily but humour me, won't you? The creature's posture reminds me of something. Shoulders up to its ears. It's all elbows. It could be plastic but not one of us wants to find out. 'Bloody hell. You must have slept all night with that on your bed,' Mum mutters. Ann stares at her and words form in a cartoon bubble just above her mouth. We all stare at the leggy creature on the bed.

'*Well*,' Ann says, purposeful, taking charge. 'Suppose I'd better try and get rid of it. Wonder how it got in here?' She can't resist framing that question out loud, but of course, Mum doesn't take the bait. Ann has gone into the bathroom; comes out with a washed coffee cup and a piece of paper, a postcard in fact with

Greetings from the Red Apple Motel in Goldtown. Mum and I move back silently to let her through.

'Right.' Ann steels herself. We all stare at the locust. A tickly feeling creeps up my arms; I hate insects, and especially one with a bright green body like a pea-pod. 'Right,' Ann says again. She pounces. She slips the cup over the creature, while Mum and I shriek in sympathy, and then Ann slides the postcard carefully under it. I picture its legs, spindly, awkward, being squashed into an even more acute angle. Gingerly, Ann lifts the cup, tightly holds the card at the bottom, walks ceremoniously over to the door. Mum rushes to open it for her. We all step into the heat of the bright, stiff morning, the smell of apples, the constant sticky-sweet motel smell of popcorn. Ann, still only in her T-shirt and bare feet, marches over to the furthest edge of the parking space, where the trees are. Mum and I trail behind, pyjama'd. We watch spellbound as Ann places cup and card down on the grass and then, like a conjurer, draws the card slowly out. There is a pause before she lifts the cup.

We step back and stare. There it still is, a trick locust, a joke? Nothing to indicate at all that it's alive, aware of us, aware of the close call it just experienced. It stares down at the ground. It makes no attempt to move away, make a sound, nothing.

'Look at the size of it,' Mum squawks. She and Ann exchange glances and Ann laughs, an oo-arr missus laugh. We march back into our motel room.

'I don't think it was a locust,' Ann announces, heading for the bathroom with her clean clothes for the day. 'Locusts are what you find in the Deep South. It was something else.'

Mum has the sense not to ask what. She's scrabbling for her last cigarette in the pocket of her rucksack. She's singing to herself. It's a line from my tape that has stuck in her head, she keeps repeating it, but she has it deliberately wrong: 'I got one hand in my toffee, the other one's eating a Dip Dab . . .' I have a temptation to say to her, no one finds you funny Nicola. I don't hear anybody laughing, do you? But of course, I don't.

'Do you want to drive?' Ann asks, jingling the keys at the car door. Mum shakes her head, pretends to be fumbling with her sunglasses, sorting out her camera strap. 'No, that's fine,' she replies evenly. 'Maybe when we get on to Vancouver Island I'll do the driving.' Ann nods, but doesn't speak. I breathe a sigh of relief: that's that ritual over with, and so early in the day, too.

The car smells of new carpet and orange peel. Of four weeks of journeying, of suntan lotion, restless bodies, heat pouring through glass windows. And of course, controversially, of Mum's endless smoking. They were disappointed initially when the guy at Budget Rentals produced a Chevy that was so unlike the Chevy of their dreams. Brand spanking new for a start. They almost wished they'd gone Rent a Wreck like Mum suggested, but Ann said she didn't want to break down in the middle of some fucking mountain forest and Mum, given that she can't even change a wheel, unlike Ann, had to agree. This Chevrolet, this white Chevy Cavalier, with its *Beautiful British Columbia* number plate is a bit too much like a Nissan Micra for Mum's taste. But hell, what does she know about cars anyway? They decide that Thelma and Louise would still have driven it if it was all the rental company had on offer, and that, after a short giggle at their own silliness with this Thelma and Louise thing, seems to do the trick.

I sit in the back, as usual, with my headphones on, and a huge bag of Fritos. They think I can't hear them, and it's not just the headphones, I'm definitely perfecting invisibility on this trip. I'm glad I brought so many books and tapes but the only thing I long for is English chocolate. Decent Cadbury's. This Hershey's stuff is nothing like it and Ann says she hopes I don't mind her mentioning it but if I want my skin to clear up maybe all those crisps and stuff aren't so good for me, have I ever thought of that, and I say I have thanks. I keep my eyes peeled for gas stations or stores which might have Cadbury's.

Being in the back, my view is sideways. It's a strain to try and look out of the front windscreen, to try to see things through the space between their two heads; the one so dark and ratty, the other so blonde, so pony-tail perky. Mum's hair, mess that it is, takes up far more space than a head has a right to. When the light starts to alter, when we're driving through late afternoon to evening, when I get drowsy, her hair plays tricks on me, blends with trees, the patterning of spiky trees on the windscreen, the endless passing trees we've seen this trip and I do begin to think there is a tree in the car with us, a dark, thin, pine sort of tree, sitting there in the passenger seat, stiff, its bark rough and flaky.

Today it's quickly over the border back to BC (they didn't think much of the States, spent ages discussing the difference of attitudes and Margaret Atwood, how friendly Canadians are, how different the Canadian border staff are, why Canadians drive with their lights on, and how sexy that guy is on *Due South* and what is his name again?). I'm listening to Alanis Morissette but I can still hear every word and keep both things in my head simultaneously so I am not, as they think, miles away, when Ann says: 'Does she eat this much at home? I mean she must have put on at least half a stone this trip . . .'

Mum's tone is defensive, initially. 'She's at that age. She's thirteen next month. Growing. You know. Didn't you eat a lot at her age?'

'No, I don't think I did.' Ann shoots back, rather bravely, if you ask me. I mean, open disagreement is unusual between them. 'I think I was only too conscious of my figure at that time. You know. My skin and my figure.'

Ann's skin and figure, for a woman of thirty-five, are – I suppose – something to be proud of. Mum looks a bit more haggard, it's the smoking, she's definitely the more lived-in of the two. And where Ann is small, neat and perky, Mum is just thin.

'And aren't teenagers supposed to be more – aggressive?' Ann continues. 'I mean, where's all the heavy sarcasm, you know, rebellious youth and all that stuff? She seems to get quieter and quieter. All she does is read. God, she even answers us politely. I can't remember being like that at her age. Not one bit.'

No, I can imagine Ann as a teenager. She would have done everything right, everything in the right proportion. You want feisty, you want rebellion? You got it. You want a thirty-something self-help manual positive-thinking no-man-is-going to-treat-me-like-that woman who runs with the wolves? Now you've got that too.

'She does seem so old, for her age,' Mum concedes, her face turned away from Ann, staring out of the window. I can tell she is twitching for a cigarette. She shifts stiffly in her seat. Alanis sings louder than ever, my finger sliding on the volume dial.

'D'you think she misses Dan?' Mum asks, always she awards Ann this special insight, this ability to know me better than she does, this magical therapist status. Ann is a social worker, but her speciality is Child Protection cases, not adolescent psychology. What the fuck does she know?

'How long is it now, since you heard from him?'

They're warming up now, their favourite topic, it's going to be a long haul before we stop for a pee-break. Mountains fly past, trees, a bloody bear could knock at the window; they wouldn't notice a thing.

'Five months,' Mum says. 'That bastard. I haven't had a penny off him, but actually I don't care. He never thought I'd manage this trip. That we'd manage this trip on my pathetic earnings from the shop. Ha.' She lets out a long sigh, a satisfied sound, like she just had a drag on the longed for cigarette. 'If he could see us, eh?'

Ann gives a joyful grunt.

'If they could *both* see us. Even when we talked about it, I knew I'd never get here with John, it was just pie in the sky. This has been a fantastic trip. Fantastic scenery, fantastic motels, fantastic food.

'The only thing missing has been fantastic sex, and you can't have everything . . . Perhaps we should pick up a hitch-hiker, like Thelma and Louise, what about it Nickie? Trouble is, I haven't seen a decent one, have you?'

Laughter. Their heads duck briefly together and the space between the windscreen darkens and fills with Mum's forest of hair. I know without seeing that they are exchanging glances, rolling their eyes or something, something that refers to me. I turn Alanis up to her limit. The road is climbing, there's a logging truck crawling up ahead, I know we'll be slowing soon, amidst plenty of cursing from Ann and a long diatribe against deforestation from Mum. I wish I could sleep on demand, or do that other thing, that waking trance that Indian yogis do. I wish that locust, with its horrible stillness, its unreal, plastic quality, its uncertain aliveness and its cooped up legs, would stop popping into my head.

We stay one night at a youth hostel in Vancouver and take the ferry ride in the morning. Mum and Ann are still excited by the novelty of ferry crossings although we have done several on this trip. They get me to take photos of them standing on the deck, nearly blown away, with the cormorants in the background and a deep green blob on the horizon which is Vancouver Island. I don't tell them that their hair whipped away from their faces like that is not very flattering; but I know from past experience that these photos will get binned the minute they see them, so I don't care to spend too long perfecting the framing, the way Mum – ex-photographer for the *Wigan News* – is demanding.

Rainy damp Tofino is all they could have hoped for, it seems, and what that consists of is a tiny motel – The Sea Pen – and a slightly hippified town with its vegetarian restaurants and its Native Art Gallery that Ann wants to spend forever buying a bracelet in, and its Spectacular Views of Clayoquot Sound and every other building offering boat trips out to see the whales, the real reason we're here. They have a long discussion over this, with Ann checking out the prices in each one and Mum picking up every leaflet in the Rainforest Interpretative Centre to try to decide which one is most eco-friendly, not Harry's Charters or the Whale's Tale – *twenty-five-feet of water-hugging action* – according to Mum, but the one run by natives: Chuck's Trips. We traipse along, book our trip for tomorrow morning, a little bit of banter where Mum asks what kind of whales we're likely to see and Ann cuts in with 'I don't think we can expect to see orca at this time of the year,' just as the guy is saying the very same thing. I almost feel sorry for Mum as she draws fitfully on her seventh cigarette since we arrived here, one hand in the back pocket of her shorts. I offer her a Dorito chip but she says no.

We eat this enormous vegetarian salad in the Tofino Pot Shop, served to us by a guy not much older than me with several piercings: eyebrow, lip, nose, which starts them off on their other favourite topic; all giggling and allusion and innuendo and thinking that I don't know what they're on about. Ann slept with this guy who had his penis pierced. Apparently it's very pleasurable, for the woman especially. Mum would love to try it. She has a problem enjoying intercourse, she can't actually feel very much rubbing in the right place and thinks that a little stud would act nicely on her clitoris, thank you. Of course what they actually say is 'God tell me again' and 'Didn't it hurt?' and 'No, I'd do it again, but it's a bit hard to find out, isn't it, without asking directly? Or running your hand over his trousers and feeling for a tiny lump!' And then they look at me and splutter half their organic apricot juice all over the place before they shut up.

After the meal we drive to Long Beach for a walk. The rain has eased off and the sky is bleached to a pale driftwood brown. There are signs that say PLEASE LEAVE THE BEACH AS YOU FIND IT but they are both looking for driftwood sculptures or razor clams to tart up their sea-themed bathrooms back home. They walk ahead of me, arms linked. Mum calls over her shoulder: 'Poppy! Look at this!' but I pretend not to hear. The sea is one of those great elemental seas, big and browny-green and rolling, a sea like I've never seen in England, or anywhere come to that, and that's what I will take, that's all; that one moment, that great tongue, the sea. I don't need photos or razor clams, I can just close my eyes to bring it all back; three tiny specks, one, two, three; two big specks, one smaller speck, beside the surge of the sea and fringed by an ancient rainforest and other things, small things and big things, dots on a long, long beach, a beach that seems to go on for ever. But doesn't.

The morning of the whale trip is brighter. Ann and Mum, having drunk nearly two bottles of some Californian red last night, are not at their best. I pull on my biggest pair of jeans, which are still horribly tight and cover up with a large Starbuck's Coffee T-shirt. I'm ready long before they are. I find the car keys for Ann, and Mum's cigarettes and matches. I'm surprised to feel something close to excitement. Anticipation. The Whale Trip. The high-point of our five-week visit to North America, long talked about back home in Yorkshire. We drive to the Whale Centre, park the car, walk to the quayside.

'He's okay, Nickie, look at him.' Ann nudges Mum at the young blond guide, we've just been introduced to: our Skipper for today, name of Eric. Eric they think is a bit naff. Should be called Brad or Harvey, but I quite like it. He's slight, in a faded checked shirt, with eyes which strike me as dark, for a blond person. He doesn't fuss around the eight or so passengers who gingerly step on to the boat, doesn't attempt to help the women and I like that too. He watches with an expression that might be sardonic, might be merely bored.

'He doesn't look very native to me,' Ann whispers. 'Shouldn't he be dark?'

Mum doesn't like the word native, she thinks it's un-PC. Like calling him a savage. Ann has already assured her it's not like that at all, this is their own preferred word, after all, it simply means indigenous. But I can tell by the way Mum bristles whenever Ann uses it that she isn't persuaded.

The boat, the *Clayoquot Whaler* is smaller than we all imagined. There are a dozen seats behind Eric, enclosed with glass, and a dozen more on the open deck. I glance briefly at the outdoor seats and the orange life-jackets behind them, but Ann and Mum, zipped up in their jackets, think I'm crazy. Instead I sit right behind Eric on my own, stare at his windscreen, marvel at the fact that he has windscreen-wipers, just like a car and a dashboard of pretend-wood, the veneer peeling in places. The engine erupts into life and then we're hurtling out into the water, bounding on top of the waves like a dog let off its lead.

'Blimey,' Ann squeaks, between gasps, 'this is a bit – fast—'

Our Skipper is trying to tell us something about the route we're taking and what we can expect to see today but it's impossible to hear him over the motor and over our own shocked heartbeats. I'm excited: I feel like a skimmed stone, bouncing over wave after wave, with the salt-smell and the diesel catching at the back of my throat. The boat approaches a wave, flies and lands, smacks the water with a bang.

In a while Eric, who has been talking on his radio to someone about sightings that day, leans around to tell us that something special has been sighted and if everyone on the boat can spare an extra hour we can go and look for it. Most people nod their agreement. One guy has fallen asleep. Mum is feeling the worse for the wine, she's tried a cigarette but the spray dampens the end, the wind snatches the flame from her when she attempts to light it. She doesn't appear to hear him.

Ann takes the lead: 'Great. Chance of a lifetime. I'm game,' beaming at him. My seat is directly behind Eric but I'm still surprised when it's me he addresses. 'Orca,' he announces.

'Killer whale. It's usually only the grey whale round here – you're lucky.'

The boat veers off to the left slightly, the engine picks up and the sea unpeels behind us like a tin being opened, white foam crusting the blue soup. The sleeping guy wakes up, nudged excitedly by his wife. Others fix binoculars, set cameras. Mum gives up on her cigarette, puts her sunglasses in her back pocket. Ann is poised, camera held in front of her, pony-tail quivering.

But it's me who sees it first.

'There! There! There it is!' I find myself tapping Eric's checked shoulder and he half turns, grins broadly, speeds up for a moment and then stops. The engine is quiet.

The orca is nothing more than a fin. One dark fin and a fine crescent of back. It swims, glides slowly. It is some way off. The boat is silent and so is everyone on it, we have all stepped outside on to the deck, and the only sounds are clicking cameras and film whirring. None of us know why this is mesmerising, but it is. We watch the whale intensely for something else, for a leap, a tail-flick, to see its saddle patch, for it to do something. It doesn't. Eric tells us there are three of them and when we strain our eyes we pick out the others too, further off, three black pin-pricks, in a faint line. He won't go closer, he doesn't like to, he says the orca are sleeping, that's why they are in a line like that near the surface of the water. He recognises them. It's a pod consisting of a mother, and two young females. He even knows their names.

But I'm not listening. It's that trance-state again. Willed, deliberate, the shut-down. It impresses me. Even a boat full of gawking tourists can't disturb it.

We hang around the orca for a while, taking photographs. It's obvious that people are losing interest, they didn't think the whales would just *be*, they thought they would *do* something; some of them ask to be taken to the island with the bald eagles nesting so that they can take more photographs. Eric starts the engine up again – reluctantly, it seems to me – and heads back towards the island. People on the boat begin chattering, discussing whether their lens was wide enough, what kind of shot they think they managed.

The journey back feels much longer than the journey out there and, like everyone else, I'm starting to feel queasy with the choppiness of the waves and the speed of Eric's driving. Mum is slouching in a corner seat, her face mashed against the glass, one arm protectively holding her stomach. Ann chews thoughtfully on a stick of sugar-free gum. The mood on the boat slumps and Eric turns his radio up, puts his headphones on. I curse the fact that I left mine at the Sea Pen Motel.

Then quietly, he's turning around and tapping me on the shoulder, not addressing anyone else on the boat, but pointing to something. 'Look there,' he says. He taps on his windscreen. Tiny on the horizon I see a black whale tail, fanning out. It swims away from us, the tail disappearing and then reappearing with a flick, a flourish. A gesture.

'Pretty, isn't it?' Eric murmurs. He seems moved. I'm staring at the back of his ears, at the stillness of his head, I've learned to read a lot from the back of people's heads, from their tone of voice, on this trip. I'm pleased, I find myself ridiculously pleased, that after all the whales he's seen, he still feels this way. The tail flicks one last time. Eric says nothing more. I wonder why he showed it to me, only me, and let the others miss it, but any thoughts I have on that matter are distant, barely glimpsed and can only survive for two or three minutes before diving, ducking under, disappearing.

Wedding at Hanging Rock

Justine Ettler

Justine Ettler is a Sydney-based writer who spends as much time in New York as her budget allows. She first travelled overseas at the age of six when she spent a few months with her family driving across Europe (this trip included a memorable meeting with her relatives in Communist Czechoslovakia). She is the author of two novels, *The River Ophelia* (Picador 1995) and *Marilyn's Almost Terminal New York Adventure* (Picador 1996) and is currently working on her third novel *Remember Me* of which 'Wedding at Hanging Rock' is an extract. She is also completing a PhD in Contemporary American Fiction and French post-structuralist theory. She is a regular contributor to *Rolling Stone*, *WHO Weekly*, *The Age*, *Elle*, *HQ* and *Black and White*.

∫

Wedding at Hanging Rock

Elle insists I come with her to the wedding. I'm like, I don't know, you know? I *hardly* know the bride (she's the Demi from East 77th Street right?), I probably fucked the groom years ago and won't remember when I see him (but *he will*), and I'm still jet lagged from my flight from New York.

'But weddings are a great place to pick up guys,' Elle insists.

I'm like, 'Isn't that a myth?'

And Elle gives me this weird look – she's recently enrolled in an honours programme in film studies at Sydney University and is totally into all this obscure French philosophy, you know, she does post-feminist readings of pornography (whatever that is) – so I just say, 'The only guys who try to pick *me* up at weddings are *married*.'

And Elle is like, '*Really*?' reading too much into it.

But I can't be bothered explaining. 'So when are we leaving?' I go, thinking like, next week.

'Tomorrow,' Elle says, totally cool. 'The wedding starts tomorrow at 2 p.m.'

'I can't believe this,' I say, draining my martini. 'You sure give a girl a lot of warning.' I cruise the die-hard patrons of the Bayswater Brasserie for about the millionth time tonight and conclude that there's absolutely no one in sight I could even *think* of taking back to the hotel.

'Are you coming?' Elle says, lurching towards the door.

'Sure,' I go. I mean I *am* a little underwhelmed by my current prospects, you know?

I let Elle escort me – I practically carry her all the way – back to the Sebel. Under normal circumstances I'd continue on drinking in the downstairs bar – they have an autographed photo of me up on the wall with all the other schmucks and the barman's quite cute – but tomorrow's itinerary persuades me to call it a night.

'I'll pick you up in a cab at around eight, okay?'

She gives me a big, sloppy hug and wanders off into the night.

On the way to my room I try to work out if I've had enough to drink to be able to sleep but I lose count after the eighth martini. I'm like, *so* drunk, I even forget to worry about having any more nightmares.

Naturally our flight to Melbourne is running half an hour late. We're on time – for once – which means we've got almost an hour to kill before boarding. We wander into the bar and Elle orders a beer (she's the driver) and I hoe into a Bloody Mary.

While Elle flicks through a glossy magazine I wonder what I'm doing here. I put it down to my recent trauma – which I can't even *bear* to *think about* – and the alcoholic binge I've been on ever since. I make a mental list of all the drunk decisions I've made since then: I was drunk when I met Elle at the Royalton, I was drunk when I allowed her to persuade me to fly to Australia with her, I was drunk when I made my reservation, I was drunk when I packed my bag and I was definitely drunk when I asked Ronald my limo driver to take me to JFK *asap*. My decision to go to a wedding near Hanging Rock in Victoria (you know, where the film was made) is just the latest in a whole chain of drunk decisions. I almost switch into AA mode at this point – you know, chastising myself for being in denial, picking myself up for just coping and surviving life when I could be living another way, and coming into full awareness about exactly where this kind of behaviour will lead – but I don't care. I simply have no faith. I do not deserve to be saved after what I've done. There is no God, no good, no higher power. There is just me and all my shit.

I order another drink – the cocktails here are so weak compared to New York – telling the barman to, 'Make it a double.'

I mean, it's enough to make me feel like a total alcoholic – like even *more* of an alcoholic than I feel in New York. Before coming to Australia, I would *not* have believed this was possible.

I slide my fingers up inside my cuff and check my wrists. The bandages are okay. The scabs are hard and dry. Cool – *God* that doctor was *cute* . . . I gulp my drink.

This one gives me a serious hit. In seconds, I'm calm and clear enough to remember I haven't had any breakfast and I become vaguely interested in eating but then past experiences with airport cuisine intervene and I change my mind. I pick the celery out of my drink and crunch through that.

'*Excuse me,*' Elle complains.

I'm too tired to argue it out so I just pick up my drink and take a walk through the departure lounge. I finish the celery and toss the stub into a bin. When I look up there's this real cute suit sort of staring at me – I'm like, I hope this guy isn't another psycho fan!

'This is really embarrassing,' he begins in his kind of nasal, clipped Aussie accent, 'but aren't you Sharon, the lead singer from Foetus?'

'Actually,' I correct him, suddenly conscious of my alcoholic breath and digging around in my bag for some gum. 'Foetus is the name of the CD, not the band, but yeah, I'm Sharon, *that's me* – or it was the last time I checked, any road.'

He laughs politely and gushes, 'I just *love* your stuff.'

I grunt, 'Uh,' and then ask him to hold my empty glass – I'm having a really hard time finding my gum in all the mess inside my bag. Finally I find it – thank God – and ask him if he wants some. He does, so I invite him over to the bar for a drink. You can't have too many men buying you drinks in this world, I've found, no matter how rich and famous you are.

He hesitates for around three seconds – it's obvious he's going to miss his plane. But whatever he's supposed to be doing doesn't have a chance because soon he's escorting me between the criss-crossing figures, reciting his favourite lyrics and touching me on the arm. I know it's just a matter of time before he asks me how autobiographical my songs are. I decide in advance that I'll tell him it's all true. He looks like he can handle it.

Noah ends up accompanying us to the wedding. It turns out he and Elle know the same people in Sydney – it just terrifies me how small the scene is here – and I have a great time pulling rank on the airline representative to get him a seat on the plane. Being a rock 'n' roll star can be so much fun.

We collect our hire car – I climb in the front seat next to Elle even though I'm way too out of it to navigate but, you know, a girl's gotta do what a girl's gotta do – and we follow the signs to Mount Macedon. It's like, really cold down here after Sydney. The sky is full of these amazing dramatic clouds and one minute it's sunny and the next it's raining. I'm pretty freaked about this driving on the wrong side of the road thing. I mean, I did a little driving through London but this is different, we're much more *vulnerable out here* and I *am* sitting in the front seat which means it's all much more *confronting* than catching cabs at night in London.

Things get really hairy when we turn off the main highway and head up the mountain.

'Hey,' Noah says from the back seat, as all the light disappears behind some really serious looking dark clouds. 'They should have had the wedding on Valentine's Day. That's the day the girls disappear in the film.'

I'm like, 'Hey, don't freak me out!' And there isn't even anything to drink on board.

'I bags be Miranda,' Elle says.

'I want to be Marion,' Noah says.

'Do you *mind*?' I say, putting a lot of spin on it. 'Some of us are trying to keep calm in here.'

'You can be Irma,' Elle says. 'She's the one who gets found.'

'I thought her name was Edith?' Noah says.

'Just count me out, okay?' I'm like, not in the mood.

It's only 1 p.m. but it's so dark Elle has to turn on the headlights. We seem to be going really fast and when I ask Elle about it, it turns out the speed limit here is quite a bit higher than the limits at home. I'm like, *wow!* It really *is* the Outback here. Finally we pass through this little town that, thankfully, doesn't seem to be too redneck, and soon we pull up outside this mansion with a garden which leads on to Hanging Rock.

I'm like, so fucking cold I'm ready to wear a blanket but when we arrive in the garden for our champagne – the view is totally *amazing* – I hear we'll be spending most of the day inside a heated marquee.

There are a few New Yorkers here and while we wait for the ceremony to start, I catch up with old friends. But when someone asks how things are with Robert and me I go into this total spin and end up running off into the Outback – not really looking where I'm going, not really caring – and throwing up quite dramatically at the base of a eucalyptus tree. I wipe my face with my serviette and rinse my mouth out with the rest of my champagne (miraculously there's some left in the bottom of my glass).

When I look over my shoulder I see Noah's followed me into the bush. I'm like, phew, it's only Noah. Anyone who likes my work isn't going to be too shocked by seeing me vomit.

'You okay?' he asks, handing me his glass of champagne to sip.

'Yeah,' I go, shaking my head at the champagne, thinking maybe it's time to slow down a little.

But when Noah reaches into his pocket, takes out a plastic sachet of white powder and asks, 'What about a line?' I'm like, me say no? Do fish *swim*?

'Great,' I say, thinking, trust a suit.

'Had a bit of a big day at the stock exchange yesterday,' Noah explains, a guilty look in his eye.

I'm like, hurry up, my whole being practically glued to the contents of the little plastic bag.

We do the drugs and rejoin the other guests just in time for the end of the ceremony. The bride and the groom each have a glass to smash according to feminist/Jewish traditions and soon it's all over. When they kiss, even the drugs can't prevent this choking sensation from welling up in my chest as things I'm determined not to think about threaten to burst up out of the primeval slime of my unconscious into the light of day. I'm like, no way, José. This girl's *determined* to *party*.

Ralph and I (Ralph is Demi's business partner), sneak out of the marquee between courses to smoke a joint. It's absolutely freezing outside – I'm wearing a summer suit in mint by Calvin

Klein – but he's quite cute and I'm really determined to get him off alone to see what happens.

It's getting dark so we don't go too far. We sit side by side on a bunch of moss-covered rocks and take heavy drags on the joint. Ralph's a film-maker and tells me all about this film he and Demi are working on about cannibalism and how he's just been taken on by one of New York's biggest film agents.

We make it roughly halfway down the joint and then our fingers touch and it's totally sexual. I can't wait for him to make the first move so I take the joint out of his mouth and lean over and kiss him passionately. In seconds we're making out against a tree. It feels great. Ralph's a good size for me and technically very proficient. I get quite carried away and come three times in a row. As soon as he pulls out the spell is broken and I find Robert forces himself into my mind against my will. I give in, and just look at Robert and smile and Robert smiles too, sort of sad and walks away. Overwhelmed, I start to cry.

At first Ralph asks me what's wrong, then he just holds me, while I sob my guts out against his shoulder.

'My poor darling,' I sob. 'My baby, I'm so *so sorry*.'

'It's okay,' Ralph says.

But I know it's not. 'I just want to go home,' I cry. 'Please, someone take me home.'

In the distance I swear I can hear these girls' voices calling out, 'Miranda, Mir*anda*.'

Everybody's going to keep on partying at The Lounge back in Melbourne but I'm booked to fly out on the last flight to Sydney. Noah, Elle and I slide, drunkenly, back into the hire car and commence the perilous drive down the mountain. I close my eyes – I just can't bear to know in the state I'm in – and the sight of Elle driving and taking turns swigging from a bottle of whiskey with Noah is just too much for me right now.

I relax a little once we get on to the highway. It's so flat, I can see the city in the distance, its tall buildings glowing and blue. Eventually I just give up. I pass out in my seat and leave the rest of the journey up to fate.

Monterrey Sun

Jean McNeil

Jean McNeil is from Novia Scotia, Canada, but now lives in London. She has lived and worked in Cuba, Brazil, Mexico and Central America, where she wrote the *Rough Guide to Costa Rica* and is an author of the *Rough Guide to Central America*. Her first novel, *Hunting Down Home*, is published in the UK by Orion.

∫

Monterrey Sun

October 15, Toronto

Yesterday Julia asked me to go to Mexico with her. I said, Are you serious? She said, I'm sick of slinging overpriced food at overpriced people. I want to get away from the restaurant, from the city. Just for six months or so. Come on, it'll be an experience.

I said no. We only met six weeks ago. She's older than me; her girlfriend can't go because of her job, that's why Julia asked me. What would she think of us going to Mexico together?

Today I saw this sign. It was locked to a fence outside one of the houses squished between the Vietnamese mafia cafés on Dundas West. Someone had painted on it in yellow free-hand capitals:

BE BLATANT

BE EMOTIONAL

RISK EVERYTHING

I was sure I had never seen it before. I just went on to work. This afternoon I got back to the place and it was gone. I retraced my steps, then I knocked on the door of the house where I thought it had been. A tiny old Chinese woman came to the door. I asked her where the sign was but she just shook her head and smiled beatifically. She didn't understand a word of English.

November 26, Raleigh, North Carolina

We left last week, on the twentieth. We came this way because Julia wanted to drive through the Carolinas and Georgia; she hasn't been back since she was fifteen and she wants to see them again.

We haven't actually seen much of the country so far from the Interstates, just one unbroken procession of starched poplars and sycamores lined up outside the window as if for inspection. We're both really bad at in-flight entertainment. We either talk about ourselves or make up stories about the weirdos we will meet in the South (Julia assures me the South really is full of extremists and idiot-savants, just like Faulkner says). But all our story lines are pure *Dukes of Hazzard* or low-grade Flannery O'Connor – we always have the same sinister grizzled gas-station attendant named Bobby who comes up to us and says, 'Cin I *hep* you, honey?'

We stay in the jeep from time to time but mostly we settle for Interstate chain hotels. 'We don't have to sleep at all,' Julia said at some point, and patted her pocket. 'Nose candy is cheaper than a hotel.'

'You brought coke across the *border*?'

'Relax, honey. We'll blow it before we get to Mexico. That would be like taking coals to Newcastle.'

Tonight was one of those Ramada Inn nights and we sat on blue chenille bedspreads, tractor trailers slip-streaming through the dark outside. We poured our beer into the evangelicised plastic cups we had bought in a grocery store.

Julia took the SHINE ON, JESUS one. It showed a skinny sad Jesus in a yellow velour robe. In his hands was a guitar. 'I didn't know Jesus played the guitar,' she said. I turned mine to the front. TODAY IS THE DAY it announced, with a sun leaking out of a bank of clouds that had the same shape as the state of Georgia.

'God, tomorrow we'll be in Georgia,' Julia sighed, looking out the window. 'It all looks so familiar. My father was working in Atlanta when we left the South.'

'What was he doing?' Julia still hasn't told me exactly what her father's job is.

She shrugged. 'Played a lot of golf.'

'What did you do?'

She grinned. 'Played with his golf partners.'

'You were sleeping with your father's friends?'

Julia raised her eyebrows. 'Their wives too.'

I didn't believe her at first. What would she want with these Dolly Parton women?

'They're not all Southern belles you know,' Julia said.

'Were you in love with them?'

'Not in love. More in lust.'

I propped myself up on my elbow and faced her. 'I can't imagine ever feeling lust for a woman.'

'Well that's all right.' She took a sip of beer. 'There are things I can't imagine either.'

'How old were you?'

'I don't know. Sixteen. Seventeen.'

'Jesus. Didn't you fall in love with any of them?'

'I thought I did, with one, anyway.'

'So what did she look like?'

'I'm surprised you're so interested.' I felt her eyes on me and turned away, embarrassed. 'She was a typical Southern woman,' Julia said, slowly. 'Very well brought up. *Bred*, as they say down here,' she laughed. 'She looked ten years younger than she actually was. She was so bored it frightened me. She used to have fantasies about running away to New York or Europe and I would say to her, "what then?" The scary thing is, I was seventeen and I think I was the most exciting thing that had ever happened to her. I mean, *seventeen*.'

She lay back down on the bed and looked at the ceiling. Suddenly the transport trucks had vanished and the only noise was the wheeze of the air-conditioner.

'What are you thinking?'

Julia didn't say anything, just spread her arms and legs out wide until they touched the sides of the bed. She swished them in and out, like when you lie on your back in the snow and make a snow angel. The bedspread bunched up between her legs and arms.

'I'm thinking that I hope she's happy, somewhere. I'm think-ing she didn't deserve a string of vain young women for lovers,' Julia said, still staring at the ceiling. 'Women like me.'

November 30, Savannah, Georgia

Early this morning we left the coast and headed inland through South Carolina. On our way out of town we passed Corinthian-pillared houses and then, not much further down the road, the swamp-poverty tin roof shacks.

'When I lived down here I was oblivious to all this. It's like I didn't even *notice* the tar paper shacks and the trailers,' she turned to me, a helpless look on her face. 'I can't believe myself five, six years ago. I mean, as a teenager you're trapped in some interior country like Chile – thin and authoritarian. You only see what you want to see. You just ignore the half-massacred plastic toys scattered out front. Or the seventies car carcasses in the driveways. Jesus it looks like the Third World,' she blew her cigarette smoke out into the slipstream. 'Or what you imagine the Third World to look like. We just entered our white houses like moths,' Julia continued. 'They were always this *searing* white. I guess it's called Suburban Gothic. In the cities it was always condominiums. We went to places like Bermuda or Jamaica on vacation. We still do.' She shrugged and lit another cigarette, taking both hands off the steering wheel to do it and driving for a moment with her elbows.

'Yeah, well. I've been here before,' I said.

Julia looked at me suspiciously. 'Where?'

'The Carolinas. Well, the coastal bits, anyway.'

'You never told me that. I thought it was your first time.'

'When I was sixteen I just took off,' I said. 'I stole my uncle's car and went to Florida. I just went to Key West, worked as a waitress for a month or two. I was reading all these F. Scott Fitzgerald books then,' I continued, waving my hands around in some kind of valedictory gesture to show her that was all over and done with. 'You know, like *Tender is the Night*, and what I really wanted to do was to go to the south of France and wear striped bathing suits and develop a delicate sensibility, through psychosis, if necessary. But when I was sixteen I was wearing floral dresses and had a perm. They never would have let me into France.'

December 4, New Orleans

I don't believe in the distances Julia says we are covering. Even when I look at the map. I can't believe the world really is like that, so flat and uncomplicated, that we can move from spot to spot. Who are we to be able to do this? We're nobody in particular; I'm going to be twenty in three months and she's a lesbian.

It's like I'm not interested in the places we go. They are places we pass through, like ghosts. It is the rest of the world that is in black and white; we're in colour.

Every day I watch Julia's profile. It seems to evolve, take shape, come into and slip out of focus against miles and miles of low cotton-dotted landscape. A serious profile, blonde hair, cut short, enormous blue eyes. I keep seeing this one expression: a small face with two dark eyebrows squinting in concentration. From the side, it really is difficult to tell whether she is male or female. Her face has the beautifully blank savagery of the animals I grew up with, the cunning but generous small animals of the Canadian winter: an otter, a wolverine, a fox.

December 8, Austin, Texas

When you see it on the map Texas looks huge and unnavigable and *in the way*, as Julia says. We drove over a series of interconnecting bridges and estuarine developments, by rows of wet-roofed warehouses looking like greased lozenges. The sky had a chemical burn, streaked with carmine. In Louisiana we drove through a town called Sulphur and on the other side of the border we sped through Orange.

When we finally arrived in Dallas two days ago we hit the make-up counter at Nieman Marcus. There wasn't anything of interest to see. We hung out there for an hour or so. Julia didn't buy anything. She dresses simply; jeans and a nice shirt, no jewellery, only a black plastic watch. She wears hardly any make-up, only lip balm.

We noted how the lipstick names oscillated directly from jailbait accessibility to femme-roadkill. I only remember it clearly because Julia and I argued between Sweet Nectar lipstick (for me, I was still technically a teenager) and Hellfire Nights Red (for her, even though Julia never wore lipstick normally – it was one of the concessions she made to Texas).

Even with lipstick on it was the cows being hauled and not the truckers who looked at us most kindly, their wet inquisitive eyes peering through the steel-slat trucks. The only other cattle we saw surprised us in the night with their pinto patterns and sleek eyes standing motionless beside the road, more like mechanical creatures than cattle, as if they had been planted there just to signpost us along our way.

Then we drove here to Austin straight through the Tornado Belt of the Texan south-west. We really wanted to see one. But it was too late in the year and all we saw was a sky like broiling seaweed spitting hailstones the size of baseballs. The headwinds were so strong we went through twice as much gas and Julia would pull up to the gas station, leap out of the jeep and dust off her thighs like she was a trucker or a cowboy and say, 'Hey Bobby, fillerup. The missus in the truck'll pay,' and the Bobbys would screw up their faces at her and I could tell they were wondering whether she was a boy or a girl.

She disappeared into the gas station to buy *USA Today* or some bad Texan paper I keep trying to read, the ones that dedicate themselves wholly to drifter stories and murdered prostitutes.

'What do you think?'

'Of what, that prostitute stuff?' She laughed. 'Nothing, *nada*, the usual cautionary drivel thrown at women.'

Julia really speaks that way – *cautionary drivel*. I tried to imprint the phrase on my mind, so that I could haul it out one day and impress someone the way she impressed me. Maybe she saw it on my face because she turned to me and said, 'You've tried to grow up through books, haven't you? When I was your age I had my own place, my own car.'

'I don't have that kind of money,' I stared out the window. I didn't want to look at her. 'I'll never have that kind of money.'

December 9, Nuevo León

Yesterday we saw the sun go down in Mexico for the first time. It looked different, russet, its rims sculpted, like a ceramic pot.

We were shocked by the town. I think we were expecting the second we set foot on Mexican soil we would enter into some exalted landscape vibrating with pain of a folkloric intensity. Instead we crossed into Low Rent USA – a glut of *maquiladoras*, McDonald's, liquor stores selling cheap tequila, and four-wheel drives full of Texans on sex-and-bargain-Marlboros daytrips.

The balance of power is shifting between us. Julia might be older but I can speak good Spanish. The first thing we learned this afternoon was the local version of hotel check-in (at least for unaccompanied women): sign your name, pay your pesos, run in the room followed closely by a posse of *gringa*-crazed local men, dump stuff on the bed, whirl round to pile meagre furniture against the door while I yell *¡Cabrónes!* (Assholes!) and *¡Chinga tu madre, wey!* (Go fuck your mother, punk!)

We lay on our beds and stared at the plum walls or read while the *cabrónes* lurked in the corridor. Julia propped herself up on her elbow and was reading some D-grade Kahlo bio called *Mí Vida de Dolor*. I was trying to read this massive book by Carlos Fuentes.

'I want to see Frida Kahlo's house,' she said. 'I'm going to add her to my Personal Lesbian Icons.'

'I read that Frida slept with women to annoy her husband,' I said. 'That doesn't seem like the pinnacle of lesbianism to me.'

Julia stubbed out her cigarette. She turned to me; she looked tired. 'Sometimes you take what you can get.'

December 12, Veracruz

We came to Veracruz, because we wanted to go to the beach. 'No beach here, *mí amor*,' people told me. 'It's all polluted. You have to go to the other side.'

At night gas flares from the refineries rip through the sky like comets. The city has that rage-built, nearly exhausted air of tropics port cities. Veracruz is the only place that meets our gringo expectations. It really is full of jump-ship sailors, people carrying sinister bundles, cantina-owners with toxic smiles, the wind-polished faces of harbour-watchers.

The hotel balconies overlook the pockmarked boardwalk, a hurricane-battered corniche. This evening we sat on our balcony and looked out on to the Caribbean, but it had the same dead oil-slicked look as the waters of the Gulf of Mexico we saw on our way through Texas.

'This is the kind of place where you wonder if your body really belongs to you or if it's some satellite, moored just off your periphery,' Julia said. We look out on to the palm-lined squares and storm-lit vestibules where in summer we imagine women who look like tragic flowers dance stately Mexican two-steps with sloe-eyed men.

December 13, Mexico City

We are coming into the capital city. The only thing we know about it is that it is the most populous city in the world and the crime and pollution are terrible. Car-jackings are common, so we have our passports nailed to our stomachs and some money stuffed in our bras. Suddenly we see a giant billboard set on high ground, sailing above the valley of Mexico. It shows a grey Christ on the cross, hanging and doleful. Behind him is a wild cloud-raked sky. Across the bottom of the billboard a neon message flashes off and on, off and on:

No tengas miedo.
Do not be afraid.

In Frida Kahlo's house in Coyoacán we stand looking at the canvases of some of her most famous paintings. They look a little dusty, they need a wipe. In Frida's bedroom everything is as it was when she lived here. Her spine-reforming corset stands upright on top of the bedcovers, a little ghoulish and lonely in its lack of a body.

'I just love it,' Julia says, looking at the hyperbolic canvases of self-immolation. Frida is see-through, her heart, her womb with her never-to-be-born child displayed. She's ugly, I think, with her monobrow and her moustache. Maybe they didn't have facial hair removers then, but if I were her I still would have done something about it.

'She was so gutsy,' she says, her eyes shining.

I know why Julia admires her. I say nothing. It leaves me cold, Frida's over-abandonment to pain. As if she were trying to prove to herself and to the world the depth of her capacity for feeling.

December 15, Huatulco

South of Mexico City the afternoon light pours straight down, a gilded curtain, into amoebic winter fields. The days seem floodlit. Along the roadsides of Puebla are yellow cornfields, the ancient food of the Aztecs. The maize has been raked and arranged in conical shapes that point towards a sloping equinox sun.

'I've never seen anything but that thin reedy sun of the Canadian north. You've been everywhere: the tropics, the Caribbean, Europe.'

'Yeah,' Julia sighs, something she does rarely. 'But none of them have meant much to me. I've been too many places. You get blasé.'

'I think the sun is a gift. I always thought it would release me into some kind of gilded future. I read the whole of the *Alexandria Quartet* just for the colours.'

Julia laughs. 'I knew you were going to say that. The way you romanticise everything. If I wanted to see the colours of Alexandria I'd just go there. Is that why you came here, just to see what colour the sun is?'

We are silent for what seems a long time. Then it is getting to be night, and we have to find somewhere to stop. The roads through Oaxaca state are notorious *bandito* country. There is hardly any traffic. In the twilight the mercury eyes of rabbits glitter as they flee the sides of the road.

I turn to her. 'You wanted company for the drive, that's all.'

'What?'

'I'm saying I think we should go our separate ways in Oaxaca, after Christmas.'

Julia shakes her head but doesn't look at me. 'But why?'

'I thought we wanted the same things. If I can't talk about what colour the sun is without you laughing at me I'd be better off alone.'

Julia is searching for something to say. I can see she wants to remain nonchalant. I can even tell what she is thinking, that she wants to live a life full of books, and I want to live my life through them. She will never want that, thinks it vain.

'But we've brought all these books,' she finally says, using literature as a lure – an old tactic. 'If we separate we'll never get to read as much.'

'That's hardly a reason for staying together.'

She reaches for a cigarette. I can tell she doesn't like this kind of emotion, this kind of change. It's too volatile for her. She wants everything to be easy. 'It's as good as any,' she says. 'We get along.'

'Do we?'

'Yes,' Julia nods, exhaling smoke. 'We do.'

The next three hours flatlands stream by in silence. The only other traffic is busloads of workers going to Villahermosa and the oil fields of Tabasco.

Then we leave the mountains and descend into the Tehuantepec isthmus, a place of gouged saline bays full of crustaceans. We pass through its night-sodden towns; Juchitán, Salina Cruz – whole towns of men in white cotton trousers slouching on benches outside blue cafeterias. The town squares are formal, ringed by floppy palms. At midnight these towns have the feel of smothered violence, as if everyone is just too hot and tired to bother knifing each other.

I drive the last stretch to the coast. The moon is full and a metallic light slants through the windows. The road is uneventful and I begin to wonder how I will stay awake.

After a while Julia falls asleep. She sleeps with her mouth open, shifting from time to time and uttering sleep-murmurs. She is drooling, so I take a hand off the wheel, lean over and wipe spittle from the corner of her mouth with my hair. It is about two in the morning, winter suddenly doesn't exist, and by morning we will be at the edge of the Pacific, an ocean I have never seen. Above us, I watch the moon ripen from pewter into silver.

December 16, Puerto Escondido

We arrived early this morning and we slept all day. At five-thirty I woke. The bed next to me was empty. I wandered down to the beach. The sky was the pale flesh of baked salmon. As the sunset progressed it changed, minute by minute, finally blossoming into ribbons of rebellious carmine.

I found Julia in a chair. Her shoulder still retained the heat of the sinking sun. I touched her, lightly. She turned her head and smiled as if she had been expecting me. She was reading a book she had stolen from the University of Toronto Library.

'It's really nice,' she said, without looking up. 'It's called *Monterrey Sun*. It's old, though. From the turn of the century.' She wet the tips of her fingers to turn the pages and began to read.

> *On the trees the coals*
> *of the oranges burned redhot,*
> *and in the burning light*
> *the orchard turned to gold.*

'It's just like that, in Mexico at noon, isn't it?' Julia looked up from the book and into the twilit sky. 'Everything looks like oranges on fire.'

The dark gathered around us in a pool. It was a strange darkness, marine and tropical, but tendrils of cold lapped against it. As Julia read on I felt we were being slowly immersed in liquid shadows sliding down from the summits of lime-dark mountains.

> *And me the sun stripped bare*
> *the fiercer to cleave to me.*
>
> *I bear within me so*
> *much sun that so much sun*
> *already wearies me.*
>
> *No shadow in my childhood*
> *but was red with sun.*

At night we lay in our double bed, heat-drenched. We both had a slight sunburn. The ceiling fan whirred slowly with the sound of winged insects. On the wall opposite the bed was a picture of Christ looking like a moony virgin.

'Have you noticed they look the same?'

'What?' I was half asleep.

'Our feet.'

I looked down to where our feet bobbed above the sea of the bed.

'This is really bad,' Julia said. 'You can't be friends and have the same size feet. I think there's a taboo against it in some culture, but I can't remember which one. They look like fish, don't you think? A little flat. Suspicious.'

Julia rolled over towards me.

'Your feet are covered in sand, you know,' she said. 'Just like Jesus.'

'How do you know so much about Jesus's feet?'

She put her hand on my shoulder.

Suddenly we were up against each other. We are both thin and only our hip bones and breasts touched. Julia looked at me, her eyes suddenly sharded, diamond-like from the patio light triangling through the curtains. Nothing happened, we just lay there, our skins both very warm from the sun, combining our heat like lizards, before it slipped away.

December 23, Oaxaca

This morning we woke into a troubled sky – a *Norte* had blown in, there was going to be no sun for a few days, so we headed here, to Oaxaca.

'It's the Night of the Radishes tonight,' I said. Julia scowled at the guidebook I was holding. 'The night of the *what*?'

'They sculpt historical scenes out of radishes. Religious ones too. It says here the main competition has set themes, but there's a free-interpretation one too. Last year the guy who won it sculpted a piece on the Right of Man to Free Expression.'

'How did he show that in *radishes*?' She seemed faintly disgusted by the whole thing.

I leafed through the guidebook. 'Doesn't say.'

In Oaxaca the streets are mostly hilly and narrow. It is the colours of the houses that most impress us as we walk around the town: shell-pink next to asparagus, banana, dried-blood colour, like a line of melting cherry, lime, banana and chocolate popsicles. On some streets whole rows of houses are bleeding into the sidewalk, four or five coats of paint exposed by irregular stuccoing. They look like they've been struck by some kind of building-attacking eczema.

'Here comes another patrol of Juan Travoltas.' A car of the type we have come to know as the Macho Mobile (red, blacked out windows) pulled up.

'Hsss,' hissed four squat faces behind a half-opened window of a Vega or Pinto or some other forgotten seventies car. 'Chiquitas,' they whined. 'Mira, mira qué linda.'

We ran into Santo Domingo, the main cathedral, for cover. Inside it was the temperature of a wine cellar and just as dark. Nuns lurked in the aisles like mummers.

We sat down in a pew and gazed at the giant inscription above the altar – El Verdad Rey, Nuestro Señor Jesus Cristo.

'El Verdad,' Julia repeated. 'What does that mean?'

'The truth.'

'The Truth,' Julia let out a sigh. 'You know, it's funny how everything seems questionable, now. I kind of miss the bullish certainty I had when I was twenty or so. I was so determined to get a place of my own, be independent.'

'Is that why you left your parents' house? Wouldn't it just have been easier to live with them?'

She looked at me quickly, then away, towards the gold-leaf altar. 'Because I thought it would be nice to have a lover.'

Something about that phrase really stunned me – it would be nice to have a lover.

'Didn't you want to wait for someone to come along who you really loved?'

'They're not exactly inimical.'

'But didn't you have someone in mind?'

Julia sighed, raised her voice, which attracted the alert gaze of the nuns.

'I didn't want to be pathetic.' She said it mildly. Her eyes seemed to be laughing at herself.

'I can't imagine you being pathetic.'

'Well, try to imagine yourself in a world where everyone you're attracted to is poised to ridicule you.'

'Why? Because you're gay? It's not like that any more.'

'Oh come *on*. If you grow up hauled from one town to another and then back to the sticks in Canada it is.'

'So you go about avoiding patheticness by playing it safe? By grabbing the nearest person who's convenient and making a lover out of them?'

She turned to me. She had the face of a hurt wolf. 'I'm not playing it safe with you, am I?'

'I'm not your lover.'

I don't know why I said that. It came bubbling up from somewhere deep inside me and broke the surface without me even wanting it to. Julia looked shocked then, and in her face I saw a shadow of my own eight years earlier, when I had cried because my mother had stayed out all night and she smelled of men and she took my twelve-year-old face in her hands, but not kindly, and said, *I'm not your lover*.

On our way out the nuns slid their eyes over our bodies at strange lizard angles. We walked out of the cathedral hand in hand. Girls in Mexico went around like this all the time we noticed – arm in arm, hand in hand, even with their arms around each other's waists. But at sixteen or seventeen this disappears and they're walking with a boy, leaning on him like an invalid.

She turned her hand over in mine and rubbed my wrist, kneading the place where my veins come close to my skin.

Out of a silence she said, 'It's nice, isn't it?'

It was one o'clock. Only tourists were on the sidewalks; the Mexicans collected like trout in pools of shade.

In the afternoon we went to see the radish sculptures being set up in the Zócalo. Contestants had set out Before photographs in front of their entry; in these they didn't look at all like radishes but like hairy tubers, branches wafting off them, red and swollen, like flayed penises.

Someone had set up a plaque explaining that the Night of the Radishes had replaced an earlier Zapotec festival on 23

December, when they had celebrated the *Nacimiento del Sol*, the Birth of the Sun.

The sculptors were putting the finishing touches on their entries: 'The Adoration of Christ'; 'The Coming of Columbus' and 'The Guelguetza', a display of Zapotec dancing. Each corner of the Zócalo was dotted with tiny stages where crude pieces of social realist theatre were underway showing big landowners abusing peasants. We walked past 'El Terror de los Toltecas' – the Terror of the Toltecs. Radish-relief showed battle scenes of reversed gore; red skin and white insides of lopped-off limbs.

'It's easier now that we've arrived, don't you think?' Julia asked.

'I don't know. Sometimes I think women use friendship as protection.'

'Protection against what?'

'Of not quite owning your body,' I said. 'Of having to go through the world alone.'

I felt someone clutch my elbow. I turned to find Julia, looking a little flushed.

'What's wrong?'

Suddenly Julia hauled me into one of the town's three hundred churches, an old darkened hulk on the periphery of the Zócalo. In the half-gloom I leaned against the cool stone wall, felt the damp seep into my kidneys.

Julia closed her eyes.

'How many times do you think you can make the same mistake?'

'What mistake?'

'I can't lie to you.' In the half-light her eyes seemed enormous.

'What are you thinking of lying about?'

Julia took a deep breath. 'Would you love me? I mean, *could* you love me, as a sexual being?'

'I'm not a lesbian,' I said immediately, without even thinking about it, and looked at her furtively, then around the church. The Stations of the Cross, serious in the gold and mahogany of Mexican friezes, stared back at me. In one Jesus was giving Pontius Pilate the moist look of a lover.

'I'm not asking you to be a *lesbian*,' Julia said, open-mouthed. 'Even if I was, what's so terrible about that?'

I dropped my eyes. 'I'm so tired I could cry.'

On the way back to the hostel we were sidelined by the pre-Christmas processions that thronged the streets, crowds holding coloured foil lanterns and singing carols. Between the processions snazzy pick-up trucks with illuminated fog lights hauled endless nativity tableaux. In the bed of each truck were four children dressed in blue satin. A strange woman, tall, pale, with red lips and frizzy hair, staggered into my path. I had seen this woman all night, all over the town, in different places. This time she held a giant sparkler, which she kept waving in my face. A huge star made of lights hung overhead, and strung between the buildings ringing the square was a panel of lights in the shape of a poinsettia proclaiming *Feliz Navidad*.

December 24, Oaxaca

On Christmas Eve we dine at the Hacienda, a restaurant on the outskirts of the city. Lurking in groves of poinsettias are huge steaming dishes of chicken in *mole*, the Oaxacan sauce made with chocolate, chiles and fruit that both Julia and I find too rich.

We sit surrounded by kaleidoscopic Oaxacan gentry, girls with huge satin bows in their hair and women in cerise dresses.

'I haven't seen *cerise* since the 1978 Sears catalogue.'

'It obviously escaped and is living as a fugitive in Mexico,' Julia says. She is in her habitual monochromes; the whites, blacks and beiges that made me nickname her Julia Armani. She looks retrograde, a silent-screen heroine in the midst of tasteless Technicolor.

Her shirt is open to show a brown chest; Julia tans faster than I do. Her lips are parted because she is laughing at something I have just said. She holds a cigarette; she's smoking more now that we're in Mexico and cigarettes are so cheap. She gives me an open look not unlike the expectation of flowers. Her face, her lines, her edges, promise some hard skill.

I stare at the slope of Julia's throat and her collarbones; it is delicate, clear. She is baring her throat at me, but it is not at all like the manoeuvre practised by small animals caught by a larger one who know their only way out is through submission. Julia's is a violent throat, the throat of a lover.

I put my fork down, say, 'I don't feel well.' Then I say, 'I've never believed in myself as a lover.'

'Oh,' Julia nods, lips pursed, as if she finally understands something she has been puzzled by for a long time. 'You think that's another kind of luxury I've had.'

Just before sunset we stumble out of the restaurant, stuffed and drunk.

'Shit, it's going to get dark.' Julia scowls lopsidedly into the deserted scrubland surrounding the Hacienda. Above us is a cucumber sky, its skin raked by the coming twilight. 'We should have called a taxi.'

'Why don't we walk?'

'All the way back? That's eight miles.'

'Just to the *cruce*,' I indicate the crossroads with the highway that leads to the Tehuantepec isthmus. 'We can get a cab from there.'

The sky is turning from salmon to a red the colour of pomegranate juice, spilling over the purple lips of the Sierra Madre Occidental. In the crevasses of shadows the evening burns from blue to night, passing through stages of mauve, amethyst, navy, onyx.

The soil is the red dust of the desert. Not far south the cacti begin, the ones that produce tequila and mescal. Four-wheel drives, the vehicles of wealthy suburbanites and peripheral dwellers of Oaxaca, pass us. In the twilight they look like giant silver insects.

'I wish we had flashlights,' Julia whispers.

'Why are you whispering?'

Julia grabs my forearm and holds her hand there. 'I don't know. But I think there's something moving across the road.'

We peer into the darkness, where brown forms, like very thin waves, have begun to skim across the road.

Julia is wearing leather sandals. I am in my hiking boots. Corded oblongs begin to swish across our toes.

'Jesus Christ. The snakes have just come out for the evening,'

Julia says, squinting into the dark. 'They must come out on to the roads at dusk because the asphalt's still hot.'

'I *hate* snakes.'

Suddenly Julia careens into the middle of the road, jumping like a kid on a pogo stick, trying to dodge them. I stay rooted to the spot while Julia yells at the snakes as they slip between her legs.

A silver four-wheel drive passes, tooting its horn at us and managing to crush two snakes. We can see their splattered forms, like flat bicycle inner tubes strewn across the road.

'Why don't they have any guts?'

Julia scowls. 'The four-wheel drive guys?'

'*Snakes*. They never spill out. They just go flat.'

Suddenly the sky darkens. Besides the cacti the only visible form against the coming night are the sisal plants spindling into the sky. Against the mountains they look like bodies frozen in the posture of supplicants.

The whispering forms of snakes continue to invade the road, but we have become calm, and don't even try to avoid them any more. Julia is laughing against the red horizon, fast turning to enamelled navy-blue. The sky is full of stars now, clumped and curdled. Julia cranes her head backwards so that her eyes slope downwards, and they look clear, infinitely mobile and limbless, like salamanders. We smile at each other and at the sky, and as the snakes converge from all directions, we twirl towards each other with the mistaken grace of intoxicated ballerinas, and kiss.

Touching Tiananmen

Gail Jones

Gail Jones lives in Perth, Western Australia, and is the author of two collections of short stories, published by the Fremantle Arts Centre Press: *The House of Breathing* (1992) and *Fetish Lives* (1997). She has travelled extensively in Asia, from East Timor to Afghanistan, and is a particular afficionado of train journeys (the Re-Unification Express in Vietnam, the Trans-Mongolian and the Trans-Siberian). Gail Jones also fetishistically adores certain European cities, especially (like everyone else) Paris and Venice.

Touching Tiananmen

It is a rare kind of fear, and an experience common to many travellers, that one awakens in the night in a state of absolute lostness. Furniture in the room is mere strange monuments, dimensions of windows and walls are false or incalculable, and the surrounding darkness seems simply to confirm displacement. It is a riveting shock: one sits bolt upright, like some monster in a movie, new to the very world.

Anna sat thus, lost in space. Her heart banged in her body and she watched, half-dreaming, the vague room of her small hotel bevel and shift and fail to settle around her.

'China, Beijing,' she whispered to herself – as though the words themselves might fix things finally, and in fact they did. The room halted and stilled; Anna adjusted her vision to the darkness, saw her luggage in the corner, recalled the position of her room, the face of the hotel manager (perpetually smiling), the façade of the hotel (fifties-totalitarian), the situation of the building in relation to the city centre, the highway, the bicycles, the many statues of Mao. China, Beijing – no delusion at all but an actual city, inveterate and substantial, and in which she now sought her annual vacation.

Like most cities it had been pre-empted by many versions. When Anna was driven that first day away from the airport she almost expected a skyline of pagodas. She had imagined vistas of lacquered roofs curled imploringly to the sky, tier upon tier of them. Some prospect rather like a willow-pattern plate, but one coloured scarlet and with embossed lettering of gold. Trailing cranes. A pond. The bow of a neat bridge. Mountains unreal and without perspective. And there was, or so it seemed, no origin to this vision, it was simply a confederation of cultural clichés, derived from who-knows-where and mysteriously insistent.

She sat in the rickety airport bus and saw through its glassless window not pagodas at all but a dense green wood of unfamiliar trees from which issued the drumming of millions of hidden crickets. And further on, into the city, rows of tall grey apartments, most of which were unkempt and in various states of dilapidation, and beside them public buildings of truly ostentatious ugliness. These had a state sponsored gigantism, a quality also evident in statues and posters of Mao which, unmet by the recent Soviet-style iconoclasm, persisted in their confident, moon-faced presence. Mao smiled hugely everywhere; he beamed from hoardings and school yards, in stores and on buses. Or he gestured to the future in marble poses. Something severely utilitarian governed Beijing; Anna felt almost deceived; she wondered where the exotic decoration was secreted.

There were of course touristic dimensions to the city; and within the first week of her visit Anna had trudged dutifully in and out of imperial palaces (noting that opulence for which revolution was finally the only response), climbed arduously and achingly a few kilometres of the Great Wall (recalling Kafka's perverse version within which he alleged it to be the foundations of the Tower of Babel), gawked inside temples (touched by the melancholy of the mere handful of monks who now attended them, by the Mao-looking buddhas, also gigantic), and searched out those few stores whose task it is to supply Westerners with trinkets and superfluities (ah, the brilliancy of cloisonné, the statues of jade, embroidered silk nightware and ornaments of lapis and coral).

But she remained somehow disappointed. Alone and monolingual, she was aware that she dealt merely in pre-visions and exteriorities. She knew no Chinese people, and walked among them like a kind of object, conspicuous but inhuman, inaccessible to them as they were to her, without insides, a doll. And when she had accomplished one by one the tourist locations, she was left curiously unsated and felt almost a physical hunger growing within her.

Anna did not leave Beijing at her travel-agent appointed time. She lingered, without particular cause or purpose, moving first to a smaller and less expensive hotel (that of the fifties-totalitarian façade), delaying her flight to Hong Kong again and again. She became suspended, as it were, in her own unidentified species of longing. Days were spent in the hotel room, lying behind shutters in the false luxuriousness of her new silk lingerie.

Then she began tentatively to venture, down the *hutongs*, or backstreets, in which were to be discovered little buildings, whole little communities, that existed almost in the crevices of the modern city. Below looming apartment blocks were remnants of shanty houses made of sticks; and away from the Chairman's smirking invigilation lives recovered their unbureaucratic disorder. Communal televisions blared loudly at squatting groups. Hawkers pushed handcarts of peaches or spinach. Tailors worked outside at ancient treadle sewing machines and old men and old women meditatively smoked. Children dragged toys or engaged in mock battles. Everywhere were bamboo birdcages placed to entrap crickets, and meat of extraordinary redness hung on hooks at windows.

As Anna lost herself there, irretrievably foreign, she felt the gazes of others resting upon her, like the lightest of touches on the nape of the neck, like a lover's caress. And when the gazes at last accumulated to the point of disturbing her, she would make her way back to the main roads, and there trace a route back again to the hotel.

The city became gradually stranger and stranger. At first, appearing both pagoda-less and high-rise-full, it had seemed comprehendible. But Anna began by degrees to perceive its particularities. The bicyclists of Beijing, seven million or so, moved processionally everywhere: in their inordinate numbers and slow-moving continuity they gave the city a kind of animated and silken effect, recalling a rippling of fabric, a perpetual motion of undulation. And the sound of crickets, which had at first seemed simply a quality of the forest, became ubiquitous. Even at the very centre of the city Anna could hear them. They were an invisible presence, rising, every now and then, to murmurous notice.

Human language also seemed somehow to have altered. Initially Anna had thought she understood the shape of Chinese, its intonations of enquiry, of affection, of polite conversation; but the more keenly she listened the more the language was complicated, the more sounds and circuitous patterns it contained. Her hope of achieving a tiny vocabulary of a few pragmatic phrases faded entirely away. She found herself feeling muted, without language at all. Only in her dreams did she speak Chinese, and then it was of some imperial and antique form, denoting not equitable discourse but that of a foreign devil somehow evilly collusive with old regimes.

As the language multiplied so too did the people, and Anna became overwhelmed by the sheer number of different faces she saw around her. The old woman who sold iceblocks from a tub-on-wheels at the corner, the man who each morning led a Mongol pony dragging a cart filled with watermelons, the youths at the hotel who smoked illicitly in clusters and then jerked to attention, mock deferential, as she passed: all these people now seemed possessed of captivatingly individual features. Anna found herself staring, as though some secret would yield itself if one of these faces opened up to her.

She had never before felt so irreparably lonely.

One Beijing day, a day in which that loneliness hugged her closely like a net, she re-visited, on impulse, Tiananmen Square and the Forbidden City. In the square itself all was festive and bright. Family groups sucked on ice creams and children flew kites that trailed dragon shapes with fantastical tails. Photographers had set up stalls covered over by umbrellas and with old-fashioned looking cameras snapped groups of people in what to Anna appeared exaggerated poses.

She stood behind one photographer and looked with his vision: a family of five – parents, apparently, with their over-indulged product of the One Child Policy, a girl of about seven, be-ribboned and be-frilled, another adult, perhaps the aunt, and an old woman in peasant black, the putative grandmother. Behind them, in the distance, was the threading apparition of Beijing bicyclists flowing westwards and eastwards, and beyond them the crimson gates of the Forbidden City, surmounted by an enormous square portrait of Mao and framed at each side by four huge red flags. Anna lowered herself to the tripod's height – all the better to see photographically – and noticed then that the parents were gesturing to her. They were calling her over to be included in their family snapshot and the photographer turned around to add his own cheerful invitation. Anna felt herself blush. She took a place in the group – between the aunt and the mother – and was instantaneously memorialised, there, anonymously, in Tiananmen Square. Members of the family bobbed, smiled and spoke Chinese; Anna retreated with uncivil haste.

As she roamed the square, singular and Occidental, Anna began to fancy that she was being followed. She looked back from time to time and there, indeed, was a young man upon her tracks, a man whose face had a distracted and agitated look, as though he himself was anxious or under surveillance. Anna wove a little in her path, like some devious spy, only to turn again and find she was correct in her surmise: the man still followed. She halted, summoned her courage, and walked back to confront him. The man shuffled uneasily and looked embarrassed.

'Amerika?' he promptly asked.

'Australia,' Anna answered, pleased at least that this man could converse in English. But then, quite unprovoked, he seized both her hands and with a kind of madman's intensity mumbled some sort of enigmatic slogan.

'Yoon faw, yoon faw.'

Anna was alarmed. She broke free and ran; she stumbled over flagstones and headed, heart pounding, in the direction of the

Forbidden City. When she slowed to look back the man had disappeared, absorbed into the crowd of milling people, itself unimpressed and indifferent to her flight.

From the look-out on the gate Anna peered over the square. She could see particoloured circles of umbrellas, people in holiday groups, and a contingent of Red Army soldiers, identifiable by their khaki uniforms and little caps, gathering casually at the Martyr's Memorial in the centre.

This was where, only one year ago, hundreds of thousands of students had taken up occupation. This was where a styrofoam Statue of Liberty, ten metres high, had been utopianly erected. This was where the military had murderously advanced through the darkness. Where tanks had entered and bayonets been raised. Anna found herself scanning the vista for tell-tale signs, for bloodstains or tank tracks, not knowing the square had been re-paved after the purge. Then she began to feel ill. She was aware of repressing memories derived from television: she would simply not allow herself to consciously recollect. Below her all was sunlit and apparently ahistorical. Bicycles moved along the Avenue of Eternal Peace, entrammeled in their own lanes and glidingly unreal. The sound of crickets drifted upwards from emerald coloured trees.

Anna entered the Forbidden City as though seeking refuge. The imperial buildings were so arranged as to imply security: she passed through gate after gate, through hall after hall, up and down series of steps and across numerous courtyards – architecturally it connoted an almost tyrannical orderliness. Geometrical. Severe. Contrived to express both the physical and metaphysical supremacy of each emperor.

It was also a site where Westerners were known to congregate. Anna roamed the crowds and chose to linger behind a group of German tourists whose leader pronounced on everything in a tone of schoolmasterish annoyance. The tourists were quiet and subservient, and one or two turned to smile at Anna as though she were a long-lost German. From somewhere nearby fragments of English commentary came drifting on the breeze: 'The vermilion colour of the walls is achieved by an admixture of pig's blood . . .' but Anna was reluctant to accede to the explanations of her native tongue, or to join actually or in spirit the group of Americans so addressed.

Anna drifted away from the Germans and wandered among the more numerous Chinese through the Hall of Preserving Harmony past the Nine-Dragoned Wall, into the Pavilion of Pleasant Sounds, losing herself in pagodas triumphally layered and curved, in room after room of palatial exotica. There were golden bells, extravagant timepieces and ceramic urns of exquisite artfulness. Blackwood furniture, latticed and carved, stood sombrely in corners and upon it were silk draperies embroidery-emblazoned with heavenly beings, phoenixes or brilliant clusters of chrysanthemums. Whole worlds had been carved of varieties of jade, the histories of which were related painstakingly on scrolls. There were astronomical instruments of brass, costumes of opera singers and eunuchs, and jewellery fashioned from every imaginable precious metal and stone. In one hall was a kind of funerary pagoda, perhaps two metres high and of solid gold, in which were retained fingernail clippings and cut hair of the Empress dowager. Oddities, spectacles, artifacts preposterous.

This was a peculiar alienation, to be wandering alone, excommunicated, among so many immoderate objects. Anna had visited this place before, but was now struck for the first time by its quality of obsessive artifice. Everything seemed covered over, embellished, fabricated or beautified. She felt both awestruck and suffocated, both enchanted and repulsed.

Anna made her way rather quickly through the remaining pavilions and halls seeking out the exit that was somewhere ahead, but found herself halted in a small courtyard that she could not remember having seen before. An Englishman was standing before a small stone circle lodged in the earth, and was apparently narrating a story to an assembly of old women:

One day – this was in 1900, almost the end of the Ching Dynasty – the Empress dowager was so annoyed with her daughter-in-law's, the Princess's, reforming zeal and rebelliousness, that she arranged her execution. In the dead of the night four of her eunuchs stole silently into the splendid bedroom, seized the Princess, and dragged her screaming to the well. Imagine, if you will, the cries in the night, the pleas of the woman as she was stuffed, headfirst, into this tiny hole. As she drowned, in the darkness.

Anna glanced again at the stone circle, and around it the rather melancholy group of old women, then hastily walked away.

Anna began to visit Tiananmen Square each and every day. She had no particular reason to do so, but was in some way drawn to experience again and again the disconcerting sense of a place which was historically amnesiac, which had obliterated its recent past so utterly and so efficiently. She could not have said why this phenomenon so strangely fixated her: she was simply adrift in another country, caught, after all, in the illusion of a continual, sufficient present. Otiose. Unmotivated.

She walked the large square and mingled, as though indigenous, with the camera-happy crowd at their summer-time leisure. There was always a long line of people – whom Anna assumed to be waiting to see Chairman Mao somewhere embalmed in his crystal casket – but otherwise there was the pleasurable roaming of groups such as occur anywhere in public domains. She watched the kite-fliers and the soldiers, the families and the publicly tentative lovers.

And each day, moreover, she watched the young man. Like her he regularly visited the square. He was always there some-where, and some days he noticed her presence and some days he did not. Anna never approached the man, nor he she, but began to look out for him, as though to locate his figure in the crowd was the actual purpose of each visit. She would buy an iceblock or a roasted corn cob and trail between groups, leaving after an hour or two; and only once she had sighted the object of her search.

It was on, perhaps, the sixth or seventh day that the young man approached her. With no subterfuge at all he simply walked directly to greet her, as if a meeting had been arranged. He stood there before her and Anna noted that he had a kind of haunted aspect to his face. He was handsome, lean, his skin beautifully ginger, but there was also some quality of despair, of prepossession. Anna imagined for a moment that this man would become her friend, that he would guide, translate, and at last open up the secrets of Beijing.

But in an extraordinary repetition – shocking now precisely because it had a precedent – the man seized both Anna's hands and again chanted out the slogan:

'Yoon faw. Yoon faw.'

She did not break away, sensing this time that the act was not aggressive or threatening, but simply inexplicable. Yet as the man noticed that she had failed to understand his words, he became distressed.

'Yoon faw,' he repeated. And he pulled Anna's wrists downwards so that her hands actually made contact with the warm paving stones. Then the man broke into tears, released her, and left.

Anna had a nightmare in which she roamed the Forbidden City on a pitch-black night. She was entirely alone, but around her drifted the most splendid objects: ceramic vases, silk garments, carvings of ivory and jade. As she made her way through the darkness these objects seemed to flow with her, as if held in mystical orbit by her body or her movement. She came at last to a room in which she saw the golden pagoda that she recalled from waking inspection contained fingernails and cut hair. But as Anna moved closer to the pagoda – it seemed to draw or compel her – the dream instantly shifted mode and she saw enacted before her the tale of the princess drowned by eunuchs. There was the dowager Empress looking on, and there was the struggling woman, screaming out her own doom. The four eunuchs, gloriously homicidal in ivory silk, seemed effortlessly to contain and transport the princess: they moved in dream motion, as if mounted on wheels. And though the prisoner writhed, caught in her mobile human frame, the Empress simply stood, regnant and cruel.

Anna watched the scene at first, but then became a participant. However she was not at all sure which character she played. She was simultaneously the evil dowager and the tragic princess; she was either or both; she was hideously divided. And as the woman was thrust down the well (both herself and not herself) there was a cataclysmic sound as the floating objects, their spell broken, came crashing to the ground.

So here is Anna, aroused in the night, and having uttered the words 'China', 'Beijing', relocated in that city. Awakened by lostness she now calmed her fear, becoming sensible and still. She felt suddenly a certain self-contempt and recrimination, that she had stayed so long in Beijing, wasting time and money, so aimless and indulgent. She sat in her bed and thought of her wanderings, of her visits to the square, her mis-spent days.

Then, quite unexpectedly, she realised what it was that the young man had been saying; she solved the riddle of his slogan. The young man – and how could she have missed it, how could she have been so obtuse – had been saying 'June four'; he had been commemorating the date upon which the Tiananmen massacre occurred. Anna had idiotically misunderstood.

Anna lay back on her bed, swathed in silk. She resolved to leave, to fly to Hong Kong. She closed her eyes, longing, passionately longing, for Orientalist clichés, for a city wholly of palaces, pagodas, bowed bridges and trailing cranes. Without history. Without the square. Without the young man, whose image she could not now eradicate.

Leaving

Bidisha

Bidisha was born in London in 1978 and, within eighteen months, found herself making the yearly journey to India with her parents. This annual trip, from which she would return thinner than she arrived, having given the local insect population the banquet of their lives, put her off travelling for good. Now studying at Oxford University, her favourite route is from restaurant to bar. Her first novel *Seahorses* was published in 1997.

ſ

Leaving

He said:

Where is my mother in my time of crisis? When I want her syrupy tea and her chipped cups, her rattling saucer with its antique spoon. When I want the fat ginger tom asleep in my lap, and her old videos, the embroidery, the tea-cosy – these all must wait as she treks her way past river bank and mud hut, as she digs a walking stick into red earth and peers across a foreign horizon crimped with palm-tree silhouettes. Nepal, Thailand, Indonesia, Tibet – what was wrong with Hereford and Hampshire, with Devon and Somerset? What did the Lake District do, to drive her so far? And Dad sits alone at home listening to the World Service and wearing brown jumpers. Big Sis, too, has folded up her oven gloves and burnt her apron. Occasionally she sends me photographs, poignant two-line postcards. Her love's still with me, always will be, she says – but even love gets dimmed when you're here in London looking at black roofs and thickly woven smoke offset by shit-spattered paving stones and clogged drains.

Sis underneath a giant bronze cast of an angel, wings wide against a Parisian sun; Sis in the centre of a marble-tiled square in Rome, holding a white hat on to her head and laughing into the distance; Sis in men's overalls and walking boots sitting on a natural throne – rock and grass tufts – out on some hike or ramble. And the nice English girlfriends – one is in Brussels speaking Italian and Russian and French for Defence; one is a marine biologist chasing dolphins in some turquoise Pacific water haven; and the other one – well no need to get personal.

You see them everywhere, the smart new women. Out on the street, walking in their low heels and their bright trainers, swinging the tote bag or the jewelled purse. In the afternoons, it's hard to get past them to order your coffee or pick your chocolate slice from its display case, because they're there, ordering the feta and chicken sandwich, the salad with no dressing, the ciabatta and its wafts of Parma ham. Then they sit round and cross their legs, smoking slim cigarettes and talking about Descartes – probably. Because you, I mean I, I've left by then. I leave the café with its smoked glass and sculpted wooden seats, its engraved wineglasses and designer ashtrays. Past the blue café with its stark metal chairs, past the faux-Japanese eatery and its bamboo-garden patio.

Back in my flat. Or rather – welcome. Shrug off your coat, slip off your shoes – or would you prefer not to, because I am a young man, and you are one of *them* – the smart new women. Because you've read the horror books, the fright headlines, the True Life Stories. I'll leave you on the doorstep then, fingering the rape alarm in your rucksack. Pizza boxes, Indian take-away cartons, a few M & S shopping bags – Evian and Volvic in the fridge, Stoli and Smirnoff – two types of noodle, two types of sushi. Designer aftershave, designer clothes, a hand-made suit or two. Pop music and opera, porn and *PC Week*, Psion organiser and Post-It notes. Messages on the answerphone: Dave, Steve, Stuart, Paul – a litany of nice boy names, a lullaby, register of masculinity. Ex-girlfriends: Jane, Lisa, Amanda – nice English girls, all of them.

I have that interview to transcribe, and the dictaphone sits with its red nervous eye facing me, atop a clean lined pad. But what use are the fashion designers, the photographers? These style mags that pile up with my name in them, these are all becoming obsolete – I am wiping myself out. New shapes are in for menswear this season – write about those, they tell me. And which colours are we all wearing? Grey, teal, midnight, jet, charcoal, gravel – and what do you have? Give me that beautiful hand – even on the nails you are Rose Divine. Teen Blush, Vamp,

Scarlet O'Hara, Plum Fancy, Heather Shimmer, Spring Blossom. I'll hack off the white hand and keep it here, in a window-box packed with ice, to bring some brightness into my flat.

Working out now – seven press-ups, eight. Today on my way into the office to drop off my editor Sean's videocamera I counted twenty beautiful women, none of whom looked at me. Of course they fell into types – shy redhead with heavy hips and long hair, coarse Greek with gypsy-strong shoulders, half-there blonde giraffe-arcing past the bus stop, cockney Asian feverishly trying on shoes in Office. What do you say to these women, as they hand over their credit card, as they hail a cab? Can you stop them as they go from shop to bar, as they sail past on the escalator? You could ask them the time, or give them one compliment, and their blithe smiles will cut through you in an instant. Left there like a split pea-pod, you'll wilt on the chopping board of your admiration, as they glint on to tear the heart out of other things – other vegetables like yourself. Twenty, twenty-one, twenty-two . . .

The abandoned press-ups, the shower-gel and the leftovers, the pub. Where do you meet women when you live a life like mine? Who do these women date anyway? – I don't know. I work in the same offices as them, I go to many of the same places, the same parties, yet never see them with their pants around their ankles, retching into toilet bowls. I haven't seen any of these women badgering the bar staff for a complimentary packet of lightly salted cashews, I haven't seen one fall over, get into a brawl, covet a man, have a catfight. They are sirens of social ease, they are harlots of decorum, these women – and, in their homes, in their converted space, sit their partners, James, an architect – or Matthew, a designer.

The Nun's Tears, the Stuck Hart, the White Angel, the Witch and the Raven, the Sole Dove. We congregate here, me and Paul/Mark/Jamie/Ben, and talk about all sorts of things. Music, sport, films – we aren't stupid, aren't oafs: Bertolucci, Barnes, Breshnev. But who's there to check, to tick off? Eventually we have drunk enough, and the most courageous of us says – have you heard from this girl, did you call that woman? Has the third got in touch, did you ever see the fourth again? The phone number the fifth gave you, was it real? Her contact

address, was it kosher? Our private lives have turned into one
mammoth negative. Matthew is off making logos in his study,
James is away creating a building for the South Bank – and we
are left, overturning the great No that our hearts have become.
The Virgin and the Cobbler, the Tart and the Blacksmith, the
Mistress and the Slug: this is the kind of stuff we want.

We have plans to write books, to set up clubs, to go on
outings. Slowly we are trying to form a conspiracy, a vendetta,
a homage to ourselves. But the books, the imagery, the stone
statue of the dictator, hand upon breast and war-boot upon
blackened trench-helmet – they're already there. The men's
clubs, the factories and corporations – marked on the map,
see, hundreds of years ago. But the painful vividness of your
lipsticked mouth and your coloured lid – Berry, Dusk, Damson,
Rose, Tulip, Forget-me-not – to capture and freeze them, to stick
them on a pin and put them in a glass case would be my goal. If I
could run around the town with a great butterfly-net and scoop
you all up . . .

Too nice a day to mooch about the flat so I buy another
sandwich. Raw and dripping meat in mattresses of bread – that's
what I like – preferably killed slowly and with bare hands by a
man in leather trousers and a jerkin – but instead, look here, a
tuft of lettuce, a pin-smattering of garnish, some odd modern
herb – and studs of seeds in the fragrant bread. I've always said
it – Prêt à Manger undermines one's masculinity. Forget it – I
renounce it – I'll sit in the park, in Red Lion Square, and listen
to London from beyond that fringe of lonely trees, the last left
in the area, boxed in with black rail and This Square Will Close
At Dusk signs.

Sudden spike.

Was that her?

Caught me off guard. But – to maintain some distance – there's
so much men can say about women's hair. The colour, the way
it falls, what it hides, the way when it's lifted up – she rounds
the next corner of the square – is it her?

There he sits, an ordinary bloke. I am sitting on the bench
opposite him, wearing my sun hat and a long white summer
dress, not the 'her' he is talking about. Writing this story in a

notebook with green Biro, in my modern-day romantic get-up. Although he is as readable, as open to psychological exploration as anyone who thinks they're alone in a park, eating a sandwich, I feel sorry for him. There's a great stone statue of two horses in a riot of passion or fear or some other Great Emotion between us, as well as a circle of vicious bushes and some wilting yellow flowers.

There he sits, an ordinary bloke. And here I am, an ordinary writer writing ordinary things, lusting after his sandwich and burning in the sun, thinking about a story I have to write. Travelling, journeys, feminism – I arrange my hat and dream of lipstick. Thelma and Louise – Cindy and Barbie. Yesterday I travelled between Oxford and London – from one to the other and back, in six hours, just to pick something up from the office of a library there. Last week I went to Sheffield for a book reading. The week before, Birmingham, Brighton. All on the train. No musty jeep, no motorways, no highwaymen, no cactus plants in the desert. No guns, no rapes, no robberies. No pit-stops, no fusty motels, no sexy hitch-hikers. Just the sandwich stall and the fat tourists, the grim guard and the fumble with the ticket; the giant screens and the Main Concourse, the Underground sign and the train-departing call.

I was the shy girl at school. The one who loved corners. In the dark was where I flowered; I unfurled green leaves when the door was closed. Locked in the toilet cubicle, I reached up to the sky. Behind a large hardback, something in me budded into colour and life. Once there was roof over my head, and four grey walls, I blossomed, but the searching eyes of others – the magnifying-glass stare they gave me, through their mascara and my huge spectacles, made me shrivel and burn myself out. Just left a spot on the carpet, a singe-mark by the wall, a puddle on the chair. So these recent journeys, alone and on the train – they mean a lot to me.

At university I discovered that I could wear knowledge like a coat-of-arms. From over the hill would come the battle cry, the goat's horn guffaw of the rowing team, the rugby team, the football team. But there was an army of us, too, and we held up that banner of learning. The myopic and hunchbacked polyester set, calling our parents every evening and spending our money on blotting paper for our fountain pens. Thursday night was trumpet practice, Monday afternoon was chess club. The Christmas party, the May Ball, the autumn celebrations, the formal dinners – we slicked on orange foundation and pink gloss and bought hard satin dresses, sat lining the walls each holding a glass of undrunk white wine. The popular people frightened me, the good-looking people who turned my legs to quivering stalks if they were near me. They were like a pack of horses, glowing in the dark, glistening with their skin like that, shaking their manes. I couldn't walk down the high street on my own. I couldn't hail a cab, buy a bus ticket, ask for a book in a shop. I couldn't return garments, do the weekly shopping, ask for no salad in my sandwich. I couldn't walk around a museum without tripping; I couldn't sit on my own and eat a sandwich in a square in the capital.

But it's funny how things change. Now you'll find me here, in the thick of it all. Own flat, work, friends. I can go up to the bar and order my drink. What's more, I can order two drinks and carry them back to my table without falling over. Until three months ago, I'd never taken an overground train. And now – I look at the maps, at the lists of times and the long columns of waiting trains, and know: I can go anywhere. To the north coast or the south, to a cottage in acres of green or a stony townhouse in a cobbled district. I can hire a bike or a car when I'm there. There'll be a shop where I can buy food for the two, three, four weeks of my stay. A tea-shop where I can drink Earl Grey and watch people. Once I would have stayed indoors. I would have gone out every evening, sure, but only to rent a video. Again. And then I would have dialled for my crispy fried duck, for my chicken tikka or my beef satay. Because the outside world, as they never stopped impressing upon us at school, is a big and scary place.

Look at him opposite me. He's finished his sandwich and for a moment juggles with the plastic casing, trying to get it shut and stow it back in the Prêt à Manger bag. Because he's noticed me, and he wants me to know he's a good citizen. He leans over and throws the lot into the bin, a neat small package compacted by his great hand. Which is something men don't notice. You women out there, reading this on the coach, at the desk, in the bath – ever compared your hand with a man's? Even you who work out, who spend days in the garden, or playing the violin, or typing – doesn't matter how strong you think your hands are, place them beside a man's and your sweating palms become what poetry knew they were all along – lilies, rose-leaves, and your thigh flank is probably only two-thirds of his; he weighs double what you do. So this is why he shouldn't be frightened of the Smart New Women.

This morning, before seeking solace in the green shadow of this square, I had to drop something off at an office. Beaumont Road, Beaumont Mews, Beecham, Beechly Park, Beech Garden – the park names evoking cricket and roses belonging to that most beautiful sector of London architecture: wide white streets. A thousand drunks might roll in the gutters, God smite the rooftops with a thunderly hand, a little old lady might be having her purse shredded on the corner, yet you'll still turn in and, for a moment, think: wide white street. How serene, how pale. As I was coming back, walking slowly towards the bus stop with my hat and a bottle of water in my hand, I don't know if I saw a mugger or not. Don't know if I saw a thief, a rapist, a killer, a dealer, a regular nutter. What I mean is – there was a man in a metallic blue Porsche parked on the opposite kerb. There we were, I walking and he sitting talking on the car phone, both of us on the street and nobody else there under the angry sun. And suddenly it was put into perspective. Small female walks street alone. Between us two, though he wasn't yet looking at me, I felt a flicker of connection light up and slowly burn into fullness. He saw me and called out – I carried on walking. He put down the phone and started the car. He called out again – I ignored him and walked faster. The car cruised beside me like a shark swimming in London's static heart, he constantly calling, and then – then – he told me I was very rude! Can you imagine? I was very rude!

The point is this: men can go anywhere. In the car, on the phone, with the credit cards in their jacket pocket and the passport in the glove compartment. Nobody asks where they're going, when they'll be back. They can sail, they can drive. They have the money power and the social permission – because, after all, who must they ask permission of? In the shining blue Porsche he could have gone anywhere – and knew it. With the gold signet ring glinting against the open window he beckoned: beckoned to the girl with the useless purse strung over her shoulder like a kitten's toy, a doll's purse. Taking a walk. Asking him permission to take a walk.

So when I step on to the train with my purse and my chequebook and a novel and a magazine in my bag, and when I order room service and test the unfamiliar shower, I feel good. When I hold a hand aloft and a cab stops and I give an order; when my food arrives; when I tip the waiter. When I look at the streetfinder and find my street. When the night bus is already waiting when I arrive. When I give my phone number or receive a fax. When I make arrangements.

I am leaving things behind and I love it. The blue Porsche in the distance, getting smaller. The little hurts and little hatreds, the heartstrung memories – now I can leave. I can buy a place anywhere in the world.

He said:

I thought that was her. The third girlfriend. The One – whatever that means. The one whose answerphone I call insanely in the middle of the night. The one whose favourite bar I go to as often as I can. The one whose name I don't mention. The one whose name makes me wince if it's said by other people.

When we went out to dinner I was jealous of the food she ate. I wanted to thrust a fork into the gloating centre of her moules marinière, I wanted to flatten her sorbet in my rage. The wine bottle had the pleasure of touching her glass. Her glass touched her lips more times than mine did during that hour. I wanted to take home her cutlery.

Her phone rings late into the night, but she has moved out and on. She lived round here, in a small immaculate flat with art prints on the walls. She had a small black rucksack and listened to the radio all day. She drew pictures for a living. She had dark brown hair that fell just to her shoulders. Those are what I remember, and assembled together they make a stringy bouquet of attributes. They make a small and feeble homage. But that's what I'm left with – a bag of bones, some relics.

We had a fight; she was due to leave the country; she did

indeed leave the country. What I had wanted to say, then, in that final call I made, three hours before she was to leave for the airport, was: well, it was the stuff of padded Valentine's cards, it was the stuff of sugared almonds and pink carnations. To grovel in the dirt and beg, to clasp one's hands and kneel in beseechment, it's difficult to do. And, whatever she was feeling about me at that time, however deep it may have been, half her mind was on other things. For all the hurt or joy that centred around my dim existence here, part of her consciousness was levelling its telescope upon – I don't know. New things, distant things. A national air which smelt different to Britain. Different brand names, a new transport system. New coins to sort through, new customs to observe. A different cultural canon. Small things like that.

Do you know the feeling when someone you've loved leaves the country? Say, only two or three months ago, for instance? With whatever half-tender kiss-off they give you, with their dismissive flip of the white hankie – they know and you know: you've been left. You see the sad old men shuffling in their brown shoes at grown-up parties. The women with their knee-length skirts and their glasses strung around their necks. He left me; she left me. I came home and s/he was gone. I called and the phone kept ringing and that's when I just knew I'd never hear from her/him again. He wrote to me once he got there. She sent me a card. We never saw each other again. That's what you'll hear, if it's late enough in the evening, if they've had enough to drink. All the shock bubbles up to the surface and spills out.

She left me, and the next day I went out, and saw that London was a single shade duller. The newspaper man, the commuters on the train, the girls in the cafés – one shade duller. I sat down in Chez Dolores on the first really hot day of the summer, and opened my paper against the season's white front. But I couldn't read. I couldn't sit, drink my coffee, watch strangers enjoying the weather. I didn't want to go home to be alone and read magazines or play music, I didn't want to go to buy clothes, I didn't want to call my friends. I wanted to leave.

More than anything else I felt total anger: that she'd had the presence of mind to book the ticket, to pack her things. That she didn't need help from me. She'd already arranged to stay somewhere when she got there. And I felt jealous of the luggage-handler, the air steward, the porters, the cab-driver.

The shadow passes across his face as he sits looking at the ground. He doesn't know what he looks like but he's right about some things – one shade duller is what he's become. I've no doubt that within the week he was out at parties and clubs, out with his friends. Because that's the industry he works in. There are launch parties and gallery openings and private viewings every night. There are intimate drinks parties where you meet thirty-five new people, there are informal soirées where the greatest deals are struck. London makes this possible for the man about town – and he is, despite his private thoughts and private fears and private whatnot, one of the faces, one of the men one sees, one notes.

Incidentally, the woman of the 'is it her' sequence is in fact her. She's come back for a couple of weeks because she's helping a friend with her MA exhibition, helping to curate it. She's staying with that friend in a great and beautiful warehouse by Old Street tube station. The area is a swatch-sheet of greys but the warehouse, which is new, has massive windows and rich wooden floors. The kitchen worktop is the colour of granite. The bathroom has enough space for a wide chair, books and plants. Two cats spend the day asleep, curled around each other on the long sofa. Tea and coffee are always being made – songs are being sung all day, in the warehouse.

She is walking finally down the third side of the square, but he doesn't see her. She is wearing a red fitted T-shirt and black trousers with flat black sandals. There's a simplicity to her appearance which is immediately noticeable. Something in her small, basic slimness, her neat and shiny hair. She has perfect skin. She appears to be thinking of nothing, but her mind jabbers to itself constantly, with cold and ecric echoes:

She says:
Separatism is my ideology. Separatism is the way forward. Autonomy and separatism. To keep apart, to be alone, to travel, to walk, to take the bus. To not answer to anyone else. To have no message on the machine wondering where I am. That the coins in my wallet are mine, that the book in my case was bought by

me, that the T-shirt I saw today was purchased for myself alone, that I walk by groups of men and that they seem like different columns of shadow, that they seem like pillars with masks – that is my triumph.

I have seen Paris. I have bought my apartment and I have started my job. On my desk in my office, which overlooks changing groups of beautiful people, is no framed broad face or manly chest. There is a picture of the view from a Virginia bus. There is a photo of New York. There is a snapshot of Madrid. And I am in all these photographs, alone and smiling. Letters arrive for me from addresses all over the planet; I travel all the time and now I am back in London, my first city.

There have been many, many lovers. In hotel rooms, in coaches and planes, in my apartment, in the apartments of friends. In my wardrobe are fabrics of every type and colour – chocolate velvet, burnt orange silk, cranberry brocade, midnight cotton. I am so young. Every morning I look at myself in the mirror, after washing my face and taking my vitamins and, as I'm smoothing on the moisturiser, I repeat it to myself – I am so young. The world waits upon my doorstep with its heart on its sleeve and orchids in its hands.

In the next few months I will be in Dresden, Berlin, Rome, Istanbul, Munich, Budapest. In the next few years I will live in New York for a longer time, I will see Washington, I will try Venice and Vienna. Without anyone to clutch at my cuffs or weep by the front door. Without anyone to whom I owe the fidelity of letters, without any teary-eyed person begging me for more information, bleeding dates and times out of me.

When I travel, all the minor histories and all the petty dramas are sunk into the shrinkage of the land. As the plane soars into spongy blue the things that tore at my heart quiver and cry out and perish away, the people I burned for in the night get smaller, become like blots, then pin-points. And when I get to my destination, I make enquiries – the gym, the shops, the travel arrangements. I get my money and put on my flat sandals and go to explore the town. I always have money with me, I nearly always know the language, or some of the language. And I map out to myself every unfamiliar street – dodging past heavy men with their unwieldy maps and their dullard stares, reclaiming the streets that time or history or culture have withheld for so long. The cathedrals, the galleries, the museums, the shops, the temples, the bars, the clubs – I rake them over with my eyes and make them mine. Later, drinking alone and looking at my newest sky, adding this piece to the ever growing differently-blue jigsaw in the dome of my consciousness, I think not of the past but of where I'll go next, what things I'll see tomorrow, what people I'll befriend. What lover I'll take.

To take a lover. Before, it was the domain of bodiced women at the opera – a younger lover, a lusty squire, a thrusting knave was theirs for the night if they didn't mind the jibes afterwards. If they didn't mind the gossip in the servants' quarters, if they didn't mind how their sagging skin looked against adolescent haunches. They would pay for it, I suppose. But for me to take a lover – I could do it every night. I am a healthy and fit person. I can pin arms and shoulders against beds, I can break and make grips, I can knot limbs. I can cause sudden or slow pain – but of course they are not to realise that. The classes, the white kit with its changing belt, the leotard and the sprung ramp, the musty gymnasiums and modern fitness rooms of the world's richest places: that also is my territory. I am capable: I can run for miles, I can chop wooden blocks with the side of my palm and break a shin-bone or a collarbone between my thumb and forefinger. In my thigh-muscles is the force which splinters bone marrow.

There was someone, when I lived here. There was indeed someone.

Indeed. I like the way she says that to herself – so decisive. Who knows what other things she thinks, in the privacy of that book-filled bathroom? As she sinks down beneath thirty inches of bubbles and aromatherapy oil, what silent things creep into her brain? At the corner she lifts her arm and the cab stops. Old Street, she says, and then she is off.

This summer I'll be going to America with my best friend. Staying with her mother and her aunt, and later another friend. We'll hire a car and take it across the country, eating breakfast in a new place every day.

Every morning I wash my face and look at myself in the mirror. Today I thought: the world is waiting on your doorstep with a rose between its teeth and its heart on a silver platter. Soon I'll have to pack. But it'll only be a few things; the rest, I'll buy on the way. Those will be days of radio songs in the moonlight, of whispered secrets, of house-parties and beer. Every twelfth hour will bring about a change of scenery, the sky one or two shades more lilac, more blue, more hazy-grey – who can tell? Who knows what things fate hoards to hurl at me, when I finally alight in that country?

I get up and smooth down my dress. A breeze is passing through the square but he doesn't notice. I wait for him to look up and see me but he doesn't, so I leave him sitting there alone.

Okay So Far

Ali Smith

Ali Smith was born in Inverness, Scotland. She won the Saltire First Book of the Year Award and a Scottish Arts Council Book Award for her collection *Free Love* (Virago 1995). Her novel, *Like*, was published by Virago in 1997. She lives in Cambridge, has done a great deal of travelling and hopes to see a lot more of the world.

∫

Okay So Far

We have come a long way. We have travelled half the world in less than half a day. We've watched films above the Atlantic, we've seen motorways from the tinted windows of Greyhound buses and we've gone back and fore in trams and taxis to and from and round the streets of several cities new to us. This is our first rail journey here, and we are so sophisticated now in our travelling that the inside of the train is far more interesting to us than what's beyond the window.

Inside the train the seats are covered in green leather. They have headrests that are just too high for either of us. Each double set of seats has its own disposable litter bag hung on a small bolt below the window. There are different rules about where you sit and even how you get on the train; an escalator took us from the neat queue in the station to the correct platform, a few people at a time, and each carriage had its own specially designated destinations. And now here we are, in the right carriage sitting in the right seats.

We have been on this train for four hours. You are still reading the newspaper you bought in the city we left, reading about which films are showing in which cinemas and telling me what we could have gone to see if we had stayed on there. I am watching light from the woods with their shaded patches of pockmarked snow, or light from the winter-empty small towns decrepit with backlots, as it smashes and changes and slides on the green leather headrest in front of me.

A small girl stands up further along the carriage. She looks about nine, and she pushes her arms into the sleeves of a jacket. The man she's been sitting beside, the man I thought was probably her father, doesn't even look up. She looks far too young to be travelling by herself. But she is, and she comes down the aisle with her jacket shrugged on over her worn sweatshirt, rumpled like a child who's just woken up and come to the breakfast table. As she passes our seats she looks straight at us, at me, looks straight at my face, my hair and my clothes. The train slows to a halt and she goes past with the other people waiting to get off.

The train begins to move again. Was that girl travelling by herself? I say.

Looked like it, you say. I think she liked your boots. She was watching us over the back of her seat. Didn't you see her?

No, I say. I didn't even notice her.

You settle back behind your newspaper. She watched us for quite a long time, you say.

I look at my boots, then I stretch my legs out under the seat in front and settle down to doze. Last night we stayed in a Comfort Hotel. There are Comfort Hotels everywhere and we can only just afford them; tonight when we arrive we will be staying in a French version, a Château Comfort. Last night you pulled the covers back, you turned the pillow over so we couldn't see the cigarette burn in the pillow slip, and we lay gingerly apart on the narrow strip of bed avoiding the faded stains and bloodspots left by all the other people. You were lying with your back to me, and in the half-dark lit by the street outside we listened to the rain on the window and the television noise coming through the walls, and we fell to playing one of your games, the one where I have to guess about who's dead and who's still alive.

Kenneth Williams, you said.

Oh, I know this one, I said. He's dead, he's definitely dead.

Right, you said. André Previn.

He's still alive, I said, at least I think he is. Isn't he?

Which, come on, which one is it? you said, he has to be either alive or dead, a pound if you get it wrong.

He's alive, I said.

Right. Arthur Askey.

Dead.

Saul Bellow.

Alive.

Katharine Hepburn.

Alive. Just.

Um . . . Frida Kahlo.

Dead.

Nena.

Who? I said.

Nena. Nena who sang Ninety-nine Red Balloons.

Oh God, I said, I don't know. She's in purgatory. No, she gets a special medal, a special place in heaven reserved for people who completely disappear after they've given themselves over like that.

What do you mean, given themselves over? You mean she's dead?

No, I mean gave herself over, I said, made up the, the, you know, backdrop to times of our lives.

The backdrop?

Yeah, you know. The cultural backdrop.

Oh, the *cultural* backdrop. So. She's dead, then? you said.

No, I was just—

Dead or alive? you said.

Christ, I don't know. Alive.

Hah. Lucky guess, you said.

Anyway, how do *you* know for sure she's alive? I said. How do you know she's not dead? Maybe she died earlier this evening. Maybe she's right this minute, how do you know—

I know everything, you said. Now. Ginger Rogers.

Alive, I said, and you turned with your face so close to mine that I couldn't see you properly, you were so close; you made a triumphant noise, two dollars, you said, that's two dollars, altogether that's twenty-eight you owe me, that's fourteen quid. I looked right into your eyes, we were laughing, and I said, Ginger Rogers will never die, she lives forever, she's an immortal and I'm paying you nothing, and we were both laughing, and I open my eyes on the train with you next to me, your newspaper folded on your lap, because I hear you saying something, you say it again for me, Where do you think she was going by herself?

and I say, Who? That girl, you say, the one who was looking at us, the one who got off at the airport stop.

Was it an airport stop? I say. Then she was probably going to the airport.

Yes, you say. Brilliant. But why? Why was she going to the airport? Was she meeting her mother? Was she meeting her father? Where was she flying to? Was she scared of flying?

She didn't look scared, I say, and I think to myself how that small girl, though I only saw her for a few moments, looked like she wouldn't be scared of anything. I think about when I was that age and wasn't scared of anything. I try to remember her looking at us, seeing us so easily together, I imagine what you and I must look like together, then I think of her looking at complete strangers with that blank nine-year-old directness. It takes me by surprise that I'm a stranger with clothes and boots on that can be looked at and decided about.

I decide someone was picking her up from outside the station, waiting in a car to take her home. Then I remember something I haven't thought about for years, my father in the car we had when cars were still like metal shells, and instead of going straight home we drove round by the football field so he could see if there was a game on, and I was leaning against the door and the door swung open, and he reached over from the driver's seat and wrenched me back in by the arm, the car swerving towards the kerb as he caught the door by the window winder and slammed it as shut as it would go, though air and light still came in the crack where the door didn't fit.

Maybe her father, I say, was coming to pick her up at the airport.

No, you say, I think her mother. Her hair needed combing.

Right, I said. So she's obviously been staying with her father and now she's coming home to her mother after a weekend of unwashed clothes and uncombed hair. She stays with her father every third weekend. He lives in Toronto and her mother lives in Montreal. Well, near Montreal, at the airport.

Okay so far, you say. Keep going.

They split up, I say leaning back in my seat, probably because of the French English split.

And she goes to her father's house every third weekend, you

say, and he takes her to that diner we went to behind that burnt-out cinema and they have the same thing to eat every Sunday.

Burgers, home fries, onion rings and ice cream, I say, since that's what we had when we went there.

Well I don't know, you say. I'm not so sure. She didn't look miserable enough to me, to have parents in two different cities.

Yet another place is veering towards us, its lights in the seeable distance, and you are already flicking through its guide book. I shut my eyes. God help us, my father says in my head. Sit away from the door. So I huddle towards the gearstick, I can't remember the make of the car, I think it was green. God help us, eh? he said again, and nudged me with his elbow. And for God's sake, he said when we drew up outside the house, not a word to your mother, we won't tell her, don't tell, eh?

I didn't. I didn't tell anyone, not for years, not till I tell you, tonight, in our next hotel. In my memory I am not telling, I'm sitting on the kerb by the car racing bits of stick across the sky in the puddles and looking at the road, which has the same kind of surface as the one I nearly hit, the one sliding beneath the car an inch from my eye as I hang upside down over it. Some roads have smoothed tarmac that melts in the sun in the summer, it comes off on your feet. My other road, the road I now think of as mine, the road I so nearly grazed, has the kind of surface that could take the skin right off a face.

This latest hotel is a bit old-fashioned, flouncy, a bit flowery, but comfortable, not too worn. We have a back room which means we won't be kept awake by the noise of the traffic. We have spent the evening deciding which things to go and see tomorrow on our one day here, and now you are lying on the bed surrounded by discarded books and half-unfolded maps. It is very warm in the room; the air-conditioner is blasting out hot air and we can't get the window to open. You have almost no clothes on; your clothes are in a pile on the floor. The words rise to my mouth, right to the tip of my tongue, how very lovely you are, lying like that, but I don't say them, I sit on the bed and tell you an anecdote instead, about how when I was small I nearly fell out of the car and my father leaned over and caught me just in time.

I had bruising round my wrist from where he caught me, I say, you could see his fingermarks. It took a fortnight to fade and all the boys at school wanted to know how I got it. I told the teacher my wrist was sprained. I told her what my father told my mother, that I'd fallen out of a tree on to it. The teacher let me off sewing and knitting for weeks.

You don't say anything; your eyes are closed. I suppose you're asleep and you haven't heard me. I lie back on my side of the bed. I look at the cornices on the ceiling. This house used to be someone's home. This used to be someone's room, and this is the strangest thing about travelling, that when we get back these rooms and these cities will mean more to us than they do while we're actually here in them; the carrier bags with the names of museums, art galleries, shops on them will mean more than this does; this lying in a room in just another place breathing its warmed-up air.

I put the light out, and it takes me a while to realise that you're not asleep at all, that the slight noise I can hear above the air-conditioner is you, controlling your breathing so that you won't be heard, holding yourself still so I won't feel any movement of the bed. Later, after you've stopped crying, and when you're in my arms for the first time in a long time, you tell me this story:

Before, every year in the trades fortnight we would go down the east coast, to Filey or Scarborough, Whitby and Whitley Bay, places they could take the caravan. It was just me by then on holiday, eventually there was just me left to take, my sisters all got too old to want to come, and that's how I try to think of it, the three of us, all still together; my mother, my father and I in a kind of companionable nothingness where nobody spoke much, nobody said anything; my mother smoking, her elbow out of the open window and her cigarette-air blowing into the back of the car where I was sitting with my legs stuck to the car seat in the heat listening to Tony Blackburn on the radio, that song about beach baby beach baby give me your hand, or Gilbert O'Sullivan, that song he had about how good his children were, do you remember? You could tell something sad had happened to the people in the song but the song never told you what, and my father driving with his shirt sleeves rolled up and his shirt undone, and the caravan lurching along behind the car. And then there was always the time when we'd get to the caravan site and my father would put up the awning, he'd be in a foul mood, my mother warning me, leave him, he's putting the awning up. There was this one year, we were in Scarborough, and my parents met this couple, you always met people on the caravan sites, and their daughter had died of something, cancer I think. She had really loved riding horses and even though she'd been in this, you know, great pain, she'd still insisted on going out for a ride on a pony, they didn't tell me about any of this, I heard them talk about it days afterwards. That summer the weather was like you imagine when you imagine good weather. I had a kite, it was shaped like an eagle, I ran about so much I got brown all over, people kept thinking I was a boy and I didn't mind, I liked it, I was eleven, not old enough to mind, still young enough to be pleased about it, and anyway all the boys on the site wanted to be my friend because of my kite. That day I came back to the caravan and my parents had met the people whose girl had died, they were all sitting together on those folding seats and talking. My parents had been waiting for me to come back; we were going to a beach. They all looked at me, and then my parents said goodbye to the people, and when I was getting into the car my mother gave me this big hug, when we got to the beach she and my father insisted on buying me a bucket and spade, the expensive ones, even though I was eleven, too old for spades and buckets.

Now you've fallen asleep, your breathing deep and regular and your head on my arm. I love your head. I know your head well. If I were sitting behind you on a train, and I didn't know you were on the train, I would recognise you by your hair, the way it shapes into itself like that on the back of your head. I feel the weight of your head on me. We have come so far. It frightens me to think how far we have come and how fast we've gone, how little we've noticed of it. I swear on this gravity in the dark that from now on I will take small steps, I will take care, I will look at each indifferent rock, notice each leaf I pass with you.

Then I fall asleep, still wearing all my clothes. When I wake up it's morning and you are already awake, up and dressed and ready to go. You smile at me, your face is closed and fresh.

Come on, you say.

It's another day. There are three galleries to see before five o'clock. We had better get moving.

Bloke Runner

Bridget O'Connor

Bridget O'Connor was born in London. She is the author of two short story collections: *Here Comes John* and *Tell Her You Love Her*, both published by Picador. She is working on a third collection, *Bury His Heart in Dagenham* and is also writing a novel. Currently she is the Northern Arts Literary Fellow based in Newcastle-upon-Tyne.

ʃ

Bloke Runner

Here she was convalescing in the darkest corner of North East England. Home. All things H. Hysterectomy: five syllables.

Already she felt the other Bloke Runner's puffing on her neck. Particularly, panting on the inside car, the hot brown tobacco breath and watermelon scent of Ulricka Carr. Top Hustler. Red Ambition. Feral Understudy at Bloke Runner Date-A-Mate Agency. After her – Dorothy found it hard to breathe here – commission.

The Doctor (simply coded NG: No Good) said, 'Miss Gregson, Dorothy, I want you to think about the amount of stress in your life.' His stress on stress. Soft sibilant rain. *Stress*.

Or, she inferred, as he timed her heartbeat, she'd hear five more syllables: by-pass sur-ger-ry.

Ta*xi*!

It was a young woman's game. Clues. Catalogued. Later. Sitting up in the soft spineless bed, holed up in the cheapest bedsit in Newcastle, all trace of general anaesthetic gone, the lump furniture shuddering on the wet, grey, brain-coloured walls: *He* lived alone with an Alsatian dog and drove a cab by day; couldn't help with her suitcase as he had this real bad, he grinned, back. 'Oh *yes*,' she'd joked, 'well no tip for you!' caught his eyes crinkling, boxed in the mirror, flit: a good pair, well spaced, flash of brown, eyelashes with white on them, as though some of his eyelashes had been Tippexed in. It was this detail that sent her off (she was riffing on all things white), drugged still, and all things beginning with H: hospital, hysterectomy, . . . home, and by then, he'd heaved the cab round, tooted off down the street. That was an **A**, she realised, dreamily, lugging her own brown paper bags and suitcase into the bedsit with en-suite (a toilet in the corner, a sink), that smelt of pine disinfectant and somewhere in the room a thick pink band of roses, that sent her head swimming . . . roses on the carpet, the walls, crawling across the bed counterpane, black stems filing straight out like ants . . . She felt weak then, a symptom . . . post operative depression . . . but had to get out her laptop computer and log him in.

Taxi driver. Twenty-five. Geordie. Dog: Suzi. When she should have coded, she usually coded, at *least*: TD. TF. NE. DG. SZE.

A train shot by the window, a snake.

And . . . she was being shot *through* pain. She was back in the maroon-smelling taxi-ride. Through the plexi-glass divide she saw light edge around him, saw his cheek bulge again as he turned with the wheel towards her, grow bright, silver, white. Like the sheen on a real pearl. And she'd *let* him, she winced, get away.

And, she'd let her rival, that Routine Hacker, Creepy Smiler, Ulricka Carr, tap a way through!

'Geordie,' Ulricka Carr read, in sunny south-west London. Her pointed red nails froze in beg-mode, for a moment, above the key board. 'Jee-*zus!*' Usually, she'd hack Dorothy's unscramable codes: screens of marching yellow ants: Sanskrit mixed with capitalised personal insults; cod Greek. 'Twenty-five.' Finally, Ulricka crowed, Dorothy's *fucking lost it!* She shook out her mop head of loose red curls; closed her curiously flat light-grey eyes. Snorted. Snuffed up, as she waited for the screen to fill, a celebratory coin-load of speed. Read, through the beat of her speedy eyelashes: 'Taxi driver. Has dog named Suzi.' Hmm.

But, even she could not have foreseen: **A**.

During the night, doubled up, in rose-strewn delirium (the air sprouting here a leaf, there a fully-blown pink cabbage rose), Dorothy tapped out **A**. It flashed on Ulricka's turned-on screen. Then, a little elongated, flashed back along the scarred ginger varnish of Dorothy's rented dressing table. A green pyramid. A slash. Bouncing from the triptych mirror. In the morning, clear, Dorothy rushed to **Exit**, to snuff that laptop flat, but too late: already characters had whizzed off down the electricity line to Ulricka Carr's bleeping, silver screen. But perhaps, Dorothy thought, bending as the pain charged, I've got away with it.

A =: Ulricka read, chewing. She had time to walk round the room for a needle, tap a vein, before: ANGEL.

It flashed. She coughed up her breakfast croissant, bared her tiny plastic-coated teeth all over the room. 'I've,' she screamed, 'fucking hell, I've done it!'

It *was* a young woman's game. In seconds she was out thigh-deep in honking London traffic; right arm slashing down to a shaved bony knee: *TAXI!* Already she saw 'him', manacled. Sold. Saw herself stepping on to a plane. White linen suit. Heels. Destination? Havana. Hand luggage? Gold.

TAX-*I!* Dorothy screamed. While Ulricka Carr was battering, denting the counter of Date-A-Mate Agency like a cold steel wave, Dorothy was outside the hospital up north, semaphoring, waving taxi-cabs down in the slanting yellow rain, her insides still carving out sore, popping the so *lyingly* named 'pain killers', leaking thin black blood into a sanitary towel as large as a nappy. Swearing at herself, sweating, signalling outside the hospital, waving each cab down. An Angel! One in three million. The top price, she sobbed, the highest price *ever* paid for a man.

And *she'd let him get away!*

TAXI!

Her sore . . . What was left of her sore insides? She'd lost her edge. Grip. The grip on her edge. She went to kennels. Chiropodists. Swung round the ring roads. To each taxi firm. She criss-crossed town. Munched with the crowds outside Fenwicks, blinked just her slow eye, the other lizardly darting. And saw, in the Eldon Shopping Centre (momentarily tranced by the smells of bread from the Breadery, chips from the . . .), the scent around *her*, a colour in the air, the pink fug of blood; smelt roses and saw her Mam taking shape on the crowds; smelt her cheap rose perfume sprayed over sweat . . . Roses sprouting out along the carpet at home, up the greasy stairs . . . A tan raincoat. A headscarf in full faded pink bloom. Saw her trudge away, coalesce into the shining white lino. 'You coming home, pet?' Inside, Dorothy screamed like a kid: 'Poor, poor, poor Mum*my*. Here now!' Tax-*i!*

'Please,' Dorothy practised, 'Fat Iris, ah, per-*leaze!*'

'Iris,' Ulricka Carr, said, salivating, fizzing spit, 'give *me* the job.'

She'd lost it.

Finally. Fatally weeping, Dorothy'd dialled the Date-A-Mate number on her pink mobile Bloke Runner's emergency phone, connected with Fat Iris, Chief Capitan of the core agency, begged for more time, 'Honey, I'm on a live one, oh please Fat Iris, please, just give me a week.' The static tensed on the line. Recoiled. 'Iris?'

'Suuuure,' Fat Iris said. Her voice had an echo boom like the transatlantic. Even after she'd replaced the phone. And though Dorothy had been, until that (very) wet moment, the no questions asked top scorer: had brought down in her time fifteen hundred commission-rich, mate-worthy men, Fat Iris, after only the *one* drag on her fat Fag of Thought, gave that CSF, that Chomping Speed Freak Ulricka Carr, that . . . *Red Ambition*, Chief Understudy to the Stars, permission to jet up to Jesmond immediately, get in the race. 'Dorothy's burnt out. Find that fucking Angel, Ulricka, go!'

'Miss Gregson, I want you to think about the amount of stress in your life.'

Dorothy replaced the receiver. 'Sure'? The word, the lead weight in it, dropped into her head. Then sweat rolled off it. It was really time, she told herself, to get out, go. But the price on *his* head. She stuttered: the ma-ma-money!

She, Dorothy 'Dot' Gregson was, had been, *the* top Bloke Runner for Date-A-Mate Agency. She'd won trophies, earnt wacking commissions. Saved them up for? If not the Bloke Runner's dream mansion, top reward, in Havana, a palace in Jesmond. A not-to-be-like-Mammy's (scent of urine/scent of old) retirement home. Soon. After the next catch, or the wedding after that. She'd been to so many weddings, the study in her freezing-cold, high ceilinged South London flat, was racked with pastel-coloured suits; stacked with boxed net'n'veil wedding hats. Tax deductible. The walls were papered with Polaroids of smiling brides. Pictures of grooms wearing a slight bedazzled cast to the eyes. She'd bloke watched them all. Run rings. Run all those good men down. There she was smiling out too. Most of the grooms unknowing, the hook in their foreheads, on a taut silver line to her.

'This isn't a line dear,' they said, often, 'but you look so *terribly – familiar.'*

She was.

Over pink pond water, Pimms, glacial wedding cakes, it was said there was something so, just *so—.* 'Haven't we met before?'

Yes and no.

She was behind them, lightly disguised on a train, across the Atlantic, queuing for the Chunnel Tunnel. She had bright red hair, mouse, brown. Eye-glasses like owls. Librarians. Her coats were reversible, tan, green. She was the one with the clipboard, the newspaper with two tiny peepholes cut out of text.

Bloke Runner.

She'd tap in unseen: *Seen on corner of Harley Street: one Dr Timothy O'Brady. Obstetrics. Filing for divorce. Ex-wife blonde, so client brunette/new brunette. Shops regularly in Tesco . . . drinks (mod) vodka and tonic, takes 6 a.m. from Brighton to Edinburgh.*

She'd sat behind him, noting the cheese and tomato sandwich. Four quick bites, gone. Note: bolter. Coffee: two sugars, *Daily Telegraph.* Rude to small children. Snores and is CLU: Check Lifter Unconcealed. Noted, at 10.25 a.m., looked at the legs of women and even two v. young girls. Recommended only for Desperate Overhauler's. 'Of which,' Dorothy would say, at Light Joke Time at Bloke Runner recruitment seminars, 'there are *some.'*

In essence, what a Bloke Runner did was find the bloke out. Provide the information. Habits, horrors. Spot the rift in his current squeeze. The crack of opportunity. Quick! Timing was everything. Get in *now.* Dorothy was, she'd always thought, like Moses was parting the sea: keeping it wide wide, till the waves crashed in.

'The key to my particular success,' she'd say, at Regional Award Ceremonies, scruffy at Christmas parties, moths flying out of her wallet, 'is my LHV. That's,' big-mouthing, 'Long Haul Vision.'

She took the long view and always, with no question, flung the weedy ones back in, or she'd log the 'possibles' deep in code, aware her colleagues, those other Bloke Runners, fledgling

Ulricka Carrs, would attempt to hack on in, steal her leads. She'd cruise the 'possibles' every couple of years: Honolulu, New York, Basingstoke, on a double reccy: update, upgrade, or simply no grade, and keep up, en route, with all the current trend-setting magazines: style cyphers, all read on train journeys, in darkened carriages, on planes. The key to her success, her plump accounts, was patience: 'That's PAT . . .' No secondary sourcing. Unlike the other Bloke Runners she'd not uproot a baby B. Bs also equalled the Bewildered. The agency was growing harder. They'd throw a B to a lean and hungry woman in her forties threatening legal action *as a snack*! Ruin him before he was ready. Before he was full grown. It was really time to get out, go.

'Miss Gregson. I want you to think . . .'

It *was* a young woman's game. She, Dorothy Dot Gregson had finally, fatally, dropped her guard.

Ulricka Carr jetted off through clotted London clouds, Midlands smog. Her plane zeroed in on the dropped silver satin ribbon of the Tyne and Wear. Ulricka Carr sniffed back a finger length of speed. She was racing, raring to go, giving the cabin crew the bad mascara eye, screaming, 'Lower. Go there. Slow.' Tilting above St James's Park she saw, through binoculars, men in black and white strip hop then swarm the lens, small as bees.

Parks. Dog owners in anoraks. Dorothy had good sharp eyes, trained to scan a park. She went to Lower Heaton, Gosforth, Fenham and Jarrow. She marched. She followed men with Alsatians. She shouted SUZI! *SUZI!* Men walking alone with leads. Untethered. One caught in her cross-hairs, her ragged heartbeat leapt: he was riding the swings, his man's body curiously contorted, lumped in the child's swing. His pale anorak zips caught the light like wings. She kept seeing the man's body arc in the cold, grey, northern park.

Dorothy 'Dot' Gregson signalled for a cab, then another and another . . . She was a starter, with a gun. Go. Go.

A Geordie, . . . she swung past roundabouts, hardly daring to blink, twenty-five . . . dog, Alsatian. *An*-gel.

Ulricka Carr signalled cabs too, bending, pigeon-toed, peering in through a slosh of grey windscreens, then, frowning, the crucifix in her forehead deepening, waving them, irritably, on.

Leaves on the windscreen . . . leaf spit, fly dust whitening, men's features swarming, swearing out. *Not* an Angel in sight.

In the bedsit, under the pink greasy candlewick of the bedspread, holding the hot skin above her non-womb down, the screwed in belly button, Dorothy dreamt about taxis. She was out there running. Then, as taxis reared and showed her their wide brown bellies, their heavy underlay, she dreamt she was eating up the road. Sucking up a whole mouth of tar, slack dripping black candy tar.

It *was* a young woman's job.

Dorothy saw, emerging from a health club, Ulricka Carr.

Dorothy was slowly cycling through Jesmond. Neck-turning. Smelling of blood; her thin hair whiplashed across her forehead. Water ran unchecked from her nose. Then. She saw, turning the corner, emerging from the fake green arch of a health club, Ulricka Carr jogging out, a small rucksack on her back, heels bouncing, her breasts bobbing, the nipples with that indented softness, a kind of sexy sore. Dorothy wheeled into a doorway. Ulricka Carr puffed by mouthing into a mobile phone. Dorothy smelt her pheromones: her ruthless air.

Ulricka took the bus. Noted taxi L plates. He wasn't 'on line'. He wasn't on tithe to a regular cab company. He didn't have a dog licence. He didn't have a ticket to St James's Park. She circled the city.

Dorothy criss-crossed the city. Then randomly like scrawl. Looking up she saw a helicopter dip its side. She imagined and one second later she *knew* Ulricka Carr was up there riding with night-vision binoculars. Dipping into view . . . Now lost in great swirls of coral and squid-black coloured clouds. Once she looked up and the helicopter blanched out a wide cone of blue. Aerial shots. And *she* should have thought of that.

Ulricka Carr dressed Geordie: a red halter-neck slip, false brown face, white neck, puffed up hair so the shape of her neat round skull showed in car headlamps. She looked the brand new dolly part. She tripped over the gleaming back alleys, her eyes agleam. Inside her bag was a mobile phone, a pile of Bloke Watcher cards, a Polaroid camera, tracking buttons: her own innovation; she would pin on any likely looking lad, any baby B, and, also, just in case she cashed in, caught the Bigg Market Angel that night, a bright pair of manacles.

Men called Dorothy 'Pet'. It sounded strokable. She'd forgotten how she liked it. Men called at her from the top of lorries. Men peeled their windows down, sang at her. One stopped and almost made her heart stop. It was him but it wasn't him. His size, his . . . but the shiny gene was absent. His star Angel quality. She left her card. 'Er, I've got one of these already, pet,' he said. 'Didn't know I were 'andsome like?'

Ulricka Carr.

Ulricka Carr handed out cards in nightclubs. She traded them for kisses, made secret notes, couldn't help a little teacherliness along the way. 'A little wet,' she said. 'A little lower,' she said. And once, angrily, *Don't just stick it in.*' Her mouth was sour with drunken tongues. Back home at the hotel, she made notes, secreted her own code for Bad Kisser. Will Never Improve. Overhaul? Perhaps. Fey? Yes, send him to decamp. Men could be groomed. The least damaged ones made over, made, for the Very Desperate Over Hauler, work-a-day.

Ulricka Carr took off her face in the rose-tinted triptych mirror. Naked, her face peered back at her. The skin sagged a little around the eyes but the eyes themselves burned (the whites were veined like a map of B roads), then singed the mirror mercury. Ulricka Carr's plump bottom lip quivered with all the planning she had to do. She popped her night pills and ran to the window and leaned her head into the soft Newcastle rain. Exhilarated. Bloke Runner.

Outside, the cars clogged. Buses swooped corners. Queues formed for taxis; drunken children screamed down the Bigg Market. Peeps nightclub ejected the same lad over and over. There he was being thrown out and there he was being thrown out and there by Mr Cheepers too, by a sign that read 'Pint Sized Cocktails Here'. He was rolling on to his back, a look up at the stars. He was screaming 'SUZI. Oh Jeezus! SUZI!'

Ulricka Carr, through her sleeping pills, through her sleepy curly head, heard the word screamed: *SUZI!* It punctuated her dream. She was showing a gang of lads how to kiss. They were like baby birds with their beaks raised. She was bending, smiling

grimly, bending. SUZI? She woke up shot. She was out among
the biker shops in Westgate Road. She was in a taxi. She was so
hot. All day.

Dorothy rushed through New Bridge Street, through the Bigg
Market, eyes peeled. She stepped out on to the road. The air was
growing thickly dark. Girls were clicking by in big hair, white,
lemon, lime Lycra tops, cold blonde legs. The air was stuffed with
hairspray. At dusk the swallows swarmed above The Monument.
Slid. They made flower shapes . . . now a tulip, now a star. Her
neck ached from looking up. A taxi swung into her vision. She
signalled automatically, peering. Felt her arm go stiff, clutched
at her chest, thought, as she sailed to the brown cobblestones,
under its wheels: Ah, Mammy – *'Miss Gregson. I want you to think
about the amount of stress in your life'* – no—

He was above her for a moment. She saw his face, and thought
she heard in the background bow wow bow wow. 'Just lie there
pet,' he said. 'Take it easy. That's right.' She struggled up on one
elbow. 'Your name, please?' He was tanned, gold. Then, sinking,
she saw Ulricka Carr . . . her spiked heels, her curls and wet
little lips, and finally, red fingertips sinking into the cake of his
arm. 'What a lovely dog,' said Ulricka Carr. Then, Dorothy sank
through the ground.

An Angel spread its cold white wings over the earth. Gold and
red ivy had grown in a beauty queen's sash across its shoulder
and cold stone breasts. Crocuses had budded around its feet. A
sparrow bopped on the Angel's nose, staccato-pecked inside the
flared nostrils where brown bogeys had already grown under
thick pads of greenish fur. Ulricka Carr looked at the name
written in stone: Dorothy 'Dot' Gregson. RIP. 'That,' Ulricka
Carr said, 'is Rest In Peace.' She smirked like a Soap Star.
Then turned on her spiked heels and marched out. Through
the sodden cemetery gates. To Havana. Gold. Retirement Home.
To the revving taxi-cab, where 'he', pale and bearded now, was
still manacled in a splash of light to the wheel. Ulricka Carr
looked in at the grey swaying face of his dog. Frowned.

Already she felt the other Bloke Runners panting on her
neck.

Big Things

Margo Daly

Margo Daly was born in Sydney in 1964 and grew up there and in north-west New South Wales. She has been based in London since 1991 after stints in Adelaide, Melbourne and the Blue Mountains. Before leaving Australia she co-edited *My Look's Caress: A collection of Modern Romances* (1990), and published short stories, book reviews and teen fiction in various magazines. Since 1992 she has worked as a travel writer and researcher as co-author of the *Rough Guide to Australia* and contributor to *Rough Guides* to France, Europe, Thailand and *More Women Travel*. She is currently writing her first novel.

J

Big Things

Mickey loves Big Things. She has always wanted to see the Big Banana again. She would like to see it *looming*, a bright yellow giant banana she can drive right up to herself. It's still Mickey's favourite fruit.

That first time, we lay down on the back seat because all the cars were honking at us, and a man was doing V-signs with his fingers. He was half hanging out of his car and yelling at Dad, and Mum was screaming from the front passenger seat at Dad too. We pressed our fingers to our ears and we closed our eyes tight. When we opened them, still lying flat on our backs, all we could see was yellow. There it was, like a giant banana had just landed from out of space. Mum stormed off to get herself a cup of tea, to calm her nerves, she said, while we walked through the banana with Dad. He carefully studied the diagrams and boring writing about banana-growing, the way adults used to, with their hands held thoughtfully behind their backs, to show they were really paying attention. He was the same age then as I am now, and I never do that. Ever. No one else my age does either. Is it with the hands out of the way behind your back, you can peer more closely? Maybe he just needed glasses, and that's why he was such a bad driver too.

Normally there's an explanation for everything. I had my eyes thoroughly checked before I got my driving licence last year and they assured me I didn't need glasses. Not even very weak ones? I cajoled.

In the kiosk Dad bought us each a choc-dipped frozen banana on a stick, and one for himself. Mum was sitting moodily over her tea, pretending she didn't know us. It always seems extra mean if mothers do that. I guess Dad was pretending he didn't know her too, because he didn't buy her a banana. Even now, when Mickey and I reminisce about the peculiar chewiness of those first frozen bananas, contrasting with the crunch of the icy chocolate, pronouncing it one of our best taste sensations ever, Mum gets this look over her face. We ate the bananas in two minutes flat, standing up and gazing out of the kiosk window, being mean back to Mum and ignoring her, giving only the bananas our full attention.

Dad took us into the souvenir shop where everything came in one colour: banana colour. The shop was even banana-scented, not real banana smell, but the smell of those pale, chalky inch-long banana sweets. We got a packet of those to share, and a plastic ruler each that said THE BIG BANANA, COFFS HARBOUR NSW in the centre, with four tiny photographs: two different views of the Big Banana, and one of rolling surf, another of the banana plantations that covered the hills behind the town.

Mickey still has her ruler. She makes a list of All the Big Things in Australia, underlining it sharply in red against the line of colour photographs. She would like nothing better than to be a postcard photographer. Since her divorce she has been doing photography at night school; she has learnt to drive. She ticks the ones she has seen, the Big Pineapple and the Big Merino and the Big Cow and the Big Banana of course. If the list wasn't in alphabetical order, that would come first, but there's the Big Apple, and the Big Ayers Rock which is actually smaller than the real thing, but never mind. She'd like eventually to see all the Big Things in Australia, and photograph them in full glorious colour, and I'll write little pieces to go along with them, and any other stories we find along the way. We'll send them to the *Sydney Morning Herald*, where Grandad used to work as a printer. I throw that one in for Mum, and I can see she likes the idea. Something to brag about to all her sister-in-laws with their happily married accountant children with big houses in the suburbs and two children apiece.

It's a sort of popular culture quest, I inform Mum, following the well-blazed trail all the way up the north coast to Queensland. I'll be using my Fine Arts degree at last, I add hopefully.

That's the tentative plan. If things go well, we'll keep going. If not, we'll come home to Mum . . . and failure? It's been lurking around the corner waiting for me to turn thirty. I've only got a couple of months left. Mum says I've been frittering my life away overseas, what have I done with my degree and where am I going with my life? A series of dead-end jobs to finance my travelling. She doesn't say it but I know the worst thing is I've broken up with my boyfriend, and he was such a lovely bloke she says, such beautiful blue eyes. What would she know, she's always a sucker for a pair of beautiful eyes. Dad's for instance, and they didn't get her very far. All alone at thirty-two.

When I tell Mum what I am planning and that I am taking Mickey with me, she strokes Mickey's hair so tenderly, like it is still blonde baby hair. I just watch, feeling left out.

You will look after your little sister for me, won't you? she says. For a moment I think Mickey will struggle away, put on one of her scowly faces, say that she's perfectly capable of looking after herself and not so little any more, but she just sits dreamily nestled next to Mum, with Mum stroking her hair, and I'm sitting in Dad's armchair feeling like I'm Mickey's suitor or something, though she looks about five years old. I've always sat in Dad's chair and they've always sat on the couch together, and I'm like, who will look after me?

I'm leafing through the photo albums while they're in the kitchen making some tea. Inseparable or what? Mickey hates doing anything on her own. I only have to look at the photo of Mickey when she was nine, with that ridiculous feather cut, and it makes me want to cry. How can I explain, the way she's peering out from under that great fringe like a miniature Farrah Fawcett from *Charlie's Angels*, so hopeful, as if everything's going to be great. The way she's losing her blondeness, you can already see the darker roots coming through, not a baby any more, not as cute as she thinks she is.

But the photo that really gets me is the portrait of us when she's three and I'm five, me dark, she fair. Our faces and smiles are identical, with such white pearly teeth. The photo must be from the time when they touched up colour photographs. Because surely they've made her eyes bluer, mine browner? The contrast is striking, hers are practically violet, mine like a cup of coffee with just the barest hint of milk. My eyes don't give anything away, only my mouth is smiling, whereas hers – you could swim in them, like two great pools of emotion. I can feel Mum and Dad outside of the frame, beaming their love at their two daughters, Lena and Mickey, born almost exactly two years apart. Mickey is the one who is most kind. But she is also the one with the temper. Lena is the clumsy one but she is best at school. Still waters run deep, they mutter, looking at my eyes. Fountains overflow, they hint, comparing Mickey's. They talk in this kind of code all the time.

When Mickey threatened me with her fists when I was twelve and she was ten, and nearly as tall as me already, I rode it out with a supreme holding in of breath and an inability to act. Fear passed for arrogance, a statue of stone you can't hit against if it won't hit back. Mickey says the worst thing about me is when I go all quiet. I can damn people for days not speaking to them. Knock knock, Mickey says, is there anybody there?

Mickey is slack-jawed when I turn up in the 1976 poo-brown Toyota Corolla. We're driving that *thing*? she says. Well, at least it's not a Volvo.

We pack our stuff up that afternoon, we're impatient, we want to head north right away. Mickey asks me where my P plates are, because I just passed my test in England. I knew she was going to say something, rub it in. Technically I should be on P plates, but I've got three months to drive on my British licence before I'll have to take the Australian test. How would I look, turning up to the interviews I'm planning to do with a big 'P' sign on the front and back of my car? I protest. Only seventeen-year-olds have P plates. Provisional: temporary or conditional. You have to drive ten kilometres slower than anyone else.

I reckon she should be on P plates too because she got her

licence two years ago and she hasn't driven since. That shuts her up.

Mum becomes a waving speck in the rear-view mirror. She's petrified of us driving, well she would be, wouldn't she? It's like, are we overcoming our fears, or hers? They're all so mixed in together, when do her fears leave off and mine and Mickey's start? She never learnt to drive. The teenage years without a car, patronising uncles driving us to family dos, dropping us up the coast for a holiday. Friends' fathers taking turns to drive us home after a night out. Even in the world of teenage suburbia, all the other mothers, not just Mum, didn't seem to drive. But daughters drove and fathers taught them how, or brothers. I thought that was the only way to learn. It never occurred to me that you could pay for lessons. Then Mickey wrote to me and said she was learning, that she was going to drive before she turned twenty-five if it killed her, and by the time she'd got her licence, I'd started lessons.

What do we know about cars anyway? Only what we've picked up from our exes, our Dad a long time ago, and any other men who have come our way. Not even our own well-developed prejudices, but second-hand knowledge and other people's intolerant attitudes, after years of being passengers. Mickey has it in for Volvo drivers. Her ex-husband always used to say what selfish bastards they were. How they would walk unharmed out of any accident. He didn't notice me flinch. What they're really driving is tanks, Mickey says, made out to look like a smart car. A car that would crush anything in its path.

Getting out of Sydney is hell. A hot afternoon and we've hit rush hour. When I learnt to drive in London, the traffic was so slow, the streets so narrow, it wasn't very often that I worked up to any speed. Stop and start, stop and start. Now cars are whizzing up either side and when Mickey points out where I should be going, I'm too scared to change lanes. Shit and fuck and Christ accompany every turn of the wheel. I keep getting in the wrong lane and cars are honking at me and then I have to turn the direction of the arrow, until we're lost, quite lost. Mickey says she won't drive until we get out of Sydney. *If* we ever get out of Sydney, she adds. Then signs are indicating the Sydney Harbour Bridge, and Mickey says that's the way to go, right across it. Right fucking across it, all that blue water below, it's dizzying thinking about it. I hold my breath. There are all these signs and lanes going off and diverging, and big red crosses above to indicate the contraflow. I cling to the wheel and somehow get us across and then we're on the freeway. Mickey says if I just keep in the left lane I'll be all right and she passes me some water, and I stay in there for a long time, clinging on but then I have to overtake a truck, I really have to do it, it's going so slowly I'm crawling, I check all my mirrors like they showed me in London, I indicate and then I pull out and put my foot on the accelerator and I just go.

North Coast the sign says, and the freeway is carved out of solid sandstone and I'm in the middle lane and driving fast and we just look at each other and grin. Whoopee, Mickey yells. She winds down the window and lets the fast air stream her hair, she hangs her half arm out, cooling it in the breeze.

Mickey, don't do that, I protest. You know there's a law against that.

No I didn't.

Well there is. Too many people lost their arms in the seventies or something. Mum would freak if she saw you. And you kind of look like a hoon.

Mickey smiles, repeats the word. A hoon.

We leave the freeway at the first central coast town so Mickey can get behind the wheel. She can't be any worse than me, I figure. And anyway, she was the athletic one and I was the clumsy one. But I reckon her temper will be something to behold. Talk about road rage. After a few shaky blocks Mickey gets the feel of the car. She heads back on to the freeway calmly and quietly. Her only comments are scoffing at other cars, *What a bomb* and *Volvo driver* are frequent exclamations. She doesn't seem to notice the endless stream of guys in the middle lane who slow down and drive beside her momentarily to get a better look. They can't see the old pair of Adidas blue trainers, the ones with white stripes, holding down the accelerator. Or the Levis she's had since she was about twelve. They're probably staring at the tight baby-pink midriff T-shirt with the cute saying on it. Her long hair is parted in the middle and sitting unkempt on her head, held back by a pair of cheap sunglasses that I bet she bought from a petrol station or somewhere. Probably useless as eye shades anyway. Hideously ugly but they look great on her, of course.

Mickey always instinctively knows what is groovy. And now the fashion is not to look like you're trying. At least that's what I read in a magazine on the flight from London: trying to look cool was deeply uncool. Too late: I'd tried hard to get the latest looks before I left the city they were saying was the fashion capital of the world. The sort of outfits that Mickey throws together without thinking is the cool look, though trawling through her wardrobe, you'd be deeply unimpressed. From all these odd bits and pieces, Mickey creates these head-turning ensembles that I could never dream up.

Like a dolphin with its sonar, Mickey can pick up on the echoes of my mind. She'll always say something with oblique references to what I'm thinking about. I'm not saying there's anything conscious about it. Sometimes I think there's a twinship because our birthdays are so nearly on the same day. We are Pisces, the fish. Mum and Dad are two crabs, can you believe it? One little fishie in each crab's claw. Crabs eat fish, don't they? She's launched into the story of when we went travelling, on that big summer train trip when I was at university, and she'd just finished secretarial college, just before she started her first office job, the one where she met her husband, the accountant.

Your absurd quiffed hair! she says. You'd dyed it jet-black, I think you were in your Goth/Rockabilly stage, weren't you?

And your lipstick, dark purple, what planet did you think you were on?

Am I meant to laugh or cry at this point?

City chicks out in the bush, she chuckles. We were so young.

Maybe she's forgotten how she said something to me about the way I appeared to people and, mortified, I scrubbed all my make-up off and pulled down my stiff hair and spent the rest of the week feeling plain and unnoticeable. Mickey was used to being *au naturel*, that's how she met her husband. Just her own sweet quirky self. Not all armed with university degrees and expensive clothes and make-up, and a diet regime and trying to think of the right thing to say and reading the right books and listening to the right music. I didn't think I had any natural charms.

We make our way up the coast. I swerve off the road but we're all right. I can't reverse-park forty-five degrees like you have to in country towns. I practise on a deserted street with Mickey guiding me. She's better at clinging to curves too, taking the road. I'm too hesitant. She gets all the windy roads, though we don't always know when they're coming, and we can't always stop and change drivers. Once, coming down a steep winding hill, this huge truck is so close that I can't see the driver, only its blind front in my rear-view mirror. I imagine the driver is a crazed loon with a grin like Jack Nicholson, all evil intent and sex mixed in.

What do I do. What do I do? I cry.

There's no way I can pull over. Mickey can't see in the rear-view mirror, she doesn't realise the enormity of it. What if I just brake suddenly, tons of truck rammed up our arse. Mickey can't understand what the panic is about. She looks across at me. Calm down, she says. I hang on to the wheel in pure terror and take the corners. Then we reach the bottom and the road straightens and widens until you can see far ahead for quite a way, and there are no cars. The truck honks from behind and overtakes in a rush. It's even a friendly kind of honk, and a hairy, tattooed arm waves. Mickey waves back. She has no idea how close we just came. No fucking idea.

I like it better when she's driving, especially on curves, because she has to keep her eyes on the road. So I can say things and she can't turn and look at me, even at my profile. Eyes straight ahead.

I hope we meet some guys, I say tentatively.

Look into your heart, Mickey says. How can you let yourself be hurt over and over again?

Steady on. I'm making a simple statement about wanting to have some fun. Who said I'm going to be hurt? F. U. N. Your trouble is you can't forget the accountant. It's been two years.

I don't say it, that maybe I'm like Dad, living in this ridiculous state of hope, believing things will always get better, that the next plan is the one that will get me rich, or even happy. How can I explain it to her, why I am like I am?

Just listen to me, will you? You know I used to fall over a lot when I was a kid, I learnt to fall easily, to pick myself up quickly and pretend nothing had happened.

Yeah, she says, So?

One minute I would be tumbling down the stairs at school then I would be miraculously righted, walking along. That way, people didn't laugh, just stood astounded at how I could pull myself together so quickly. It hurt, it fucking hurt. I have scars all over my knees to prove it. I never stopped falling.

So I was so sure on my feet and then I fell over and now I'm too afraid to fall again?

Something like that Mickey.

Well one day you might permanently damage yourself. Think about it.

So might you, I say. You might just permanently shrivel up and live with Mum for ever.

Hah, last word. She doesn't speak for at least half an hour, then just to tell me it's my turn to drive.

Mickey is infuriating. She refuses to fill up the petrol tank. There's all these things I don't know about her coming out. After a few attempts to get her out of the car with the petrol pump in her hand, I'm stubborn enough to make us wait for the attendant to come out. I feel silly when it's a woman, I don't know why. I feel like pointing and saying it's her stupid fault, my sister's fault. But I like *men* to do stuff for us. I can tell Mickey does too. The women attendants must think we are dunces. When there's no attendant on the horizon, I fill it up myself. One day I will just sit there and *make* Mickey do it. But she is the master of windscreen cleaning, a legacy from her past relationship. He drove, filled up the tank, she passed across sustenance and liquids, made cheering conversation, and when they stopped, she cleaned the windscreen. She *is* good at it, I'll give her that, I don't have the technique mastered at all. But sometimes I wish we could just swap roles between being petrol-tank filler and window cleaner.

When we get within ten kilometres of Coffs Harbour, Mickey instructs me to pull over. We're on the middle of the Pacific Highway for Christsakes, does she know how many fatal accidents they have on this road every year? She insists it's her turn to drive. It's true, she is a better driver than me, at least this way she won't have to lie fully reclining on the back seat hiding in embarrassment and fear, other cars honking at me. No that's not it, she says, she wants to be the one to drive up to it. Rites of passage. Visiting the sacred sites of her childhood from the position of control. Her behind the wheel. Like everything will fall into place. She is going to have at least two choc-dipped bananas and practically buy up the souvenir shop. She hopes they still have those scratch-and-smell fruit T-shirts, she's going to buy a twelve-year-old's size and wear the tiny shrunken T-shirt stretched provocatively across her chest. Then we'll have some fun, she says, grinning and turning to me and winking.

Eyes on the road, for Christsakes Mickey.

Coffs Harbour is even more built-up than we remember it. A string of dingy, decaying motels as you come in from the south. Plenty of vacancy signs and boards outside giving away rooms at $40 a night. Still way beyond our $10 a night camping budget.

The Big Banana is on the other side of town, I tell Mickey. That's where all the banana plantations are, covering the hill-sides. Making you feel you're already somewhere tropical, though it's still a long way to Queensland.

Except the hills are thinned of their plantations. This side of town has been developed, all these posh motels, resorts really, compared to the shoddy affairs on the other side of town. Mickey would have kept on driving on to Queensland if I hadn't told her to turn her head to the left. The brakes screech and she does a quick turn without even really look-ing in the rear-view mirror or indicating; luckily we're in the left-hand lane, but even so cars screech behind us and honk their horns. Mickey drives into the car park, not looking at anything else but the banana. The banana hadn't *loomed*, and now the banana looks more like an afterthought to the asphalt car park that is swarming with people, children clutching various yellow-shaped objects. In the scrawny plantation behind, a fun fair toboggan ride streams through the banana plants. Mickey parks up. There's a certain violence to the jerk she gives the hand-brake.

WELCOME TO THE BIG BANANA, the sign says. Mickey doesn't say a word. She just walks up to it, shaking her head. I trail behind.

It's so small, she says. It's so fucking small.

Mickey looks like she wants to cry. I'm disappointed too but at least there's still the choc-dipped frozen bananas and the souvenir shop.

C'mon, I motion to the kiosk. Inside I order for Mickey, she's speechless really. Unusual for her to go quiet. More my ploy. We walk back to the car silently, eating our frozen bananas. Mickey throws her stick to the ground.

Mickey! I cry.

She turns to me, real hatred on her face. Don't rubbish Australia, she says sardonically, muttering under her breath, I've never even left the fucking place. I don't know any better.

Aren't you going to take some photographs? I ask. She shrugs, curls her lips, opens the car door. The driver's side.

But Mickey, I wanted to write something about it. You can't have a story about the Big Banana without a photograph.

She gets in the car, puts the key in the ignition, winds down the window, pokes her head out.

You coming?

Mickey! I stamp my foot.

Get in, she commands. There's one other place we have to see.

What about your T-shirt? I wail.

After the Big Banana, Dad drove us through the centre of town to the Pet Porpoise Pool, for a live dolphin show. Mum got a cup of tea from the kiosk and sat drinking it in the car. There was a native animal menagerie in the grounds. The photographs Dad took, small square and black and white, are blurred. He didn't realise the camera was on its last legs, not seeing properly. My shape merges with that of an emu; Mickey crouches down to pat a kangaroo and blurs into it. Only our grins are bright white, blinding happiness, not knowing any better. After we've seen the slivery dolphins perform, it's the souvenir shop again. We both choose water bubbles. When you shake them, the arching, flipping dolphins are covered in snow flakes.

Mickey parks the car outside. There's no shade. It's so hot in the car. She just sits there, staring at the souvenir shop. Her shoulders start to shake. After a while I pat her on the back. It's as much affection as she ever gets out of me. I am no good at being kind. Let's go for a swim, I suggest.

I don't mean the beach either. I read in the guidebook Mum bought us about these fantastic waterholes on the Bellinger River, as you head inland for Dorrigo, the road winding uphill through forest to the New England Plateau. There are too many people on the coast anyway.

I was hoping the waterhole would be deserted, but it's the school holidays, and a mass of little boys are dive bombing from the high flat rocks. Only the tiniest boys hold back, watching with a mixture of awe and regret as the older boys, who are only eight or ten at the most, jump fearlessly. They seem like such fierce little macho bundles already, such tiny Aussie blokes. There are no little girls, in fact we're the only females around. Mickey strips down to her bikini easily and slides into the water from the low rocks, smiling back at me like a ten-year-old as I sit down to peel my clothes off down to my one-piece. I scramble along the rocks into the water quickly, half crouching, so the little eyes won't peer at my body, but the little eyes are too busy marvelling at masculine pluck and daring to be remotely interested. Mickey has turned away, swimming on her back, looking admiringly up at the diving boys. I practise my long easy strokes, keeping to one side of the hole to avoid them. Wishing it was more peaceful, I flop on to my back and scissor lazily, watching the green trees overhanging the swimming hole. If I close my eyes the leaves dapple the strong summer light on my eyelids, light and shade. I open them and watch the boys jump, probably with the same impressed yet fearful expression as the six-year-olds'. My fear is that the boys will hurt themselves; the tiny boys know that one day they will have to prove themselves at this task.

I don't have to prove anything any more. I still fear the searing pain of belly busters and the scary gap between myself standing up and the water. I can dive sitting down, easing myself into the water which is then soft, not a hard sheet of glass to crash against. I practise my strokes, they are strong and sure. I dive under the water, rise up laughing near Mickey's face.

The shrieking plunging boys demand *Watch, watch, watch.* The six-year-olds' eyes are big and gazing obediently. One sucks his thumb absent-mindedly, one shivers, his towel over his shoulders, fringe stuck up in odd directions. I like the vulnerability of little boys, but it doesn't last long. I wonder where their mothers are. Mum would never have let us swim in a waterhole by ourselves. But then we were city kids. And girls.

Watch me, Lena, Mickey says, clambering out of the water. I'm going to jump.

Mickey, I whine. Don't. You'll hurt yourself.

Mum will kill me if anything happens to her. Mickey climbs up the rocks and she looks absurdly large in the queue, like an overgrown little girl with her long thin body. She waits her turn patiently as the boys jostle on the rock. There's definitely a feeling that she's invading their territory, *a girl.* Though *they* probably think she's old enough to be their mother. With a shock I realise she is. My little sister. I'm looking up towards her waiting, she's smiling at me, waving. It'll be ages before her go. I turn and do a few side strokes; this lazy feminine stroke is Mum, easy, languid in the water, big and shaky out of it. Breaststroke was Dad, slow and lumbering like a great hairy beast, sometimes with a laughing child clinging to his back, me or Mickey, like a hippopotamus carrying a bird that he can't shake off. A close-up view of the red moles on his pale back. Mum watches laughing in her aqua-blue one-piece with a proper mother's bra built in, her costume the same colour as the blue PVC-lined pool. Me on Dad's shoulders, Mickey on Mum's and wrestling each other. The first one to shove the other into the water wins. Her eyes are so blue and fierce, I'm frightened, but she's grinning at the same time. I believe that's what warriors do. And though she's still smaller, she wrestles me off my human perch and I fall crashing into the water.

I move on to the faster strokes, I throw my face into the water and swim and swim as if I am merely physical, blotting out memories with sensation. The plunging of curved hand, crooked arm, one, two, three and then breathe, turn head and one, two, three, turn and breathe. I lie on my back and move lazily and fast, strong arms back one after the other, and legs kick kick kicking, looking at the diamond droplets woosh into the air and fall.

She's calling *Watch me Lena, watch* but when I turn my head, all I see is the water closing around her. She springs out again like a jack-in-a-box.

You weren't watching, she says, and ducks me under the water as punishment. I missed it. I feel unutterably sad. The little boys are leaving the waterhole, drying themselves on their beach towels, folding their towels into turbans, draping them around their necks, tying them around waists, putting their thongs on their feet. It must be lunchtime. The sun is high in the sky. There's one last child trailing along, he looks back at me from under his blond fringe. So trusting and hopeful. I put my head in the water, cry into the waterhole. Maybe we made the Big Banana into something great because it was such a shitty day. The day Mum gave up on Dad. She wouldn't go with him on his next trip. Said we weren't going either. He would kill the lot of us. Dad said I could go if I wanted to. Mum said no way. Gradually it got to her holding Mickey in front of her, Dad with me by the arm, and them arguing, hostages in tow. If we'd been bigger and stronger, Mickey and I could have taken them out to the swimming pool in the back garden and put them on our shoulders. They could have thrashed it out, out there, the loser splashing into the blue depths.

The boys' voices die off through the rainforest. I watch Mickey swim across the waterhole and clamber out on the other side. She throws herself on to the sunny rock as if exhausted, lying sleeping on her front. I float on my back and look up at the sky. A colourful bird swoops across the water. I climb carefully up the rocks overlooking the pool. I stand there, looking at the water far away, at Mickey sleeping. Gripped by fear, tantalised by the potential swoop through the air, the glide through the dark, now still water.

The next day, Mickey drives the winding route to Dorrigo. We do the Skywalk, the wooden walkway at the level of the forest canopy. We gaze at the rainforest remnant, learn the names of the trees. The area was once heavily forested, but most of it was removed for settlement, and for the timber of course. In the interpretative centre we look at photographs of the Aboriginal people who once lived in the area, looking strong and happy, with white smiling teeth, and then later, staring sullenly at the camera, fully dispossessed of their land and spirits. It's so depressing, Mickey says.

We stop at Armidale, have a drink in one of the pubs on the mall, with their gracious iron-laced verandas. University town, Mickey says. Maybe I could go to university here.

We head south-east to Tamworth. Mickey hardly even turns her head when I point out the giant Golden Guitar. The capital of Country and Western music. Of tack. Right up Mickey's street. I suggest we go into the museum and check out the waxwork figures of the great Australian Country stars I've read about in the guidebook, the McKeen sisters in red corduroy A line skirts with matching waistcoats, but she's not interested. We could even hang around for the annual Country and Western Festival in a couple of days time, I say, and check out the rhinestones and the ten-gallon hats for real. I howl a bit of *Satin Sheets to lie on, Satin sheets to cry on* but she only shrugs. We camp by the Peel River on the outskirts of town.

Though it's the wrong time of year, we head west, to be encompassed by solemn heat. Mickey doesn't question me as to where I think I'm going. From Gunnedah, the rich, black soil plains stretch out. If we keep going, we'll be in cotton-growing country. Mickey stares serenely out of the window at the unchanging scenery. I drive like a maniac, without hesitation, but not with any real plan. I swear if anything gets in my path. Fucking caravans most of all. And trucks too. I overtake them all. When it's nearly dark, we find a caravan park to camp in for the night, in some dusty anonymous town beside another brown, gum-lined river.

There's a natural beach by the campsite. The water is surprisingly icy, it makes us catch our breath. Afterwards we sit on the sandy crescent of beach and watch the local Aboriginal boys and girls effortlessly swing out into the water from a car tyre tied to a rope. Mickey wants to have a go, but I won't let her.

You're just like Mum, she says.

Am not.

Are, she ends, and gives me one of her big sighs, but she doesn't try to go on the tyre. Mickey is really physically fearless, one day she might have an accident. I just don't want anyone to say it was my fault.

I go for a walk in the town while Mickey tries to get a campfire going. I see her from a distance, bent over through a haze of smoke, the river-red gums and the long brown river behind her. Her hair is wet and matted from the swim. I bring her back a packet of her favourite biscuits, choc-chip, to make up. It was me who said we weren't allowed to eat junk on this trip, so I've broken my own rule. Mickey can eat as much rubbish as she likes and never get fat, but Mickey won't eat it if she has to eat it alone. She needs the company, and she's always trying to persuade me to eat it with her. But I would get fat, and with all this driving too, I would get a fat bum and a fat waist, and the worst thing would be I wouldn't be able to fit into all those new clothes I bought in London and, besides, who would love me, at thirty, if I let myself go?

We put the billy on the grate over the fire. I've also bought real coffee in paper sachets. I make us two cups of coffee, and we sit looking at the river, munching on biscuits, the two of us clicking, the underlying tensions of being together easing away.

I miss Dad, she says abruptly. Do you?

We hardly ever talk about him. We get too upset. Maybe she knows what all this is about. Where we're going. If I'm not too scared. My eyes water. It's the bloody smoke from Mickey's fire.

Neither of us has men, I say, my voice catching. We don't have a Dad and we don't have a Grandad or a brother and we don't have a boyfriend or a husband. We don't even have a son.

All we have are uncles, Mickey says. She lights a cigarette. I don't trust uncles.

Mickey, I squeal. I thought you'd given up.

I found them in the pub last night.

They're Marlboros. You used to smoke B&H.

I just felt like one, she says. It sort of suited the river and the woodsmoke and now the coffee and the choc-chips.

Maybe she doesn't realise how much the cigarette smoke reminds me of Dad. How hard that is.

I make a point of creating a big space between us in the tent. I face my face to my own tent wall. Tonight Mickey reaches across and pecks me on the cheek goodnight before we switch off the lantern. I'm embarrassed.

I snuggle into my bag, trying to get to sleep, but I can't stop thinking abut Mickey. How I pissed off overseas and Mickey stayed home. It reminds me of the little piggies song Dad used to play on our pink little toes. This little piggy went to market and this little piggy stayed at home, this little piggy had roast beef and this little piggy had none. And I've come wee wee wee all the way home. When I left I'd been twenty-five. Disgusted that Mickey had got married to the accountant. Not being able to understand her need for security. They made an odd match. She spent most of her time interior decorating from what Mum said in her letters, and working on their garden. He said she didn't have to work. Her tomatoes were just juicy and ripe when he said he was leaving her for the new secretary. I kept pleading for her to come over after the divorce, to come and see me, to see the world.

Mickey declined. Mickey wouldn't leave Australia, leave Mum yet. Everything, she said, would happen in its own good time. It was her theory, her way of life, to just let things fall into place, while I planned and strained. In the end we were in the same position. Mickey would not get out there and try to meet men either, while I smiled and flirted like a loon at anything in trousers. The right one would come along when she least expected it, she said. She merely acted how she felt and everything fell into place. Or fell to pieces. Being unemployed, Mickey was offered cheap driving lessons and she took them up, and then these free night classes in photography. It just fell into place that she could team up with me and go off travelling. But I was the one who had the idea and bought the car and if it wasn't for me . . . I'm crying into my sleeping bag, the same ones we've had since we were kids. Green on the outside, leopard-skin print on the inside. Mum and Dad used to zip theirs together, snuggle up inside on their airbed. Mickey and I, resolutely separate inside our own bags. Mickey wanted to but I said no, I don't want to be that close.

I love Mickey. I love Mickey more than anyone else in the

whole world but I can't kiss her on the cheek. She doesn't know, she doesn't even know.

Soon we will pass the spot. Maybe she's guessed this is what I'm up to but she hasn't let on. In the end, Mum's little fishie was Mickey. She bargained for Mickey staying with her while I went away with Dad on his trip. The winter school holidays. I wanted to go, but I felt like I'd been sacrificed too. Mum was sick of Dad's mad schemes. Dad said I was big enough to come along and give my old father a hand, see what I thought. He always acted like he valued my opinion, even when I was small. Maybe Mum had stopped listening by that time. We were going on a real adventure together, heading west to check out a business he might buy, his latest scheme to get rich quick.

Dad never did have a great sense of direction and he got so lost and it was so late and it was raining but we were nearly there and there was nowhere to stop, and the highway was only two-lane with crumbling edges and there was this slow slow caravan in front of us and I screamed at him not to overtake it because I had learnt how to be a front-seat driver from Mum, and then this truck was heading towards us and he moved back into the lane and the caravan screeched to a halt and the truck swerved and our car went straight into the back of the caravan, Dad's side and he hit the wheel, and he was dead. I didn't feel anything. I came out in one piece. And there was no more new life. There was a completely different life.

I could pretend I haven't known all along. Drive right on past. How would Mickey know anyway, she wasn't even there.

Stop, Mickey calls, stop. I screech to a halt. We don't even park the car, we just sit right in the middle of the highway. There are no other cars around. The sky is a clear blue, not a rain cloud in sight. It was a different time of year, a different time of day. There is still a dent in the sign that the truck went into. I remember sitting and staring at it and wondering when someone would come to help. The sign says WELCOME TO WESTVILLE. Underneath has been added Tidy Town of the Year. No cars come. No one is exactly flocking to the town where I was heading with Dad. Where he would finally be a big success. The sky is high, fine and dry. I notice glittering along the sides of the roads. Broken glass, bottles thrown from cars. Further up there's a huge burnt-out truck tyre.

We would have hated it anyway, Mickey says. Dad did have some dumb ideas.

I know what she means. I laugh and it turns through a snort into crying. Mickey reaches across the automatic transmission box and gives me a sideways hug which I accept awkwardly.

Let's go back to the campsite, she says. You got any of that special coffee left?

Mickey swings out across the river on the old tyre and I watch her, two steaming mugs of coffee beside me, with her cigarettes and lighter. Maybe I'll even have a cigarette. I feel like it. I light up and wave the cigarette at her as she leaps off and plunges into the water. Whoopee, she cries.

Zoo

Gaby Naher

Gaby Naher, born in Sydney, Australia, in 1967, fled her home town on finishing school. She studied languages in Zurich before moving to Paris to continue her studies and work as an au pair. Back in Australia, Gaby completed a BA in Communications at the University of Technology, Sydney, before moving 'overseas' once more. She worked in the publishing industry in London for nearly six years and in New York for six months. Currently living in Sydney, Gaby works as a literary agent and is completing her second novel. Her first novel, *The Underwharf*, was published by Penguin Australia in 1995 and Hamish Hamilton in the UK in 1996.

ʃ

Zoo

Someone said the polar bear was deranged. Another that it was hysterical, running amok, but the woman knew better. She knew that the bear was just trapped. The woman had been on a visit to a small zoo and had observed this so-called polar bear hysteria for close on two hours. There was something about the bear's frenzy that held her there; in the hazy heat of summer the woman pressed herself right up against the glass that formed one side of the pool. The bear, whose fur had turned a lurid shade of lime from the algae in its water, would place her massive haunches against the edge of the pool and draw her legs in tight. Then in one explosive movement she'd propel herself outwards torpedo-like. On her approach to the opposite wall, she'd twist around to greet it with her back, slide her haunches into place and push again. As the woman watched, the whirlpool the bear created with her own body carried her with it until they were two mutually reliant entities. The bear's energy alone, it seemed, would shatter the walls of her pool.

Now the woman is moving there's no question of stopping. In the small rental car she screams past her street without a thought to the sleeping man. It is only when she is heading due east, almost at the outer ring road, that she thinks of the overnight bag she was going to take with her, and then, as an afterthought, she remembers she was to bring the man with her too. But she can buy a toothbrush and a spare pare of knickers en route, she reasons. And the man must be tired, after his flight; he'll be grateful for the rest she is affording him.

She turns on the radio, jumps from station to station – there is only one band. Channel-hopping is better than staying put and her left hand hovers between the gearstick and the radio's dial. The car is small, but powerful, and the woman finds herself breaking the speed limit without trying. She's singing now, echoing the airwaves' unique babble. The woman sings the words of songs she's never even heard before – she sings in tongues.

After an hour on the road the little car feels like home, despite the antiseptic odour that exudes from the cardboard Christmas tree hanging from the rear-view mirror. But that's easily dealt with, and with barely a thought for the environment which she's paid to protect, the small, cut-out thing goes shooting out of the window and away. Even the garish fabric of the car's interior appeals to her, it has that quick and easy feel to it – the fast food of upholsteries. Beyond the car, the grey urban blur falls away at the outskirts of the great city. The blue green world that flickers at the corners of her eyes as she stares forwards is a buffer zone, a cloak which she draws in close. For the first time in days, the fist that resides in her abdomen is tentatively uncurling.

With the tiny sunroof open to the blue sky above her and the wind playing in her newly loosed hair, the woman could be going anywhere. And without a destination, anywhere is exactly where she is going. She makes a quick decision . . . the decision is not to decide. She will simply go.

The woman is comfortable in the car; if she were able, she'd purr. At times she accompanies the radio some more, but mostly she's practising the tolerance for silence. The car is her instant kingdom and she a born ruler with a sure hand on its destiny. If she does not wish to stop then so be it.

Ever since the woman heard from her ex-lover, the one she left behind, polar bear hysteria began to encroach. On the same day she received his news, at work they told her she was to be promoted – a director. There wasn't a tinge of lime in her ebony hair, but she became captive to her own manic energy, just the same.

In the office where she worked in marketing, she progressed through her schedule of calls and faxed proposals at a terrifying rate, by turns impressing and completely confounding her colleagues. At times she spoke so fast that they could not understand her. It seemed she'd learnt a foreign language in her sleep and spoke it without thinking. But her staccato rounds of phonecalls and subsequent, rapid-fire instructions to her colleagues were punctuated by hourly trips to the emergency stairs. After a few laps of the one hundred and twenty strong staircase, her pulse quieted in her body and she could once again think.

And after work she would take to the city's streets in a pair of old hiking boots, convinced that she could take in all of South London on Monday night and East London on Tuesday. There was the occasional greasy spoon halt for hamburgers or kebabs – anything that she could eat while walking – but essentially, she had become pure movement. She was a tightly wound coil, spiralling, pirouetting, dancing a manic tattoo around herself. In her mind, she would throw her knees high, her long legs casting crazy shadows in the pale glow of dawn. She'd walk whole city blocks in the blink of a wakeful bear's eye.

The woman liked her work – they wanted to make her a director – and she cared for the man who would come on a plane from across the world. But when she let herself think of the man or the job, her chest contracted and her lungs failed. When she imagined herself as one of the charity's directors, with her own flat, a spacious office and speedy but green company car, a hard, cold fist formed in her belly. And when she tried to imagine herself with the man, her body roared at her from deep down inside.

When the man arrived she had been only too eager to curtail the romantic, candle-lit dinner that he was so in favour of, and at which they were to discuss the future. She had wanted him at home and fast, and with his clothes off. She had wanted him more than she'd ever wanted anything before. He had been flattered – why not – and eager to oblige. He'd told her that they should spend more time apart if this is what it did for her libido. But that was only after the second fuck that he'd secretly struggled with. And after the third, when she'd come but he hadn't, he started to watch her with a weary combination of awe and concern.

Before he sank deep into sleep, he'd told the woman that living on her own was dangerous. Living with him she would be safe. He said that her zeal, her appetite, was simply unnatural.

But the woman did not mind her new condition, even if it did prevent her from sleeping. What she could not tolerate, however, was lying in a small double bed and playing at sleep like a child. The problem with practising stillness was that it took so much effort it made her body shake. But for the man she would try . . . for an hour at least. She timed herself by glancing at the luminous green digits on the clock after every third breath. When her hour was up she crawled from her bed and on to the ledge of her high window, from which she could watch the dawn creeping greyly across the South London rooftops. Even dawn was too slow.

Before eight she was pacing Acre Lane with the residents of the halfway house on the corner, and stopping periodically outside the car rental office to peer through its glass front for signs of movement. And when the office finally opened and she was inside and filling out forms she had to apply her full powers of concentration to the elderly man as he spoke. His words formed so slowly that she feared it would be days before a sentence emerged.

When the paperwork was completed, she was to just make herself comfortable. She was to wait. The woman tried this, each leg taking its turn to be the one to jump up and down as one hand played a staccato rhythm on her thigh. When she wasn't playing drums on her thigh, she was twisting her thick pony-tail this way and that – perhaps the hair's smoothness against her fingers would quiet her?

When the car eventually pulled up in front of the office, the elderly man honoured her by leaving his desk. He saw she was nervous and wanted to give her his own considered instruction about the car and how she might tame it. He showed her how each of the lights worked, and how to access the spare tyre in the boot. It was only when he started to explain the difference between leaded and unleaded fuel, and the change in the London air over the last few years, that her immaculate manners dissolved. She offered a quick, Yeah, thanks, before speeding away. In the rear-view mirror she watched the man's bony hand suspended there, as if the car's roof were still warm and solid beneath it.

But there are reasons to vary from every plan. The petrol gauge sitting on empty is an excellent reason. Finding something to eat is a close second. But the woman doesn't want to stop, not in the true sense of the word. Like a mirage, a vast service centre appears up ahead, spanning the motorway and pulsing with the traffic's energy, its form indistinct with the haze of fumes. As she approaches the shimmering mass, it reveals itself for a moment – a space craft and the cars driving right up into its belly are bringing their earthly prizes home.

Petrol first. Then she leaves the sanctuary of the car, steeling herself before heading for food. But the inside of the service centre is not too bad at all, in fact, the woman more than tolerates it. The colours of the carpet and the vinyl booths in the cafeteria are so lurid that lingering is an impossibility. The woman is soothed by her fellow travellers' unease, by the shared need to maintain momentum. She feels no hunger but eats, regardless; the food looks and tastes synthetic. She eats to remain part of the road's momentum, not for sustenance. She thinks of the man in her bed back in London – he's probably up and searching for her by now. When she moves to the public telephone to call him, the fist inside her forms a tumour just above her pubic bone.

When she pulls out on to the road again, the blue sky has been replaced by a dense mist, a mass of off-white fur that isolates the motorway. Now she's really in outer space . . . she and her car move through the atmosphere seamlessly. Through the mist, her headlights fix on a sign that instructs her to stop for regular rests; but to the woman, the delays are more arduous than the journey itself.

She's reached a near meditative state . . . all she needs to do is keep her eyes on the road in front of her, her hands on the wheel, and every now and then guide the car smoothly through a couple of gear changes. The mist has joined behind her, obscuring the past. Before her, the future is little more than the bright, pale cones illuminated by her headlights.

But when night falls, the woman's eyes smart and she sees small, flying objects where there should be only darkness and beneath it, the road. One small shape comes flying so fast that she brakes and swerves but fails to avoid it. She does not feel the impact, nor does she hear it. She leaps out of the car into the silence of the evening street, but finds nothing, no small bird, no soft, child's plaything. Nothing but the certainty that her control is slipping.

She drives slowly now, until she reaches a village. It's a place with grey stone cottages and slate roofs, with pretty flower borders and the warm glow of light seeping from behind drawn curtains. On a slow crawl along the high street the woman finds a quaint, olde worlde bed and breakfast.

'What's a nice young lass like you doing roaming the country-side alone at this hour of night?' the proprietor in her bold red tartan wants to know.

But the woman just bites her tongue and smiles. Asks to pay her account in advance.

Her room is alive, seething with peach-coloured flowers, the bed is awash with frills and tucks. But once the woman has taken a shower, brushed her teeth with a finger and washed out her knickers, she feels oddly at peace there. When she crawls into the high bed and lies quite still in the darkness, her body no longer roars. And almost before she can think of sleep, it is upon her.

The pale light that steals into her room early in the morning is like a warm hand come to shake her. She is bolt upright in the bed even before the day's first bird call sounds, low and spectral behind the house. The woman is across the room and at the window in an instant – her car is where she left it the night before and the town is quiet as a grave. If she cranes her head out of the window and peers down the road, she can just make out a vast, dark mass that lies silent and waiting. Already her body is coming alive, is beginning its daily practice of screaming at her.

The guesthouse door clicks shut silently behind her, but the woman senses she is being observed, none the less. With her boots tightly laced and two dry biscuits from the tea tray in her pocket, she strikes off through the sleeping town.

At the bottom of the road the dark mass reveals itself as the lightening sea. But the roaring in her body does not abate as she moves towards the dunes on the edge of town, indeed, it heightens. From the top of a high dune whose ascent makes her body sing with effort, she can see up the coast for miles. To the north, pale sand runs as far as the eye can see, forms a natural causeway leading to a scattering of islands that lie exposed. Down the coast and marking the edge of town, a vast, granite-coloured castle monopolises the sea front, sits up, high and proud, on rocks that rise from the very ocean itself.

It's settled then, she'll head north. With the energy racing through her body, she'll easily reach the islands by mid-morning. In direct contrast to the place she grew up – a beach that was a field of scorching heat, and an ocean of dumping waves and the occasional shark out back – England lies benign, open before her.

Walking up the beach, her stride sure and long, feels even better than driving. At least in walking she's moving her limbs and pushing forward. Later, she thinks, when it's warmer, she'll remove her boots and feel every particle of sand as she passes over it. The sea to her right is taking its colour from the sky, the greenish-blue of one is infused by the brilliant blue of the other; together they form a vast cocoon for the energy that's coming off the woman in waves. For the first time, perhaps, since she has lived in England, she feels completely alone. Up and down the beach, way out to sea, and in the farmers' paddocks that border the dunes, not another human being stirs. Her only companion is the occasional, big-faced brown cow, and the odd, sweeping, diving sea bird.

And while the islands themselves don't actually draw nearer, other landmarks in the distance reveal themselves. Up ahead she can now discern two golden, stone pinnacles, reaching for the eggshell-blue dome of the sky. They appear as sentinels, flanking the mouth of a vast estuary that lies between the woman and the causeway. Now she has company, the sentinels become her guides and witnesses.

The woman stands at the foot of the southern pinnacle, its warm surface grainy like sand, and estimates that it's still two kilometres to the northern pinnacle. In between sprawls a wide estuary, a sea of sand scattered with small islands of water. She can't walk due north, taking direction from the other pinnacle, because there's too much water in between. She plots her course inland now, veering north-west; if she walks in about half a kilometre, she can make her crossing and head true north again.

The woman savours the new perspective that her change in direction has afforded her. She takes pleasure in the subtle movement of the cows as they graze the blue-green slopes skirting the sandy bay. She feels part of nature, at once powerful as the sea and light as the clouds. And she enjoys the way the damp sand beneath her clings to her boots, laughs at the ground's greedy sucking when she lifts her feet. Her own walking soundtrack has now almost entirely replaced the roaring in her body. As the sand grows stickier, grows mud-like, her pleasure only heightens. Pulling her boots up out of the ground when they sink is a challenge, not a chore.

And when the sand sucks and her feet are buried to her ankles, she just stops to roll her jeans high and to change her bearings for further inland. After ten minutes of walking through pale mud that now reaches the top of her calf, the woman halts for a brief reconnaissance. Behind her, her disappearing footsteps are testament to what she has achieved and proof of her own exertion – to turn back now would mean it was all for nothing.

And so the woman plods on. She finds that singing stills the new, unfamiliar tremor in her chest. She sings because she won't acknowledge that the tightness there, the tremulous fist that roves around inside her body, might represent fear. The first time she loses her balance and is pitched forward on to her hands, her legs have been sucked in, right up to her knees. Here, the earth has its own appetite. The mud is reluctant to release its hold on her now, and she no longer thinks of it as sand. She is a wrestler, each time she has hauled herself free and beaten her adversary, she is pulled back to the ground and must struggle again; victory is utterly illusory.

When the mud reaches up to caress her thighs and she can no longer roll her jeans beyond its sucking grip, she turns again to assess a possible route of retreat. But the picture has changed dramatically now – not only has the mud claimed her footprints, but further out, the incoming tide has covered the mud. Again she goes to move and is pitched forward, on to her hands – she is singing 'Jingle Bells' and doesn't miss a beat as she struggles to drag herself upright. But extracting her legs from the mud is getting harder; her boots weigh like concrete beneath her.

In a skilful balancing act, the woman removes first one and then the other sodden boot – they fit snugly on to her hands. Now she can crawl forwards and although this involves sinking to her elbows and mid-thighs, she takes some small satisfaction from her own resourcefulness. She begins to make rules for herself: no looking back; sing, continue to sing; and keep moving no matter what.

But she does permit herself to gaze, longingly, at the blue-green sloping fields as she executes each forward move. She might be playing solo Twister, for the contortion involved in each new positioning of a hand or a foot. The cows take little interest in her plight and this is somehow reassuring – it can't be that serious, can it? Upon occasion, one glances in her direction and she imagines it has recognised one of her songs from the farmer's transistor radio at milking time. But she is still a kilometre from the true shore; when she allows her thoughts not her heart to instruct her, she accepts that even the cows cannot hear her.

When she stops to breathe between songs, behind her she can hear the insidious lapping of the sea . . . can almost feel the tickling tide at her toes. Now she debates the likelihood of being picked up by a wave and carried all the way to shore, versus the possibility of sticking fast in the mud and watching the sky disappear for ever as the tide comes rushing in over her.

She tells herself that this is not the worst of times. The worst of times is the polar bear's pool. Here she has fresh air and a clear sky overhead that is actually colouring. Here she has blue-green hills and cows and the sea. Here she has a limitless horizon. Here she can breathe – even if her breath does come fast and gasping.

She is tired now – what she feels is the collective fatigue of the last weeks. Now the strain of co-ordinating all four limbs to achieve momentum is nearly beyond her. The sea is coming, it will carry her. She has always loved the sea. She should at least turn to greet it, she will turn to greet the sea. And with the last of her strength, she pitches herself up on to her feet. Now, with her arms outstretched like a tightrope walker, she turns herself around to face the water.

The woman is surprised to see that in places the water has already crept past her. In places, the water is flush up against the blue-green paddocks. Inadvertently she has crawled up on to a rise – the sea is still two or three metres behind her but on either side it's rising fast. She looks down at her poor, bloodied feet only to realise that she can actually see them. To register that they no longer plunge deep into the mud.

Part of the estuary now, the woman is reluctant to flee it. Where the water has crept up to cover the mud, it is already reflecting the beauty of the sky. There is the occasional patch of grey sand, and all around it, pools of clean, bright water.

Almost without her knowledge, her legs have started to move again. Now she is backing up the muddy slope and her legs feel light without the pull of the earth to constrain them. She turns, slowly, to face the fields again and the cows who continue to ignore her. Her feet are blue, with bright red slashes, her socks are long gone. On her hands, her boots hang down like dead weights, lumps of sodden earth. She could take them off and throw them on to the grass if she wanted, so close has she drawn to dry land.

She is some way up the grassy slope before she allows her legs to buckle beneath her, and she sinks gracefully down on to her bum. The woman crawls around to face the estuary and watches the tide cover the last of the mud with an audible rush. The shoreline is dotted with signs, warning signs. From where she sits she can decipher the word QUICKSAND. Lying back on the grass, the woman looks up at the sky and realises that the bell-like sound that envelopes her is laughter. Her own laughter. She is laughing so hard that she begins to choke. To the farmer who has just crested the hill above her, she looks like a crumbling mud ball and sounds like a choir of angels.

Even as he is drawing towards her, all well-intentioned concern, she is fixing on the northernmost pinnacle through streaming eyes, and fumbling with her boots. And when the farmer finally draws in line with her, she has almost regained her stride.

'Miss, Miss,' he is saying. 'Are you all right Miss?'

But she is still giggling, tries to nod her head in response.

'Miss? Miss, can I help you?' he is asking, reaching out for her crusty sleeve. 'You must look out, Miss. You must take care. This is a dangerous coastline . . .'

But she is still laughing and he lets his hand fall away. Under her breath she repeats the word dangerous again and again. Her eyes are fixed on the northern pinnacle, and despite the aching in her legs and the dead weight that is her arms, her body has gone quiet. The only roaring in earshot comes from the surf as it rolls on in.

It is July, Now

Kathy Page

Kathy Page was born in London where she still lives. Her stories are widely anthologised and there is a collection, *As in Music* (Methuen 1990). She has published four novels, including *Frankie Styne and the Silver Man* (Methuen 1992) and is currently working on her fifth novel, about a religious cult, and a new collection of stories, *Paradise and Elsewhere*, which takes place in a variety of countries and cultures, both real and invented. Morocco, Mexico, Estonia, Finland, as well as remoter parts of the UK, have inspired recent fiction. She won the *Traveller* writing award in 1992.

∫

It is July, Now

I ride the bus to the airport so as to keep the expenses. It takes an hour and a half and then the plane is forty-five minutes late. Well naturally, I do not take kindly to extra work at weekends and for two weeks the Director has been plaguing me to inspect the flat and before that he rejected one I had found myself, which was with someone I know: one room only and landlady *in situ* would not be suitable – they are used to having personal space, he said. A flat is a flat, I think, four walls: if one of us has lived in it, it will do for her. I did not make the inspection, but told the Director that I had. Some of the people in our Academy, I told the Director when he suggested I have a visitor in my department, are the foremost experts in their fields; it is a joy to hear them talk. But many of the foreigners who come do not even speak their own languages correctly, let alone have a proper pedagogical method or good manners. They all say that they are very interested in us and would rather be here than at home, but it is my view that some of them come here because there is unemployment in their own countries and they are inadequate to secure positions: so I am against it.

'Even so,' he said, clicking his pen in and out, as he does, 'there is nothing to be lost.' So it was decided.

Just as I am convinced that she has missed the plane I turn around and the person sitting on the bench behind me, wearing a dark red coat and no hat, can only be her. The coat is far too long: it will trail in the mud; the shoes will be soaked through. And her hair is cut short about her face, so that she looks like a child, but with very shiny lipstick on: the fashion, perhaps, where she comes from, but to my mind not a good one. Fashion is an odd thing. There, where they have freedom, they follow it. Here, where there has been none, we are all individuals.

'Good afternoon,' I say.

'Hello.' She stands up, her gloves fall on the ground, she bends straight down to pick them up, forgetting to offer her hand.

The Director also said that I should invite her to my home. A glass of wine with cheese was the done thing, he told me.

I have a whole house, in fact, only a minute from the city centre but built in the country style. Three floors, four rooms, a garden, gables: I had it painted ice-cream pink last summer. It is large enough for my daughter Katrin and me not to get in each other's skirts. She has a job at the City Hall but they won't allocate her a flat because there is enough space here. Still, I have my own study in the attic, with waxed floors, fresh curtains, a good rug, a proper office chair and a telephone extension. The house is mine – nationalised, of course, but I have the proofs and it is just a matter of time – and even you, I thought at the Director, cannot compel me to have someone in it if I do not want. He is young, very clever. Before, he was a scholar in a garret; now, he has been given a laptop computer, whereas I am paid nothing extra for being Head of Department, though it looks good on my CV, which we all have to make these days – and eventually, when the country is sorted out, it may lead to something.

The visitor's flat is in an anonymous district on the outskirts of town, big blocks with numbers and no names and because I haven't been there before I can't give good directions. The taxi driver is Russian and loses patience so I decide it is better to walk. She has some boots, she says, but they are right at the bottom of her bag, should she get them out? I tell her no.

'This isn't what I imagined,' she says. 'What sort of place is it?'

'It is typical,' I tell her. Finally we arrive. The stairs to it smell terrible: still, I think, it will probably be all right inside.

'I have never seen so many cats,' she exclaims.

'Actually, I have a cat myself,' I say, as I try to let us in – the lock is stiff – 'it is on penicillin at the moment,' I tell her, 'extremely expensive, an import. People can look after themselves. But pets are helpless, they can't manage: we must take care of them!'

Finally the door opens on a narrow corridor with a room either side and the bathroom at the end. The place is extremely hot and dusty – I go straight over to open a window, but when I get it to open I see there is an old cupboard and some rotting rugs on the balcony, and the remains of a seagull in the middle of it all. I remember also that I told the visiting lecturer on the phone that I had inspected the accommodation and that it was comfortable. I want to escape. But she walks around, trying everything, even opening cupboards and flushing the toilet. She says the television does not work.

'In any case, it would be incomprehensible,' I tell her.

'Well, not the pictures,' she points out.

'The programmes are of poor quality. It wouldn't interest you. Here are your fees for the three weeks.' I give her the envelope. She looks at the money, puts it back in the envelope without counting it, undoes her coat. She has on a pair of close-fitting black trousers and a soft brown jumper that clings to her shape. She stretches her arms and rolls her head around.

'What next?' she asks. It is dark by now. I take her straight out to look at the shop and the bus stop and tell her that I will meet her at Kaarmanni Olletuba at eight for supper; the Academy will pay. Just then my bus comes. Anyone will know where it is, I tell her as I get on.

She wants me to write some phrases down for her.

'Really, there is no point in language lessons,' I say. I have put on my suit and a brooch; she too has changed and it is a cream knitted dress now, with flecks of grey and red in it and a roll neck. 'You will learn nothing in such a short time, it is extremely complex grammatically.'

'I'm not talking grammar –' she says, 'I just want to be able to point at a sandwich and say please. Or, for instance, to say "Can you give me directions to" rather than just barking the name of a café at some poor woman in a bus, do you see what I mean, Piret?' She has a habit of using one's name all the time.

'You are here for just three weeks,' I say. 'Everyone can see that you are a stranger; they won't expect it of you.'

'That's not the point.' I am not used to being argued with.

'We have a great deal to do,' I say, firmly. We push on and cover the necessary arrangements. I am ready to go then but she is drinking her soup like a snail.

'Well, Piret,' she says, 'tell me about yourself.'

'Here,' I tell her, 'we do not have small talk. We get to know each other slowly.'

'I see.' She plays with her bread and looks around her as if she was trying to commit the place to memory. 'Could we have more wine?' That uses up the money I saved by coming on the bus.

Life is hard, I tell her while we drink it. It cannot be legislated against as you are always trying to do in the West. You have a deal – good parents, bad parents, dead parents, a good country, a bad country or in-between. However it is, you use your talents to carve a way for yourself, you just make the best of it. Some people go under. Some people complain too much. Others are too kind . . . Drink makes me talk. When we at last emerge there is a strong wind blowing from the sea; the thermometer in the square shows minus fifteen. 'What is your word for snow?' she asks.

At home, Katrin is still up, eating milk pudding and watching the Finnish television channel, very loud, and reading magazines at the same time. The magazines are dreadful. What is your wildest dream? they ask. Do you get enough? How do you rate on the passion scale? She is not an intellectual, though she could have been, perhaps it is to spite me. She is particularly difficult these days. You resent me, she often accuses. It's not my fault there's an accommodation shortage . . . At least, I tell her when she complains, you have a mother, which I did not have for very long – all I remember is her brushing my hair, and coming to me in the night. I dream of that still once in a while; it's only natural. My father of course was away in the war, then died in it. Mainly I grew up in the orphanage – it was harsh, but invaluable in teaching self-reliance.

I didn't ask to be born, Katrin is always saying. You think you've done such a lot for me, but you haven't. I want nothing from you. You've never really loved me, it's only duty . . . She becomes impassioned. You think he would have stayed with you, happy ever after, if not for me, she says. Don't you? We make our meals separately now. After all, she is twenty-five. Some of what she says is true, but not all.

The visiting lecturer comes to the Academy on Monday morning. Apparently she left the bus at the wrong stop the night before and had to walk several kilometres through the snow and there was some problem with the toilet in her flat, which flooded; also drunken men banged on the door – but this is normal, I tell her, in the district where you are. She has on jeans and a silk blouse and the boots she wears are very odd. She spends the morning photocopying and uses most of the paper for the term.

I do not normally go out with subordinates, but a visitor has ambiguous status so I accept her invitation to attend a concert. 'Let me treat you,' she says. 'Treat?' 'To treat is to pay for, but really a matter of taking turns,' she explains, 'of showing you'd like to provide even if you can't. It works out the same in the end.'

'Here, each of us must keep to her own economy,' I say. 'It is simply too stressful otherwise. It is almost rude to suggest such a thing. You will embarrass people; they will feel that they have to return the favour when they simply cannot afford it.'

'I'm sorry,' she says and her face turns red.

The National Symphony Orchestra puts no one to shame, though the auditorium is unexpectedly full of children. I don't know why this is, I tell her in the interval. I expect they have offered the tickets free – for so-called educational purposes – and because there are so many choices these days that they cannot fill the hall. To my mind it is far too young; I did not introduce Katrin to classical music until she was seventeen, and not to jazz, which is more sophisticated, until a year after that. This accounts for these people who clap at the wrong time: they are the parents of these children; they have been forced to come, and have never before attended such an event in their lives; they simply don't know how to behave.

'Did you enjoy the music?' she asks suddenly.

As we leave she says, 'May I ask you a favour? I need to call home, and none of the boxes does international calls, or am I missing something? But the phones at the Academy would do it, I think. Do you possibly have a key? Or maybe you have the right kind of telephone yourself, at home?'

'It is urgent?'

'Very,' she says. I do not feel I can reasonably refuse so we go to the Academy, which seems eerie without students and colleagues being there. It is hard to find the light switches; I give up and wait in the dark on a bench in the corridor while she uses the departmental phone. I can hear her voice but not the words; perhaps she is whispering. It rises and falls and there are long silences, exclamations, laughter once or twice. It is not business, and not very urgent either. It is twenty-five minutes before she emerges, a half smile on her lips, eyes shining. When Katrin wears that kind of face, she always avoids questions, and goes straight to her room. I am angry.

'You have dealt with the matter?'

'Oh yes, thanks, Piret,' she says, smiling.

I cannot sleep at all that night. I keep thinking of Karel, who was Katrin's father. We were both students. It was the last year when we grew close. In summer we were both sent to do compulsory training in medical studies, so that we could fulfil our obligations if war broke out. It was in the forest, lectures all day, anatomy and so forth, but the nights were mainly our own and they were long, warm nights. We swam in the lake together, while others drank and sang patriotic songs; we despised them. Out there, beyond the reach of their voices, the water was smooth and cool as glass and afterwards our bodies were like silk. At this point I remember thinking that so long as you knew someone else who thought like you, anything was tolerable. Across whatever horrors you could hold to that connection. When we got back he came every night to my flat. It was not deliberately that I became pregnant but I do not believe in interfering with what is meant.

'But I do not believe in being trapped if there is something that can be done to prevent it,' Karel said. He took up a post in the north before she was born and I never heard from him again; I don't even think of him often now.

The cat climbs on to my bed. It is wheezing when it purrs, but otherwise it seems all right. I smooth down its fur and it stretches out flat with its ears back; it is very comforting. I can hear Katrin snoring at the other side of the house. She has done so since a child. To start with I tried to cure her of it by waking her, but gave up.

Next it is the Post Office. I have told her the directions, but she insists on being taken. She insists also on having her letters weighed: they cost four times what they would have. Just put the stamp on, I tell her, are they going to sit at the airport weighing each one? 'Maybe that's why your last to me never arrived,' she says, but the fact is I did not get around to writing it. I excuse myself from lunch. There are some cheese pies at home and I want to check the cat: the vet said that since it was a virus the medicine might strengthen him but the cure was down to his natural resistance. Katrin often says I care more about that cat than I do about her, that I never made a fuss over her, though of course that is not true. It is an instinct to be tender with children, it happens whether you will it or not. She simply does not remember. Children who have their parents take things for granted. She says that I love that cat in a way I never loved her. She says that the money I spend on the cat, added up, would get her a plane ticket anywhere in Europe. She means Paris: a Frenchman came with a trade delegation. She has many boyfriends. However, I do not allow them to stay in the house.

'This country is supposed to be *liberated*,' she tells me. 'There is nowhere for us to go. You are greedy,' she says, 'a greedy, jealous old woman . . .' Sometimes, when I get in, I have a sense that someone else has been in the house, though there is never any proof. I feel the cat knows too.

Towards the end of her last week, the visiting lecturer waits outside in the corridor for me to finish my Level One class and asks for the fourth time now to go to lunch together.

'Somewhere cheap,' she says, 'we'll go Dutch of course.'

'But actually, I am going home today,' I say. 'Dutch?'

'Well I can't,' she says, 'it takes an hour each way on the bus – you could stretch a point.'

'Is there a reason?' I say. 'Is there some particular academic matter you wish to discuss?'

'No,' she says – her voice very even – 'there isn't. Just some food and a chat. For the sake of itself.' None of my regular lecturers would suggest such a thing.

'Perhaps,' I say, 'I can organise it so that we go out for a drink on your last night, along with the Director, who would be interested to hear what you think about our students and their progress; I can ring him this afternoon and make arrangements.'

'No,' she stares at me, 'I was asking you, Piret, whether you wanted lunch, with me, now.'

'I have told you.'

'You,' she said, 'take the biscuit.'

'The biscuit?'

'This is a one-way street,' she says. Again I query the idiom. 'There is no point in language lessons,' she says then, and her voice turns hard: 'seeing as we are never going to communicate.' She turns and walks off.

It is very upsetting. Then, when I get home I walk straight up to the cat's basket to pick him up. Katrin has fed him in the morning and the wrapper from the medicine is still on the table. But he is lying there dead, his body stiff and his fur cold. My whole skin shrinks and I run back to work. I have a meeting arranged with the Director. He tells me he is going to Stockholm at Easter, for a month, paid for by the Ministry for Education; would I please take over his administration while he is away?

I tell him that the visiting lecturer is going well. I ask him for more money for books, and whether we could set the exam later in the year – after all, I say, we can make up the rules how we want them now. He says that he will note my ideas. But he has already closed his notepad and started putting things away in drawers while I am still talking. I stay in my chair. He stands up. So everything is fine? I try to stand up too but my legs will not do it. And I try to say in a brisk, businesslike voice – oh yes, absolutely – but I cannot do that either. I say nothing at all for a few seconds, and then the words blurt out of my mouth:

'Actually, I have bad news. My cat is dead, I am just going home to bury it.' But I do not want to. I do not know how to go about it, I do not want to touch it. I have had that cat for six years. He turned up on my doorstep, very thin, and I took him in. He has slept on my bed and sometimes I used to talk to him. The vet cost more than my food for a month, just for one injection, but I did not begrudge it at all. Not at all! This is how I feel. It was of course the wrong thing to say to the Director; his brother died in a labour camp, two-thirds of the way through twenty-five plus five.

He puts his hat on. 'There are plenty of cats,' he says. 'You can get another one.'

I pull myself together and think how there is a chance Katrin will get home before me, and perhaps she will wrap it up and deal with it. She's a practical sort and it would be easier for her since she didn't love it.

I decide to have the afternoon off. I need some groceries and am walking up the main street when I see the visiting lecturer on the other side. She has her hands stuck deep in her pockets and that, I think, is because she will keep leaving her gloves on the desk by the copier. One of the brass buttons is missing from her coat. I stop walking. I want to turn and go away, but instead I just freeze, watching her peer into the shops as if she had never seen things before. And it seems to me that she looks sad. And suddenly I know what it must be like to be unable to speak or understand a word of the language, not even guess at it, to get everything half-right or wrong. It must be like walking around with a shell around you which no one could get through, hard outside but very, very tender beneath.

At that moment she sees me, crosses the street, shouting 'Piret! How are you!' even though it is only hours since she asked the same thing in the corridor, and even though we parted on a bad note. I do not understand, and again I find myself saying something unintended:

'You?' I ask. 'How are you? You have not been lonely on your visit here, I hope?' She laughs. I burst into tears. It is very embarrassing.

She takes hold of my arm. 'We'll go in here,' she says. I am crying so much that I can't see where she means. It turns out to be the new place, Palace Café, with a pink marble floor. It is very warm inside. All the crockery has a broad gold rim. The coffee is strong, and they serve it with chocolate truffles on a saucer.

In the middle of the ceiling hangs a huge chandelier, a strange thing made from liqueur glasses and bits of welded kitchen implements, and the chains from sink plugs: post-modernist, perhaps. I find I quite like it.

'This is a very expensive place,' I say, 'for tourists only.'

'Let's have something else,' she insists, 'brandy, pastries, whatever. Look,' she says, opening her purse. 'This is worth nothing at home, I'll only have to put it in the airport charity box.'

When everything is there on the table and the waitress has gone, she asks: 'Are you going to say what was the matter out there?'

'No. There is a great space,' I explain to her, 'where nothing can be said. It is not personal.' There is silence and she bites into a pastry, filling her mouth. She dusts her fingers, swallows, looks up.

'These,' she says, 'are the best thing I've eaten since I came here. They remind me a bit of something I had in Greece but those had mint in them too.' She smiles lightly, as if none of the things that have taken place between us had ever been.

'We have mint ones,' I find myself saying. 'At Easter.' Again, it is not intended, but the feeling is of it slipping out, rather than jumping.

'Do you? Does it grow here?' She pats her lips with a serviette. I wonder how old she is. Anywhere between thirty and forty, it is hard to tell. Like me, she has no wedding ring.

'I have two types in my garden,' I tell her. 'It dies and then comes up again, very reliable. Of course, you can dry it for winter . . .' She takes a lemon cake, I a cinnamon biscuit.

'The biscuit,' I say, and we laugh. I tell her more about my garden, how I prepare the soil for carrots, and how I store them. I tell her about the different kinds of daffodil bulb. Every now and then, between mouthfuls, she asks me to clarify: you have to put those under glass I suppose? What time of year would that be? And I think: how easy these things are to say! The content, I sense, is not the point at all. Yet at any minute, I think also, she could ask me something I don't want to answer. At the same time the feeling of waiting for this to happen is almost a pleasure and I am somehow disappointed when finally the bill comes and it has not occurred. They bring our coats.

'Can we go back to your house?' she says.

She does not at all mind burying the cat for me, though the ground is still frozen, so it has to be a shallow hole. I watch from the kitchen window as she stamps the earth flat. Afterwards we drink some wine and she goes home in a taxi. I pay for it because she has spent all her money in the café, but I don't mind.

Two days later, I see her to her plane.

'Life goes on, Piret,' she says. We embrace. I watch her through the passport control. 'I'll write,' she calls at the last minute.

But no letter has come and it is July, now. The peonies were particularly good this year, the lettuce was early. I have not replaced the cat, but I planted a new lilac close to where it is, yet not so close as to disturb it. Death is always such a shocking thing: it makes one reconsider life. Once, here, that seemed endless; now it feels shorter all the time. I would like someone from outside to tell these things to.

Sunflowers

Kathryn Heyman

Kathryn Heyman was born in New South Wales in 1965 and has lived in most of the Australian states at one time or another. Before working as an actor and playwright, she was a deck-hand on a prawn trawler in the Timor Sea and a competent hitch-hiker. She was lured to the UK with the promise of a European theatre tour, which gradually shrank to a tour of Ireland and Greece. Kathryn is currently the Writing Fellow at Glasgow University. Her first novel, *The Breaking*, was shortlisted for the Stakis Prize for the Scottish Writer of the Year. She is currently working on her second novel.

Sunflowers

I always forget what a shock it is, when I first look down and see this smooth slice of land, clean edges like a bite-mark. There's blue, even up here I can see the movement in it, and then a clear sharp edge. A line of brown, slightly smudged, blurring into a yellow patch. And then a big wide yell of green. Something happens in my chest and deeper too, maybe near my womb, some jumping. There is not land, and then there is land, it's as clean and simple as that. I'm swallowing hard now, seeing the earth below me, seeing the continent that holds him, flat and solid. While I was over sea, it was uncertain, dreamlike. Earth is too solid. Earth swallows, I know that. I close my eyes again and imagine clouds gathering so that I will see only fluffy softness when I look again.

Sandy made the first phone call. It must have been late, because I was sound asleep and I don't get back from the restaurant until one-ish. All sorts of nut-cases get hold of my number, so I leave the machine on at night. I can hear it ringing, I can hear the voice, muttering on and on, something about 'hospital, don't worry', so I lie there in a warm half-dream and think, okay I won't. When I get up in the morning I am full of panic, knowing it wasn't a dream after all. My sister's voice on the machine sounds controlled, super calm, the way she always does. The house echoes with her voice. Binky answers the phone when I ring back, sounding nearly as tired as me. 'Put your Mum on,' I say, and she says, 'Mum's not here, she's gone up to see Grandad. I'm driving up tomorrow. Not that you'd care.' Sulky and sullen, the way she was that time when she was seven and I told her she had to clean up her mess when I looked after her. Frightened, I suppose. I'm starting to catch the fear now. When I phone Dad's number and get on to Dorothy she's got that what-would-you-care voice on as well.

'He went in yesterday, they say he's got three months' she says, and I'm trying really bloody hard to feel anything except fear, and to feel some warmth for her. Trying not to expect her to cut me off or shoot me down, and I nearly get there as well, until she says, 'We don't expect you to come. Your father will be fine without you. Sandra and Simon are here helping out, they've been very good the last year or so. Really, don't come, it's too far away.'

I close my eyes tight together, trying to get rid of the sting, before I can open my mouth. 'I'll get the first flight I can.' The words are squeezed out and I hear Dorothy give a little sigh before I hang up. There's only one hospital in Fremantle, so it's easy enough to get hold of the number. Harder to ring it. In the end, I sit on the floor staring at the phone for about three hours before I fall asleep, tipping sideways on the hallway floor so that my head rests on the stairs, the edge of the first stair digging into the soft base of my head. Spit covers my chin when I wake up – I always lose control of my mouth when I sleep anywhere other than my own sweet bed. My fingers are pressing the number out on the keys before my head has a chance to catch up. Can you hold, and will you hold and will you bloody hold, and then his voice. Old and cracked and puzzled. I can hear him saying to the nurse Who is it? before his voice comes properly close on the line.

'Who is it?' This time he says it right into the phone.

My mouth opening and shutting. 'Me. It's me.' Forgetting my name for a moment, forgetting who I am.

'Mack?'

He is right. I am Mack. Away from him, I am someone else, Charlene. But inside his realm, it is his name for me which defines me. Mack. As tough as a damned Mac Truck. Something like that. It started so long ago, I can't remember any more.

Charlene is allowed to be soft, have an underbelly, but as Mack
– I remember now, it is coming back to me – I am hard-edged,
solid and unbreakable. It was Mack he threw out in deference to
his wife, Mack was tough enough to survive. And it was Charlene
who came back, banging on his door, asking to be let in. It was
Dorothy who hid behind the door, waiting for me to go away.

So it is Mack who says 'What are you doing in hospital you
mad bastard, trying to get a rest, or what?'

He doesn't play back though, doesn't say, At least some of us
work enough to deserve a rest, ay? Which would have been
good, or at least acceptable, because though it maddens me, it
is familiar. He, instead, is unfamiliar. A quivering stranger saying
'You've done well, all by yourself. I'm sorry, I'm sorry for it all.'
A cheap film.

I'm trying to get Mack back, hard and tough, but it's me
Charlene saying 'You've never said that,' and 'You're going to
be okay. Say you'll be okay. Please Dad.'

He doesn't though, just breathes raggedly down the line,
and after a while says 'It's good to hear your voice Mack. I
have to go.'

'Drink from the bar?' The stewardess is leaning across the seat,
her hand touching my elbow. My eyes are aching and my head
swimming but I say yes please some vodka and I take it and drink
it straight, don't even wait for the ice. She smiles and says there'll
be no more delays but I'd be happy for more, many more. They're
up to the cartoons on the video. Even better without the sound.
Tom catches Jerry, Jerry eats the cheese, Tom gets in trouble.

He wouldn't speak to me at all. For eight years, not a word. Twice
I tried to speak to him. The first time, only about two weeks after
he'd kicked me out. He didn't say a word, and I knew it was
him, not her on the phone. I know the way he breathes. I was
crying into the mouthpiece, saying 'I'm sorry, I'm so sorry, let
me come home, let me go back to school, I'll try and get on with
Dorothy,' and all my words were running together the more
I cried, not making any sense at all 'Ineedto, pleasepleasedad,
youknowiwasjust, pleasewaitplease.' He listened for a while and
then hung up. The second time was about a year later. He hung

up as soon as he heard my voice. I sent him a letter. Never heard back of course, but I didn't expect to. I wanted him to know I didn't hate him, that's all. Or to know I did hate him, I'm not sure which. He got a Christmas card every year, carefully addressed to the two of them: *I hope you're well, I've got a job waitressing in Melbourne,* or *Merry Christmas – I'm head waitress these days! Hope you're well.* I did write a letter once saying: *I didn't hate Dorothy. I just wanted some attention.* When I almost got married, I turned up on their doorstep, trembling inside. Angelo made me. Said he really wanted to meet my father before we got married and anyway I should try and heal old wounds et cetera. He was a member of AA, Angelo, he was big on cleaning up the past. That was the time Dad let me in. Never said 'Where have you been, how have you been, my how I've missed you' just 'I'll make some tea.' He kept staring at me, not knowing what to say next. Talked to Angelo instead. When we left, I sat in Angelo's car bawling my eyes out while he stroked my arm. Angelo was a bit of a dud, as it turned out. Like me.

I didn't phone before I left the country. Sent him a card instead, with sunflowers on the front. *I'm going to England. Hope you're well.* At the bottom, in little writing, almost so he'd miss it, I wrote *I love you.* After the time with Angelo I did phone once or twice, even spoke to Dorothy about the garden. But there was nowhere to go really. He had nothing to say to me. When we were kids, I was always his favourite. His pet. He was besotted with me. Dorothy changed all that. Still, kids get abandoned and worse every day, don't they? When I get there, he'll be perking up – the nurse sounded optimistic. I'll hold his hand, and he'll say 'I love you Charlene, why don't you stay for a few weeks when I get well, I could use some help around the garden.' He could, too. They plant all the wrong things – sweet peas and bloody roses when they should just stick in some succulents and kangaroo paw and maybe even a waratah bush and the whole place would look alive for once. Sunflowers, that's what I'll put in. They try to make it too ordered. Even the vegetable patch. I had to do a gardening course to get the dole. Prove I was willing to work. It was great though, I loved it – I sent a pack of basil seeds after, with a note – *Put these next to your tomatoes, they'll be insect free and taste better.* I know they won't though. Basil is for Italians.

I know it's ridiculous, of course I do. If I didn't think he was going, really going, I wouldn't be on my way back. But I can at least be there for those last weeks. Not in the garden, okay, but there, beside him, in the hospital. Saying everything I didn't get to say back then with Angelo, or even before, when I left. And to ask all the things I never asked. What Mum said before she died. Why he hung up when I called. Whether he liked the sunflower card. Why he put Dorothy first. Whether the school noticed me missing. Sandy would never say, or she didn't know. She always answered my letters, sent little cards with pictures of ducks and fluffy cats.

I've left Janine in charge of the restaurant, and I know that if I'm away for more than three weeks, things are bound to start getting messy. She's good with customers and the kitchen, Janine, but she's useless with the floor staff. Strange thing is that I don't care, not really. He knows I'm a manager but I still wanted to yell it down the line before his voice went weak. 'What are you doing in hospital you mad bastard, trying to get a rest or what? Hey, did you know I'm a manager now?' Still he said I'd done well, all by myself. I should have had some help. He meant that, and it's true. But maybe I should have asked for it. Trouble with me is I never know when to open my big trap, and once it's opened I don't know how to close it.

Ding-dong. Sweet, a sweet sound. The sound of friends ringing doorbells for afternoon tea, not of a red light flashing above your head insisting you put your bloody seat-belt on. Ding-dong. Avon calling. I keep my eyes closed so that I don't have to look out and see Perth rising up to meet me. People are shuffling, sitting up straight and clicking their belts on, saying At last and About bloody time. There's the sound of bones bending and creaking, mixed in with the clicking of the belts, the smoothing of hair. I keep my eyes closed, I don't want any of this display. My skin feels grey and I'm having trouble breathing.

There's a huge queue to get through passport control. Some blond surfer boy from Cornwall starts babbling away to me about Margaret River and how he can't wait to hang there, on and on in my ear. His mouth keeps opening and shutting and this endless pile of salty words keep falling out and I think: I don't have to listen to this, so I look at him and say in a small voice 'My father – he's very ill, I'm sorry.' Don't know why I say sorry, but the guy stops talking and he says sorry as well. I take my bag to the desk and say 'My father's ill, you have to let me through.' It's one of those efficient looking women with scraped-back brown hair and as she starts to shake her head, my mouth goes soft and my chin starts to buckle in on itself. She pats my shoulder in an embarrassed way and waves me through. Sorry.

Simon is waiting for me outside, leaning against the glass wall. It's the only place he can smoke. His face is wrapped around a cigarette.

'I'm sorry about the wait. Thanks for coming to find me though – I could have been lost in baggage reclaim for all you care.' Not knowing how to be with him, this stranger, my brother. I flick him on the arm.

'Don't start, Charlie.' He hasn't called me Charlie since we were kids. I want to hug him but he keeps his cigarette in front of him, warning me off. 'Charlie. Dad died yesterday morning. Sorry.' The words come out in a mix of smoke. Smoke signals. Everyone's bloody sorry sorry sorry.

Air is leaving my body in a rush, flowing down arms, legs. My lungs are being pressed flat, I am ironed as flat and smooth and dry as a sheet. There is no liquid and no air, anywhere, not anywhere at all in my whole body. We get in Simon's car and drive, the river stretching out in darkness below the causeway. The Casino is white and squat, lit up by the moon. My hands are folded together on my lap, like a good girl, and I can feel Simon beside me, his body pulsing. Words rise up and grow heavy and solid in my mouth.

'What time?' I ask the side of his face. 'When was it? I need to know where I was.'

His eyes don't flicker from the road. 'Everything always gets back to you, that's what you think. This isn't about you. If you come back in here, stomping around, insisting everyone notice how different or sad or special you are – just don't. I'm warning you.'

Suddenly – not knowing what to do with my hands, my mouth – I desperately want to punch him. If he weren't driving I would lean over and slam my fist right into his mouth. Instead, I pull my hands up to my face and scream into them. Simon keeps driving, not listening to the unmuffled sound of me screaming into my pillow-hands. I stop screaming and, although my face is wet, I don't know what to say. A piece of snot has travelled from my nose to my mouth and I swallow it. Simon flicks the radio on and I press my face against the window, watch the river disappear and the ocean appear like magic, like it always has.

Eventually I say 'I've been on a plane for thirty-six hours and I haven't slept for days. I'm not actually asking for a whole lot, Simon. Please.'

'Dorothy is the one who matters at the moment. She's lost her husband.' His voice never used to be this cold, I'm sure it didn't.

I open my mouth before I realise that the words will get stuck. 'I have. I have lost. Lost. My father.' I swallow some more snot. 'Why are you angry with me?' Because I can see he is, even from here, even in the dark, even now.

Simon breathes out loudly, he sounds like Dorothy, sighing away. 'Ten a.m. Does that make you happy?'

I hadn't even left Heathrow. And no, it does not make me happy.

'I'm not angry with you.' His voice is soft now. 'I'm sorry.'

'I'm sorry too. I'm sorry for it all.' Not even sure what for, what I'm sorry for, but I didn't say it to Dad so I might as well say it to Simon. With the moon shining in like this, his face all round, he looks like a child.

Sandy runs out when we pull up in the drive. The lights of the house shine behind her and she trips on her way down the steps. Her body is warm when she hugs me, her breasts cushioning me. She puts her hands on either side of my head and looks at my face, says 'Come in, Dorothy's asleep, you must be exhausted too, will I make you some coffee, or, maybe a shower?' I shake my head and say yes, yes I am exhausted, but some coffee would be fine. Binky is sitting at the breakfast bar. Her eyes travel up and down me, flick-flick, fast and cold. She says 'Hello Charlene' and then 'Nan's asleep, and I'm going to bed too.' Kisses Sandy and even Simon. She has to step over my legs to get past, so she raises her feet almost knee-high, like a pony, so she won't have to touch.

'Did Simon tell you the funeral's tomorrow?' Sandy hands me a coffee. She is at home in this kitchen, as if she has never left. To me, it is unfamiliar. The colours have changed. Funeral. I shake my head, trying to get the word to jumble about and make some sense. 'Dorothy wanted to get it over as soon as possible, I'm sorry Charlene, we had no way of getting in touch.'

I want someone to call me Mack. I want Mack back, not this rawness of being Charlene. My soft underbelly scraping the ground. Being in this kitchen makes me feel small again, unseen. Coffee slips down me, helps me to nod if not to speak.

'Simon's doing the eulogy. Dad said it was what he wanted. He talked to Dorothy before he went in.'

'Fine. That's fine.' There's really nothing else to say.

Binky breathes in and out below me, in the bunk which used to be mine. I wanted stars on the ceiling then, and moons. Those glow-in-the-dark ones. And I wanted the room to be white with green bamboo plants everywhere. Begged for it. Instead, it is pink and warm and frilly, the way it always was. My eyes are closed and inside my head I go: *My father is dead my father is dead* to see what will happen. Nothing does, except that sickness rumbling about in my mouth and in my gut. I doze in and out – pictures jump about in front of my eyelids, bright colours and flashes of aeroplane seats and toilets. Currawongs wake me up, singing away outside, and a knife-edge of sun cuts across my face. Binky is doing sit-ups on the floor. I roll over so that my face hangs over the edge of the bed and I can watch her properly. 'Binky.'

She doesn't stop sitting-up-sitting-down-sitting-up-sitting-down. 'I'm called Bianca these days. Haven't been called Binky by anyone but Grandad for years.'

'Sorry. No one told me.'

'You never asked. Too busy in Lon-don.' She says it as if it's two words of several syllables each.

I am about to ask how she's feeling, then decide I'm too tired to care, climb down and step over her. There's no bath, so I try to get the feeling of drowning in the shower instead. Power the water out, right into my face, until I can hardly breathe. It pours into my eyes and mouth, burning. I sit in the steam for ages, watching the drips run down the walls. When I go back in, wrapped in a mauve towel, Bianca is lying on her back with tears rolling down her face. There are two wet patches, either side of her on the carpet. Her mouth is open and her shoulders move up and down, but there's no sound. I kneel beside her and stroke her hand. She makes a small whimpering noise before she rolls over and hides her face. She lets me rub her back until she stops shaking. When she has been still for a while, I say 'I only left because I had to.' She gets up, pats her face and says 'I'm going to have a shower.' She does not say thank you.

Dorothy's voice echoes in the kitchen. I don't want to see her. Fear swills about with the sickness. Sandy taps on the bedroom door, and says 'Oh good you're up' as if she didn't know. 'Do you want breakfast, love?' She always wanted to be my mother. She's so much older than me, I think she thought she was my mother until Dorothy came along. Not that Dorothy tried to be my mother. Not that I would have let her. Sandy comes in while I comb my hair and shake the creases from my dress.

'No. I feel a bit sick actually.' Which is true, my guts are swirling about like crazy now.

'We all do. What about coffee?'

I know she's trying to get me out there, into the kitchen with Dorothy. And I know I should go out there and hug her for goodness' sake, but I can't, I just can't seem to make myself. It's just, if she pushes me away, I'll sink. I'm not strong enough to shrug it off. 'No. Nothing.'

'Come and say hello then.'

'Not yet. Please.'

'Simon's just arrived. It'll be easier now. Be much harder at the funeral.' She sits on the bed, arms folded. She is right. We both know she is, so I follow her down the hallway.

I'm shy in my black dress, unsure if it's right. If it's too much. Too short, or something. Dorothy is leaning over the bench, half in shadow. I touch her on the back and she turns, takes my hands and holds them for a moment. She is already in hostess mode, her eyes half-glazed. She smiles and says 'Thank you for coming Charlene' and although we both know I didn't do it for her, I mean it when I say 'You're welcome.' It is all I am able to come up with. She pours me tea and more tea and more tea. There is nothing to do but wait.

'Are people coming back here after?' I do not want to make polite conversation, but I am trying.

'The golf club. I organised it yesterday.' Simon is crisp. Early morning efficiency.

'Is there anything I can do?'

Dorothy turns her head from Simon to look at me. 'No, Charlene, there isn't.'

Before we go, Simon wraps a small box in cloth and puts it in his glove box.

'What's that?' I touch-test it.

'Dad's medals. Dorothy gave them to me. Dad wanted me to have them.'

My mouth is stale and airless again. 'Oh. I thought you would have his fob watch.'

'Sandy's having it.'

'Oh.' And there is nothing else to say except, of course, what-about-me, which would have been far too self-absorbed. So I say nothing, nothing at all and sit folded carefully all the way to the crematorium. Like a good girl.

Sandy sits next to me, on the end of the pew, squeezing my hand all through Simon's eulogy. It's hard for me to hear him, because of the buzzing in my ears. He looks small inside his blue suit and keeps twisting his neck about, trying to escape from the tight collar. After he sits down, Sandy stands up, brushes Dorothy's shoulder and walks up to the little stage with a Bible in her hand and starts to read. Her voice pounds at my head like the shower water, I can't understand at all what she's saying. Words. Just words. She takes my hand again when she sits down, but I stare ahead and make my hand fishlike. Too tired to make sense of it all. They play the Last Post on a scratchy cassette player while Dad's coffin disappears.

Outside, the sun is burning into the wall. Uncles I have no memory of hug me and call me Charlotte and say what a shame I wasn't able to do anything in the service and I say yes isn't it. Strangers pile into cars and start driving off. Everyone seems to know where they're going except me. I stand next to the rose bush, wondering what to do next. Sandy brings a red-haired woman over. Auntie Someone or other, who says 'Oh you're the youngest. The difficult one.' I stare straight ahead and wait for her to leave. Sandy's arm goes around my waist and I step away.

'What?' Sandy is, oh, all innocence.

'Nothing, Sandy. Absolutely bloody nothing. Forget it. Why didn't you tell me?'

'What? The reading? I'm sorry. It's what Dad wanted. I didn't mean not to tell you. I didn't think about it.'

There is a gash inside me, slicing deep and deep. I keep my mouth shut, stay invisible. She did think about it, I know she did.

Dorothy leans on Simon's arm, waves off the last of the uncles. She turns to face me. With the sun shining on her, the scar from where I slashed her is bright and red. It travels down her face, which is strange because I don't remember cutting like that. I only remember grabbing the knife and pushing forward, forward to the place where her face was. Blood, I do remember blood and the odd sound of muscle tearing. But it was so long ago, I can barely remember. She can though, I know that. Her hand goes up to her face and I can see her, suddenly, doing that every morning. Touching the scar. I wake up each morning easily, I do not remember this every morning, what I did. My mouth is full of saliva and stupid words and I swallow hard, watching Dorothy's scar get in the car with her. Simon gets in the driver's seat, sticks his head out of the window and yells 'We'll see you there.' Sandy nods.

'Come on.' She takes my hand again, and this time I let her. 'I'll drive you. I'm sorry you couldn't do anything.'

She holds my hand while she drives, letting go to change gears. Now and then, I wipe my face. My hands get wet and slippery. She is so big, Sandy. She fills the car up, has room for everyone. Next to her, her bigness and warmth, I shrink. Shame shrivels me. I think of Dorothy, facing Dad's coffin with her scar, and my wounds seem small.

The doors of the golf club are tinted brown glass. I can see them inside, forming a line. Dorothy hugging them all, one by one. I hug Sandy. 'I'll stay out here.'

'No you won't.' Her foot is already in the door, her hand still attached to mine so that I am yanked inside with her.

There's an orderly queue. Dorothy leaning on Simon's arm, I can see she's tired too. More tired than me. Sandy lets go of my hand and wraps her arms around Dorothy, who is stiff backed, holding herself up. Huddles of uncles and cousins are forming in the bar and I am feeling sicker and sicker and suddenly thinking I have no right no right at all. I keep my hands at my side and do a half smile, not sure of how else to get past. Dorothy puts her hands out and stops me, pulls me quickly to herself and puts a dry kiss on my cheek. She says 'I'm sorry about your father Charlene. Thank you for coming. Really.' She hugs me again and is both bigger and softer than I think of her. I look at her hands and say 'Sorry. I'm so sorry Dorothy.'

Sandy collects me a plate of sandwiches and kisses everyone. I put the sandwiches on the bar and walk out into the sun, let the heat pour over my arms. With my eyes closed, I can see yellow flames. I walk up the verge, watching the sun bounce off the street lights. Dad's house is just around the corner. Dad and Dorothy's house. Steep hill though – I'm out of breath by the time I get there. I climb the side fence and stick my face under the tap. My mascara will run and my hair will look like a dog's breakfast. Good. The garden's bigger than I remember. A new shed, and a glasshouse. Lined up by the back fence, a row of sunflowers, higher than the glasshouse. They're just behind the vegetable patch. My eyes are on the sunflowers and I walk closer and closer. Almost tread on his leeks. Their leeks. Cherry tomato plants are right next to them, tiny red dots hanging off the green. And three clumps of basil, scattered in amongst them. The purple broccoli on the edges is looking dry so I fill a bucket and splash it on. Mule-tail is starting to sprout in among the strawberries. And she needs some nasturtiums. There's a pair of too-big gloves on the glasshouse shelf, so I put them on and start weeding. Soon, it will be time to cut the sunflowers down and shake the seeds free.

And You Know This

Leone Ross

Leone Ross was born in England and moved to Jamaica at the age of six. She attended university there and then returned to London to do her Masters degree. Her first novel, *All the Blood is Red*, published by Angela Royal Publishing in 1996, was longlisted for the Orange Prize for Literature in 1997. Her work has been anthologised in *Creation Fire* (CAFRA 1985) and *Burning Words, Flaming Images* (SAKS 1996). Her second novel, *Orange Laughter*, will be published in 1998. Leone lives and works as a journalist in London and has travelled widely within the Caribbean, the United States and Europe. She still can't drive!

5

And You Know This

Amber craned her neck, trying to see over the passengers. There was still no sign of Birdie. She wondered if her friend had asked for the hover frame after all. When they spoke on the VidNet three days ago Birdie's face was tattered. Amber found it difficult to conceal her shock. 'The old girl don't look too good, does she?' Birdie laughed, a racking bark that sounded like fingernails on a smooth surface.

'No, no, B,' she'd said, 'yuh look fine, girl.'

Birdie laughed again. 'Yuh too lie. After all these years yuh goin' start lie to me now?' That was when Amber had suggested the hover frame. After all, why did they pay their taxes if not for these little luxuries? All Birdie would have to do was step in and be spirited to where Amber stood in the airport lounge. But Birdie had been just as dismissive as she'd expected.

'Hover frame? Hover frame yuh rass! Amber Bailcy, is not me one ah mash up! After yuh have arthritis ah kill yuh off! Me can still dance yuh under the table – and yuh know this!' They had both broken into laughter at the memories. Over the years whenever anyone asked if she'd spoken to Birdie recently, they'd wink and chorus 'And yuh know this!' It was Birdie's stock phrase.

'Call for Sister Amber Bailey.' The cheery mechanical voice echoed through Arrivals. 'Sister Bailey, puh-leeze access Channel Number One Zero Three.'

She walked over to the Com Terminal, trying to ignore her limp. It had stopped irritating her these days, but Birdie was right. She was a far cry from the dancer she had been. She tapped in her diagnostic code and gave her keyword to the operator. A recording reminded her that she was in Airport Jamaica 237 and wished her a spiritually productive day. On screen, silent waves stroked a peaceful shore. Amber grinned. They had made it to the year 2070 and Com Terminal messages were still like any of those old telephone recordings: cheesy and insincere.

'Girl child? Yuh dere?' Birdie's face flickered on to the screen.

'Me here, man. Didn't I say I was coming?'

Birdie winked. 'Like yuh have a choice!'

'Hush up yuh mout', gyal. So what taking so long? Man all over de long roads of Jamaica waitin' for us!'

'Me comin', me comin'. Me jus' want to tell yuh de Medic haffi give me another injection.' Amber kept the smile plastered to her face and tried to tease. 'Me only did need one. Yuh sure yuh don't need the hover frame?'

Birdie sucked her teeth. 'Me tell yuh a'ready. Me come to dance inna de sunshine. Jus' mek sure yuh have the rum an' coke waitin'!'

The Com Terminal flickered into a peaceful blue. Amber remembered how much time and money had been wasted on what had come to be known as the Big Blue Talks. It had been a joke. International airport officials from across the world had met with the wisest men and women to meditate on the relative merits of their Com Terminal screens. What low-octave frequency to insert behind the colour to soothe tired travellers. And God, the months discussing the colours. In her day – her and Birdie's day she reminded herself – they would have been too busy shooting up one another to waste time with such foolishness. Still, she had to admit that the screen did what it was supposed to do: she felt instantly peaceful looking at its depth. She walked back to Arrivals and smiled as a small, sprightly woman lowered her head and moved to give her a seat.

'Peace be with you.' The woman looked anxious.

'And also unto you,' Amber answered. She watched her walk off; the woman was trying to stop herself from looking backwards. So. This was going to be the way.

'Gyal pickney!'

Amber shook her head and turned in time to see Birdie coming towards her at a clip that a fifty-year-old would admire. Her arms were open wide. 'Yuh ready to mash down Jamaica?' she yelled. People turned and stared.

It was the same old Birdie. A bright purple, low-cut jumpsuit and orange shoes. She had tied yellow handkerchiefs all over her outfit; around her calves, dangling from her sleeves. The earrings were festive baskets of miniature fruit. The lipstick was uncompromisingly red, slightly eerie against the ash of her face. Blue nails flashed on her hands. Amber had always felt grey next to Birdie. But she couldn't hold it against her. She put a self-conscious hand up to her own tidy, braided hair, and then her friend was on her, hugging her. She felt tears prick at her eyes.

'Lawd, girl, yuh look good, good, good!' Birdie patted her ass and broke into laughter. 'Albert must have cried eye water when yuh stepped out of the house!'

'Some.' Amber couldn't stop smiling. Birdie's energy was infectious. It had been too long.

Birdie read her mind. 'Twenty-five years, eh? What a disgrace! Anyway, Miss T'ing. We goin' mek up for it now! Where de car?'

The car was sleek and mean. Both women stood in front of its green elegance, taken. It looked like a resting animal. Birdie passed one long fingernail across its bonnet and raised her eyebrows.

Amber let out a breath. 'Well, we got style.'

Birdie grunted. 'Yuh hands don' let yuh drive, right? So me ah tek de wheel! Ah wonder how fast this t'ing can go?' She climbed into the driver's seat, caressed the leather wheel, gazed at the dashboard. 'Look, look! We can hit 500, chile! Zero to 500 in five seconds!'

Amber carefully moved to the passenger side. Underneath her, it was soft and reassuring. 'Yuh know we not supposed to hit that speed until we reach,' she warned.

'Shit. A'right. Ah promise. Now. Tell me what's been goin' on with yuh.' Birdie hit a switch and watched delightedly as the top of the car slid away. She flung her arms open. 'Praise Jesus! Fresh Jamaican breeze!'

Amber opened her mouth to answer, but the sound of a child's voice interrupted her. The little girl on the pavement was tugging at her mother's hand, her high voice cutting through the warm air.

'Mummy, mummy! Watch de Post Ladies! Post ladies, look mummy! See dem deh!'

Her mother was squirming with embarrassment. 'Eleanor! Be quiet, nuh!'

The child would not be distracted. She continued to stare at them, at the green car. 'But Mummy, me never seen a Post Lady before. Me can talk to dem?'

Amber bowed her head. She had hoped to leave without this. It was too hard. She pressed her lips together. All she wanted to do was drive on.

The woman looked helpless, gesticulated at her. 'Me sorry. Peace be wid yuh—'

Birdie was having none of it. She turned the key and the engine purred velvet. She looked up at the woman and her eyes were full of cheerful defiance. 'Woman! Tell yuh pickney –' she clicked to Start '– me not no rass Pos' Lady!' She put her foot down and threw her head back. The car leapt forward. 'Yeeeeeeeee-haaaaaaaa!'

Despite herself, Amber joined in. Their relic voices wound around each other, reminding each other of their youth.

'Yuh want a smoke?' Amber wiggled the precious pack at Birdie and watched her friend's salt-and-pepper hair stream back in the wind. Birdie had always been proud of her hair.

'What? Still a sinner!' Birdie chuckled and jerked her head forward. 'Tell me is double contraband!'

'Double double!'

They shrieked with laughter. Amber slipped a plastic case from her bra and began to roll the joint on a magazine on her knees. Marijuana was a pain to get these days. Of course it was legal. Just that the spiritual majority was so uptight about it. Funnily enough, they had outlawed tobacco. At least marijuana's healing properties had been accepted back in 2010.

'Rass!' she cursed as the papers fell from her fingers. At 101 years old, she felt a limp was quite acceptable. What annoyed her most was the arthritis in her hands. Now they were ugly hands. Ugly was a word she rarely heard these days.

'What?' Birdie was looking fine. There was a shine in her face.

'De damn weed spill all over the car.'

'Just pick it up, man!'

'Birdie . . .'

'What?'

Amber swallowed. She didn't want to be afraid. 'Yuh want to talk about it?'

'No.' Birdie was silent for a moment. She moved one hand from the steering wheel and patted Amber's cashmere knee. 'Not yet, a'right? Too soon.'

Amber bent forward and picked up the papers. A small moan escaped from her lips. She couldn't help it. It hurt too much. Birdie glanced over, her face set. 'Don't worry, baby. We soon reach.'

Amber realised that her top, so lovingly ironed by Albert that morning, Albert who still liked the old ways, was soaked with sweat. She thought about their daughter, Simone. Her full mouth had been set in a thin line when she left. She shook the memory away and concentrated on feeling fine. At the Post meeting they had repeated the advice like a mantra: Be positive. It wasn't difficult yet. For now, she could pretend, Birdie handling the green car like it was part of her body, scooping them through the Kingston traffic. Birdie insisted on turning the CDMax to blaring decibels. Amber had brought a collection of their favourite oldies, and they jigged and writhed as much as they could. Lionel Richie crooning. Prince promising them Eroticity. Grandmaster Flash and the Furious Five. Amber surprised herself by remembering the entire rap and Birdie carolled out the chorus, her voice steel over cotton wool. Then they playfully fought over the rockers: who first, Chaka Demus & Pliers, or Shabba?

An hour later they stopped at a bar at the side of the road. They had breached Kingston's outer limits and the surroundings were beginning to change. Thick trees caressed each other, breeding scarlet bougainvillea. Mosquitoes swam around Birdie's head as she tried to stretch. Amber could hear her joints crackle. She wished she was able to take the wheel.

'Boy. That weed gone straight to my head.' Birdie weaved slightly.

'Yuh could never hold a spliff.'

'Kiss me bumbo.' Determinedly, Birdie moved forward.

The bar was a small, modest affair. Pink hibiscus bushes flanked its calves. Inside it was as cool as peppermint. Candy striped chairs and no Vacupacked meals on the menu. The sign outside blared it: REAL CURRY GOAT COOK LIKE YOUR MOTHER USED TO. The barman looked at them gloomily and then brightened when he spotted the car. 'Peace be wid yuh.' It sounded strange in his mouth.

'Lawd God!' Birdie rolled her eyes and parked herself on the stool in front of him. She wiggled her long fingers. 'Also unto yuh an' gimme a rum an' coke. By de way, yuh have pan chicken?'

The barman shifted uncomfortably. Amber hid a smile. He was probably worrying about the bill. The government would award him several thousand points, of course. People who came into contact with Posts were paid well. Just that it would take at least six months to reach him.

He had the good grace to smile. 'Yes ladies. We have chicken, curry goat—'

Birdie tossed her hair flirtatiously. 'What yuh want, Amber?'

Her stomach fluttered at the thought of real goat. 'Me woulda love a roti.' She looked appealingly at the man. 'Please tell me yuh have goat roti . . .'

His smile grew broader. 'You ladies know good food.'

Birdie arched her eyebrow. 'Well, look at how we old, man!' A tall frosted glass appeared before her. She took a long swig and shuddered. 'There is a God! Rass! Amber, park yuh pretty hide and put one of these down yuh neck! Mm, mm, mmm . . .'

Amber watched the man, who was taking what looked like real onions from a container. He was no more than fifty. A spring chicken, and well preserved. Given his generation, he'd probably last until at least 250. She tried to stop herself from looking too hard at his muscled arms. She leaned over. 'B, me envy the sweat on fe him brow . . .'

Birdie tried not to laugh. 'Me want to know whether him ride like the car. Look sweet . . .'

Amber nudged her in the ribs. 'Birdie, yuh too bad! Imagine! At your age an' stage!'

The other woman raised her voice, mischief dancing in it. 'Hey, Mr Bar Man! Me friend *like* yuh, yuh know!' The man turned and grinned and then went back to chopping onions. Amber writhed with embarrassment. 'Shut *up*!' she hissed.

Birdie would not be hushed. 'She want to know if yuh ride smooth, pretty man!'

'Sir, ignore me friend. De alcohol gone to her head, y'know?'

'Don' start me on the drink stories!' Birdie was in full swing. 'Me remember a certain somebody who get drunk and grab up two man one time, imagine, Mr Man, she was a little bit ah gyal, only seventeen, grab up de man dem and give de both of them piece inna de back seat of her father car!' Amber tried to put a hand up to her mouth, and they wrestled gently, playfully.

'Imagine . . .' Birdie was panting. 'Gyal, me seh, let me go! Imagine, Mr Gentleman, she married now but me know seh Albert married her because the pus—'

'Birdie!'

'—me seh the *pussy* sweet him!'

Amber buried her head in her hands. She couldn't stop giggling. The bar-keep smiled at them. Together, they watched the laughter roll over the Blue Mountains and through the bright day.

'Birdie, which man yuh love the most in yuh life?' Ninety minutes after they left the bar behind them, Amber lifted her legs on to the dashboard and left them there. It felt like victory. The car was going faster, and the wind splayed her plaits.

Birdie glanced at Amber. She had zipped her jumpsuit further down and the bones jutted into the wind. She downshifted to avoid a meandering chicken. 'Yuh can see seh we hittin' country. People out here still have dog and goat ah walk like people!' She yelled at the fleeing bird. 'Chicken! yuh ever see a car in a hospital bed yet?'

Amber shook her head. 'Like yuh ever see a *chicken* inna hospital!'

'Wid de Animal Rights Bill in Atlanta yuh see dem all de time, me dear. Chicken wid bruk foot ah get aromatherapy, donkey dat forget how fe bray all ah get counsellin'—'

Amber burst into laughter. 'Birdie, how yuh so lie?'

Her friend turned to stare at her, dead pan. 'Yuh don' believe me? Mi seh, me see fowl ah get rub down wid geranium oil!'

'Anyway, yuh changin' the subject.'

Birdie tossed her hair and sucked her teeth. 'Yuh know who.'

'Mickey?'

'Of course.'

Mickey. Amber remembered him. How could she forget? He was the only man who had ever made Birdie chase. Her friend had met him in New York one long winter, the first time they had been apart. She in London, doing her nursing training, Birdie being Birdie, squired all over the US by a rich man thrice her age. In the days when Birdie had a silken navel so deep you could drink out of it. By the time she had scraped together the money to visit, Birdie had left the rich man and was drunk on Mickey. Mickey, who pulled out Birdie's hair in ten-strand handfuls, making her count. In bed. Mickey who brought Birdie a prostitute home for her twenty-first. And forced her to prove her love by watching. Sick Mickey, with toffee eyes.

'But yuh lef' him . . . what? Seventy-eight, seventy-nine years ago . . .'

Birdie laughed. It sounded younger than it had three days before. 'Miss T'ing, ah don' really appreciate yuh remindin' me of me age!'

'Birdie . . .'

'A'right! Yes, me love him the most.' She glanced at Amber and flicked a fly off the steering wheel. The road had gone bumpy, rolling their breasts. 'Why? Because de man had the sweetest lyrics me ever hear in me life. Would ah be wid him now? No rass way. Would ah tek him back fifty years ago? No. But sixty years ago, maybe. Maybe.'

'But why? Him was such a rass idiot.'

'Bwoy, dis car ride ah sweet yuh so much yuh start swear

now?' The car bumped. 'Somethin' just occur to me. Suppose dis car bruk down? What we do? Put it off?' Birdie flung her head back and laughed.

Amber moved uneasily. 'I guess we call dem an' dem send another one.'

They were silent for a mile, each lost in her own thoughts. Amber thought of Albert. He would be drinking CoffeeLike, hating it as he always did. It was still hard to be this age, with these memories, in these times. Remembering real coffee. She could see him, so much younger than her. Only seventy-five. He had been as young as the bartender when they had met. But he had loved her.

'Yuh know what?' Amber looked at her. Birdie's voice had moved down an octave.

'What?'

Birdie reached up her hand. She did it so quickly that Amber had no time to register her intent. The hair, grey and black, once long to the small of her back, sat in the purple lap. A wig. Amber stared. Birdie's skull was smooth and elegant. She had never realised how graceful her friend's neck was. The sun spots didn't seem to matter.

'Oh my God! How long—'

'It start drop out fifteen years ago.' Birdie's voice was quiet. Shaking her smooth head, she coaxed the car up to 110. 'Me did love me hair. Yuh know me love me hair, right, Amber? But every time me touch me hair fe all dese years, every time, me t'ink ah Mickey. T'ink how him hurt me, an' how me woulda do anyt'ing for him dem time.'

Amber reached out and touched the wig. It looked so real. It must have cost a thousand points. More. 'Birdie. Me don't know what fe tell yuh—' She wanted to cry.

'Fling it out for me, darlin'.'

'What?'

Birdie's jaw was set. 'Fling. Fling it out for me. Time for me to bloodclaaht realise seh me ah old woman!' Her voice rose. 'Yuh hear dat, Jamaica? Dis is a old woman, drivin' dis car! Me too old fe have dis idiot bwoy in me head!' She turned to Amber and grinned. Amber could not remember a time when Birdie had looked so queer and so beautiful.

'Yuh sure?'

'Yes, girl. Me wash de man right outta me hair! Finally! Fling it!'

Amber took a deep breath. Let the wig flow through her fingers into the tail wind.

The injection crept up on them, like the good weed had. Amber took her feet from the dashboard, and like a child at its first step, folded her legs beneath her. They had told her to go slow. She sighed. Curiously, she straightened her fingers. The pain was still there, but now it was creaked and subtle, an old rocking chair of pain, clicking slowly back and forth.

'How yuh feel?' Amber asked.

'Jus' fine.' Birdie wriggled her slender hips in the seat. 'First time I feel like a fresh fuck in years. Me see seh yuh sittin' like one ah dem yoga man, like yuh bad.'

'It feel funny.'

'Dat's what dem seh would happen . . .'

'Yeah, but me forget what it feel like to not have to shift around de pain all the time, y'know? Yuh in pain a lot?'

Birdie tossed her head and then remembered she had no more hair to toss. 'Sometimes. De pain killer mek it all go 'way fe months, but yeah, me feel it. Me nuh feel is cancer. Me t'ink somebody put a obeah spell on me.' She tossed Amber a mischievous grin and gripped the steering wheel like a lover. 'Yuh want to go faster?'

Amber was jolted out of her fascination with the fading pain. 'No. Not yet. How yuh in such a hurry?' She hated the sound of her voice. Squeaky and mean.

'Yuh 'fraid?'

'Of course me 'fraid, man.' She shook her head. 'An' is jus' like yuh can't wait to reach.'

Birdie reached out a hand and squeezed her leg. 'Me 'fraid too, girl. But what? What we goin' to do? Cyan' change it. We jus' haffi drive.'

Amber watched the deep green foliage whip past the edges of the car. They slipped across Flat Bridge and told each other the old stories of drowning, before they had made the bridge safe. Past Pum Rock, where matching sets of stone genitalia sat mysteriously in the rocks, one on each side of the river. They had proved them natural fifty years ago, after all the rumours that the Arawak Indians had created them. Birdie giggled wildly. Pum Rock always pulled her funny bone.

Amber had come back to Jamaica after her training. Birdie never had. Birdie was the adventurous one; the one who had always wanted to see more, to get past what she saw as the parochial limitations of the island they had been born in. Amber had missed everything about it in the four years she had been away. The dusty yellow butterflies that took over Kingston once every year, fluttering and dying on benches, in mid-air, on people's foreheads. The chorus of crickets at night time as the heat dimmed and broke into grey evening. The cut and thrust of Jamaican voices on the radio. Even as she watched things change, watched the whole world calm before her as people's spirits met and relinquished the old resentments, even as technology and spirituality has combined into a new order that she could only have suspected as a child, as shiny, efficient TransVacs replaced the clapped out buses and the mad people disappeared from the streets, as Birdie wrote and then VidNetted her news of her life, a life that had seemed inherently more exciting, with its champagne chuckles and stolen romantic hours, she had not regretted staying in her country. The butterflies did not go away. Simone had only been back a few times. She was a woman of the 2000s, impatient but courteous in the face of what she saw as her mother's archaic opinions. But Amber had wanted her daughter so badly. Thanked something, God, the Universe, that fertility treatment had made it possible. Even so late in her life. It was a good life. Albert's love and his little miseries, even the arthritis that they said they couldn't cure because she had old DNA. Her grandchildren would never have swollen joints or be unable to drive a car.

Amber felt the eerie warmth flow through her. It seemed to be concentrated in her legs. They had said that each person started in a different place. Started being Post. She unfolded a limb and gazed. The calf was long, longer than she remembered.

Wondering, she reached out a hand. The skin in front of her was beaten brown and smooth. She hooked her skirt up to her thighs. They were taut. For an odd moment she felt as if she were seeing Simone's thighs, her twenty-three-year-old daughter's thighs, but even as the thought occurred, she dismissed it. No. These were younger thighs. Stronger than her daughter's ever had been. Dancer's thighs.

'Amber . . .'

The warmth spread through and through Amber. She looked across at her friend's face. Birdie's hair was growing back, like an animated waterfall. It had started at her crown, wet sable. She could actually see it pouring its way down Birdie's back. But this was not the most astonishing thing. Birdie's face was changing. Fascinated, Amber watched the cheeks change, softening and filling, moulding around cheekbones that had become too sharp with alcohol and late nights and age. Birdie was shaking.

'It happenin', Amber? Ah can feel me face an' me body stretchin'—' Birdie took her eyes from the road and sucked her breath in sharply. Her voice was a whisper. 'Jesus Chris', girl! Yuh look like yuh twenty-one!'

Amber wrenched at the rear-view mirror on her side. The crow's feet were gone, spirited away like a dream. Unable to resist, she brought her hands down to the front of her blouse. Underneath the light material she could feel her heartbeat, hot beneath her skin.

'Oh my God, Amber – it really happen like dem seh, it really happen—' She realised Birdie was near tears. The Emerald wavered dangerously on the slate road. So clean now, not like the rain-filled potholes of their childhood. Potholes had been eradicated from the world in the twenty-first century.

'Birdie, min' de car . . .' She felt as if she was speaking from a dream. They couldn't stop the car now. They had said they couldn't. She undid her blouse. Her breasts were heavy, like smooth sacks of wine. Somehow they had lifted themselves from their 101-year stoop and pressed back against her ribcage, nipples smiling. She felt along the aureole, not caring about the wind caressing her naked flesh.

It was Birdie's tone that jerked her back into reality. She knew that sound. It was like when they first met, at sixteen, when the headmistress had given them double detention and Birdie had told the fool-fool woman that she wasn't serving no detention, after all, she had man waiting at the school gate. Her face had been set the same way. It was the same face, the same Birdie, sixteen years old, defiant and untouched by time. Feeling immortal. She could feel the car slowing.

'Amber, me goin' to stop dis car.'

A metallic voice emitted from the depths of the dashboard.

'Warning. Sister Bernadine Collins and Sister Amber Bailey. Warning. The Emerald T4 should not drop below two hundred miles per hour. You are not at the designated stage.'

Amber gripped Birdie's arm. She yelled above the voice.

'Birdie, yuh cyan' stop! Remember? Birdie! Is soon time, girl!'

Birdie shook her arm off. Her new mouth was twisted. 'Ah goin' fin' somewhere to park. Who seh we cyan' jus' stop, eh? Who seh so? We could stop, Amber! Stop an' have it all over again. Dem couldn't find us!' Her voice was almost pleading. 'Let me stop . . .'

Amber swung to face her. 'Birdie, t'ink what yuh doin'! The car won't let yuh stop anyway! We would haffi jump!'

Birdie let go of the wheel. The green car exerted itself. The speedometer began to climb.

'Automatic drive now activated. You now have one hour to your final destination.' The mechanical voice was calm, but Birdie would not be soothed. All her hair was back, whipping richly against her face. Her eyes, Amber thought, were too bright. Birdie began to rise, one foot on the seat. She was trying to stand up.

Amber grabbed at Birdie's leg, amazed at how her body obeyed her. She waited for a flash of pain. There was none. Only warmth. Birdie kicked awkwardly. She was yelling. The car was going faster.

'Nobody never try to get out! But we could! Look pon yuh! Look how yuh beautiful an' strong! Both ah we! Dem wouldn't fin' us! We could jus' disappear! Me an' yuh!'

'No! No! Birdie! Look at me!'

Birdie struggled, trying to get away. 'Girl, if yuh don't want to jump, me goin' jump!' Amber held on to her with grim determination. Birdie felt like an electric eel. She had touched one at the beach when she was ten, and she knew. It had been a baby, crackling, but not enough to hurt. The wind whistled past her ears. The car was going faster.

'Birdie. Listen to me! If yuh stand up, the car top will jus' close! Remember? Dem never tell yuh?' She had a handful of purple material. If she could just stop her from standing. She hooked her legs around the other woman's and tugged at the cloth with all her strength.

'NO—'

'Birdie, ah beg yuh! Stay with me!' Amber yanked. Birdie, who had untangled a leg, crumpled. She half fell into Amber's lap, banging her hip on the gear shift. She began to cry. Amber stroked her hair. It was soft. Softer than any expensive wig.

Birdie's mascara was running. She still used mascara. Old time ways.

'Me sorry . . .'

'Hush, baby. Me know.'

Birdie raised her face. Amber marvelled at the symmetry. She had old photographs that Simone laughed at. She had thought they captured Birdie's face. None did.

'We only have one hour, Birdie.' She didn't know what to say. 'Yuh remember de butterflies in de school yard?'

'No.' Birdie's voice was as harsh as it had been that morning.

'Yeah, man. Yuh remember. Yellow butterflies. Like clouds. A whole heap ah dem. Dem used to fall on yuh face an' dead. An' yuh would get vex.'

She smiled as Birdie chuckled into her shoulder.

'Yes. An' yuh would look like yuh goin' to bawl, cause yuh know dem was goin' to dead.'

'Yes.' They rocked together for a little while. The Emerald purred on.

Birdie touched her own face. 'Is only dat me get excited, y'know . . .'

'Ah know.'

'Yuh know me did always like me looks. Me admit it, me kinda vain. An' de idea dat me coulda have it all again, Amber. Y'know. Walk down street wid dis body, mek de man dem whistle . . .'

'Dem nuh even whistle dese days, Birdie. Dat is old time behaviour.'

'Me know, me know. Just dat ah miss bein' beautiful. Ah miss man cryin' at me foot bottom. Yuh have a husband. Him 'memba how yuh used to look. Me nuh have nobody. Jus' de woman dem inna me building, an' dem all t'ink me mad . . .'

Amber looked at her. 'But dem not wrong.'

They laughed.

'But yuh undastan', right?' Birdie said.

'Of course,' said Amber.

The metallic voice interrupted them. 'Sister Bailey and Sister Collins. You have fifty minutes to final destination. Countdown will begin one minute before arrival. Peace be unto you.'

Birdie pulled herself upright. She put her head on one side and reached up and across to hold Amber's hand. They chorused together.

'AND WE KNOW THIS!'

They watched the clock, listening to the sound of their own breathing. Amber thought that she had never really heard her own breath before. Even when meditation and breathing exercises had become compulsory at school, and she'd had to do catch-up lessons with Simone. Albert would pinch her and tell her it was because of her old DNA. They would laugh. He had only been born twenty-six years after her.

'Well.' Birdie shook herself. 'Since me get back me hair an' de car doin' it own bloodclaaht t'ing, ah goin' step inna de back seat an' blow inna de breeze.'

'Careful. If yuh go too high . . .' Amber said.

'Me learn me lesson.' Birdie's voice was contrite.

Amber watched her move. It was wondrous to see her clamber skilfully across the seats. She could hardly believe it. She leaned against the back of the car seat and gazed at Birdie. The purple jumpsuit was an apology on her sixteen-year-old body. It bagged at the waist and hugged too closely at the hips. It was three inches too short. Birdie had shrunk with age. Amber looked at herself in the mirror again. They had warned her that it could be confusing, disorientating. She had never been too fond of her face anyway, supposed that it had served her, but that was all. The car continued to purr around sharp lanes. It was getting faster. Ducking her head low, she climbed into the back. Birdie tried to smile at her, as her ribcage rose and fell. Birdie was trying not to hyperventilate. 'Who yuh – who yuh—'

Amber took Birdie's hands in her own. Part of her felt serene, as if none of it was happening.

'Calm down, sweetie. What yuh want to seh?'

Birdie gulped and her breathing steadied. 'Who yuh love the most in your life?' she said. The Emerald whizzed along the road. The engine sounded as if it was speaking to them. Nearly there nearly there nearly there nearly there.

Amber smiled. 'Albert, of course. And Simone.' She looked away. She had hoped that the question wouldn't come up. It was one of the reasons she had chosen Birdie. She loved her, but she had expected the ride to be full of Birdie's confessions, regrets, denouements. Then she could hide her own thoughts.

'Me nuh believe yuh.' Birdie struggled to sit up. Her voice had changed. This was the sweet tones of the choir she had sung for, when they were sixteen.

'Sing fo' me, Birdie,' she said. She looked at the clock. Twenty minutes. And counting. She could see the sparkle of the water by the road. They were by the sea and it wouldn't be long.

'I will. Wait. Just tell me. Tell me who yuh love the most. Me know is not Albert. Every woman have a firelight in her eye fe the man who sweet her, lif' her up. An' yes, me know seh yuh love Albert. An' me know yuh choose me because me woulda talk de head off a donkey. But is your time too, Amber. Your time too. An' me fling way my hair a'ready.' Amber shook her head. All the nights of regrets, sleepless, longing. She had pretended for years.

'Tell me, Amber. Tell me which man yuh love the most.'

Amber laughed. It was a silver sound, lost in the wind and the unending mutter of the engine. She listened to the warmth running through her. One plait loped over her shoulder. No grey. Perhaps it was time to tell. They had told her she should not reach her destination bound by silence. She turned to look at Birdie. Birdie with her soft throat and her kiss me you fool lips and her dark, wise skin, almost purple, like the tree bark around her mother's house.

'Is you.' The words sat between them. She felt as if something had broken inside her newly sixteen-year-old self. 'Me love yuh since me meet yuh, and me never talk.'

Birdie's face was a mixture of horror and incredulity.

'Me love yuh since me see yuh ah cuss wid teacher in de school yard. Love yuh all de time, Birdie. Sleep wid yuh ah night time, ah giggle 'bout man, tell yuh how to kiss.' She closed her eyes as the warmth plunged and rose in her. 'Remember how me tell yuh how fe kiss?'

'Put yuh mout' on him mout', soft up yuh lip an' memba fe breathe.' Birdie sounded as if she was reciting.

The clock blinked at them. Fifteen minutes to arrival. Fifteen minutes. Fifteen minutes.

'Me never want to tell yuh now. Me never want it to be de las' t'ing yuh memba 'bout me. Mek yuh t'ink seh me ah watch yuh an' t'ink bad t'ings . . . but de injection – it makin' me warm.' She giggled. It was like being happily drunk. 'What a rass injection!'

Birdie put her hands up to her eyes. 'But why yuh married? Why yuh lie? Why yuh never talk, baby? Dis is de time fe people recognise dem t'ings. Dem wouldn't judge yuh. Not like when we was pickney.'

Amber laughed again. ''Cause is only yuh, Birdie. An' me did know seh yuh wouldn't love me back.'

The Emerald smoothed its body around the corner. The sea flirted with them from a distance. Soon they would be on the sand. They could feel its urgency. The speedometer began to rise. Amber looked over at Birdie. She was crying.

'Yuh 'fraid, Birdie?' She reached out for her hand. 'Yuh 'fraid?'

Blue nails dug into Amber's fingers.

'No. Is not 'fraid. Me dash weh me wig. Me tell yuh dat. But you, girl. Me cyaan stan' it, Jesus Chris'! So yuh regret everyt'ing, yuh waste everyt'ing!'

Amber shook her head. Birdie didn't understand. She must make her understand. She had to raise her voice over the wind. Streams of sand whirled around them, golden clouds.

Nearlytherenearlytherenearlythere . . .

'All me did want to do was tell yuh. Dat's all. Me live me life.

Nuh regret nuttin'.' She searched Birdie's wet eyes. 'Tell me yuh know what me mean. Me a'right. Me did jus' haffi tell yuh.'

'Promise me yuh mean dat. Yuh really fin' peace? Tell me yuh a'right. Amber, me nevah know. Me never give yuh anyt'ing.'

Amber reached out and it felt as if Birdie floated into her arms. Belly to belly. 'You was me friend, B. Dat's all. Dat's good.' The car roared and she felt her heart beating. Like a yellow butterfly.

'Sing for me, Birdie,' she said.

Birdie raised up her voice. It was strong and long and real. An old hymn. From hot days in Sunday school.

'You are the rose, the rose of Sharon to my heart . . .'

The sand obliterated the car. It was as if they were lost in a quiet storm. They could hear the countdown beginning.

'You gave me water that refreshes me in every part . . . you are so beautiful . . .'

The sand changed around them. Kaleidoscope colours, bright as a bird's wing filling their eyes. They held tight. And Birdie sang.

'And I love you more than words can say . . .'

Amber's final moment of consciousness was filled with the sound of Birdie's voice, filling her eardrums as the Emerald thundered towards the Light.

'You are my beloved and my happiness in every way . . .'

The little girl smiled hesitantly at her mother as they sat cross-legged on warm mats in the bedroom. The last of the lights for the Post People were fading into the distance. It was the third time they had seen them in as many weeks.

'Mummy, yuh think those lights were for the Post Ladies we saw today?'

'Probably.' Her mother reached out to touch her face. 'It mek yuh sad?'

'No. Dem look old an' happy. Like dem was ready to die.'

'Ah t'ink dem was well ready.' Her mother helped her into bed. The child listened to her mother's footsteps on the stairs. She smiled at the window as the purple lights flittered into night and a final golden bubble sank beyond the window into the sea.

Acknowledgements ∫

'Leaving', © Bidisha 1997.

'Its Own Place', © Joanna Briscoe 1997.

'Big Things', © Margo Daly 1997.

'Wedding at Hanging Rock', © Justine Ettler 1997. Extract from a novel in progress, *Remember Me*.

'Tofino', © Jill Dawson 1997.

'Lady Chatterley's Chicken', © Louise Doughty 1997.

'A Hundred Years as a Snail', first published in *Dirt and other Stories*, © Catherine Ford 1996, The Text Publishing Company, Melbourne Australia 1996. © Catherine Ford 1996. Reprinted by permission of the author.

'Sunflowers', © Kathryn Heyman 1997.

'Touching Tiananmen', © Gail Jones 1992. First published in *The House of Breathing* © Gail Jones, Fremantle Arts Centre Press, Western Australia 1992. Reprinted by permission of the author.

'Monterrey Sun', © Jean McNeil 1997. Extract from a novel in progress of the same name.

'Zoo', © Gaby Naher 1997.

'Bloke Runner', © Bridget O'Connor 1997.

'It is July, Now', © Kathy Page 1996. First published in *New Writing 5 An Anthology* edited by Christopher Hope and Peter Porter, Vintage 1996. Collection © The British Council 1996. Reprinted by permission of the author.

'Can't Beat It' first appeared in *Sport 12*, New Zealand 1994. © Emily Perkins 1994. Reprinted by permission of the author.

'And You Know This', © Leone Ross 1997.

'Okay So Far', © Ali Smith 1997.